RESURRECTION CODE

RESURRECTION CODE

a novel by Lyda Morehouse

Des Moines, Iowa

Also available from Mad Norwegian Press...

Chicks Dig Time Lords:
A Celebration of Doctor Who by the Women Who Love It
edited by Lynne M. Thomas and Tara O'Shea

Whedonistas:
A Celebration of the Worlds of Joss Whedon by the Women Who Love Them
edited by Lynne M. Thomas and Deborah Stanish

Wanting to Believe: A Critical Guide to The X-Files, Millennium
and The Lone Gunmen by Robert Shearman

Dusted: The Unauthorized Guide to Buffy the Vampire Slayer
by Lawrence Miles, Lars Pearson and Christa Dickson

Redeemed: The Unauthorized Guide to Angel (ebook forthcoming)
by Lars Pearson and Christa Dickson

Running Through Corridors: Rob and Toby's Marathon Watch
of Doctor Who (Volume 1: The 60s)
by Robert Shearman and Toby Hadoke

Ahistory: An Unauthorized History of the Doctor Who Universe
by Lance Parkin [2nd Edition available]

THE ABOUT TIME SERIES
by Lawrence Miles and Tat Wood

About Time 1: The Unauthorized Guide to Doctor Who (Seasons 1 to 3)
About Time 2: The Unauthorized Guide to Doctor Who (Seasons 4 to 6)
About Time 3: The Unauthorized Guide to Doctor Who
(Seasons 7 to 11) [2nd Edition now available]
About Time 4: The Unauthorized Guide to Doctor Who (Seasons 12 to 17)
About Time 5: The Unauthorized Guide to Doctor Who (Seasons 18 to 21)
About Time 6: The Unauthorized Guide to Doctor Who
(Seasons 22 to 26, the TV Movie)
About Time 7 (forthcoming)

Copyright 2011, Lyda Morehouse. All rights reserved.
Published by Mad Norwegian Press (www.madnorwegian.com).
Edited by Christa Dickson and Lars Pearson.
Jacket & interior design by Christa Dickson.

ISBN: 9781935234098
Printed in Illinois. First Edition: March 2011.

For Xochiquetzl and all other knights that go "squee!"

Vayomer Elohim "Na'aseh adam b'tzalmenu kidmutenu"

Genesis 1:25
And the Gods said "Let us make man and woman in our image, and like us."

Chapter 1
Mouse

This neighborhood is full of ghosts. Everywhere I look, a memory lingers. Most of them are ugly. There, in the long shadow of the Tulun Mosque, I met Mohammad the first time. Three blocks to the east, just beyond that silk and tech market, I betrayed him.

With my mind on the past, it's unsettling to see so many people on the street. The Cairo I remember was little more than a ghost town. In the forty years since I first left, the city has regained its reputation as the loudest place on earth. There are women in hijab pushing prams, men in suits subvocalizing stock tips on the LINK, kids begging for credit uploads, marketers hawking cheap plastic crap, and students flirting real-time. Electric motorbikes whiz through the narrow streets, while gear twinks scoot by on steampowered contraptions of all manner, despite a plethora of signs posted in English and Arabic forbidding anything but pedestrians.

All the activity makes my head hurt, especially before my "morning" coffee. Of course, I'm not supposed to be drinking anything before sunset, it being Ramadan, but, in my opinion, the bigger sin would be subjecting anyone to me, non-caffeinated.

I take a steadying sip and watch the sun set in deep pink and purple polluted splendor on the glassy-expanse of the Great Pyramids.

If you're unhappy, why come here at all, father?

Page's note blinks on the handheld that, a moment ago, had the *Guardian's* entertainment section. "You know, I *was* reading that," I say.

No, you weren't. You were staring morosely at the tech market.

Of course he can track my focus. Mostly, Page lives in my head via all the mouse.net bits that miraculously started working after I hung out with an angel who was probably Satan. But that's another story.

Page knows how cranky I am when I first wake up. No one should be in my head before I get my first jolt, so often he'll talk around me through various electronic devices. It's disconcerting to say the least when your hotel toaster tells you good morning in your own damn voice.

I know I'm supposed to call him Strife or some other crap-ass moniker, but he's always been my Page, so screw that.

You have no respect for me.

I roll my eyes. Track that, Page. "You sound like a teenager," I tell him. "I came here for you, you know. You asked me to, remember?"

I asked to go to Mecca. Specifically, I reminded you that you have not yet performed hajj, and you are getting up in years. This, however, is not Mecca. Mecca is precisely 1,285 kilometers east of here.

"Patience, grasshopper," I say, taking another sip. I have to crook my elbow close to my body to keep from being jostled by passersby. Too damn many people, I tell you.

Merciful Allah, I sound old.

Technically, you are "elderly."

"Oh thanks for that one, Page. I am so never calling you Strife."

"All the kids sub-vocalize these days, you know." It's Deidre. She's come to join me at the cafe. "You should learn."

I shrug. I'm not sure why she agreed to tag along on my little sojourn to the homeland. Maybe the heat is good for her hip joints too. Or maybe it's because Michael is AWOL again – off to heaven or wherever he goes – and the only apparent perk of being the mother of the messiah is that she returns your LINK texts now and then. Why I let her come, well, that one's easy. I'm a sucker for a pretty face and size six undies no matter how old we both are.

Her hair, like mine, now has a lot of gray. The whiter-than-blonde bits have come in wiry and wild, and somehow even more "I just rolled out of bed" looking. It still turns me on. Intensely.

Like her eyes, which always seem to be scanning for the criminal element that just lurks behind my own.

"Don't you start on my age as well. I can kick both your asses," I say.

I wouldn't count on it. She's still "packing heat."

Page uses my eye to highlight the silhouette of the colder steel hidden under Deidre's light linen blazer. "Cool. Do you do x-ray vision, too?"

Sure. But I doubt you'll find it very tantalizing.

He shows me her bones and a soft outline of skin and flesh, mostly blurred by layers of clothes. He's right. Not very sexy, except in a medical thriller sort of way.

When my vision returns, it's to Deidre's scowling face. "All these years and you're still looking for a peep show?"

I smile impishly and shrug. "I'm officially a dirty old man."

"You're officially irritating."

A waiter appears and deposits the Turkish coffee she ordered via the LINK. I'm weirdly jealous, even though I have full access to mouse.net which is the primary interface of Cairo – and, well, most of North Africa. But, my LINK connection is still slag, how any of my connections work still baffles me.

You made a deal with the devil.

"Oh yeah, that's right."

"That you're irritating? I'm glad we agree."

"Ha, ha." I sip my coffee and shoot her my best sarcastic side-long glance. "I was talking to Page."

"Say 'hi' for me."

"Hi for me," I dutifully repeat. Tapping the hard lump at my temple that once held the state-of-the-art wire-wizard LINK gear, I add, "Do it yourself, you've got the LINK."

You two are like an old married couple.

"What, like you and Dragon?"

"Say 'hi' to her too, will you?" Deidre says just to bug me, and picks up my handheld to scan the headlines, which Page has nicely replaced for her.

What are we doing here, father?

My eyes can't help but return to the silk market. I can almost smell the dust and rot of the Blackout Years. "We're here to put some ghosts to rest."

Blackout

I was trying to find God when Allah sent Mohammad.

Blinding afternoon sun cast long shadows through the courtyard of the Ahmed Ibn Tulun mosque. I stumbled through the shifting sand that covered the courtyard. My blood stained the few exposed cobblestones in dark, unholy spatters. I'd come here by instinct, drawn by a memory of peace and safety.

I should have known the blackout had destroyed everything that had once been good in my city.

"Hello?" my voice reverberated in the empty arcades, bouncing through pointed stone arches. "Could someone please help me?"

Since I spoke in Arabic, my words had been directed at God, who I still secretly hoped lived here within these ancient, sacred walls. My pleas received no answer, however. God, it seemed, like most Cairenes, had moved on to better real estate.

Trembling legs could no longer support me, so I crumpled to the ground, with a soft, muffled, "Fuck, goddamn, mother fuck."

Of course, it was these words that Allah heard most clearly.

Peeking around the curved edge of an archway, a boy close to my own age appeared like an angel, a shy cherub. His round face was made even more spherical by an overgrown halo of hair and wispy beard that encircled his chin. Short, willow-thin, he flitted like a nervous sparrow.

"Hey," he said, echoing the English with which I'd chosen to swear. His tone was high and light and nervous. "Are you okay?"

Given the blood that had started to seep from the deep wounds in the flesh of my backside, the only appropriate answer seemed, "No, not really. You?"

Strangely, this seemed to delight him. He crept closer. I could see the flash of a wide, bright grin on his dark face. "You really do speak English! My prayers have been answered."

At least that made one of us.

In deference to his joyful mood, I promptly passed out.

The next few weeks were lost in fever-induced haze and dreams of virgins-who-were-sometimes-men and boys-with-soft-lips and sweet songs of angels.

Music continued into my first forays into wakefulness. I heard English nursery rhymes and calls to prayer in mangled Arabic. It was the last bit that shook the final webs of fever from my brain. I have always been a word nerd, and I simply had to survive long enough to correct his pronunciation.

I woke up saying the Arabic accurately over and over and over again, and him, kneeling at my side, chanting carefully along.

"Oh hey," he said, looking deeply into my eyes as though searching for signs of intelligent life. "You're really in there now, aren't you?"

"Mostly," I said, finding my voice thick with disuse.

Dusty sunlight pierced ragged gauze curtains in sharp, bright shafts. We were no longer in the mosque, this much I could tell. The room was narrow and hardly large enough for the two of us. I lay naked in a pile of clean, fresh straw. Straw? I picked up a brittle, yellow stem in my fingers and examined it in disbelief. What, did I awake in a manger?

No, the more I looked the egg-shell white walls and acoustic tile ceiling, I reealized was an abandoned office building.

My companion smiled happily, almost goofily at me. "I'm Mohammad, by the way."

"Christian," I said, noting the irony with a cough of a laugh.

He handed me a water bottle stamped with the UN Peacekeeper's emblem, and I drank deeply.

"Christian?" He repeated. Then he shook his head, and pointed to his chest. "No, I'm a Muslim. Sunni."

"Cool! Me too."

Mohammad's frown deepened. He peered into my face. "Are you still in la-la land?"

"I don't know, am I?"

Very seriously and deliberately, he explained, "This is Cairo. Egypt. You, uh," – I couldn't wait to see what he'd come up with here – "had an accident."

An accident? Yes, that was a pretty accurate description of my life thus far, and I couldn't help but laugh more robustly this time. He backed away, nervously. I had to put poor, confused Mohammad out of his misery. So, after wiping the tears from eyes, I put my hand to my heart, "Christian is my name. Christian El-Aref, lately of Maadi British International School before, you know, the apocalypse." I may have made some exploding sounds here, and mimed the rushing of all that black water that rained down on the city when the Aswan dams broke, because Mohammad went a little pale.

I tended to forget that most people lost their families rather horrifically that day. My mother, at least, had sense enough to orphan me years before the flood. I really only knew my Aunt Fatima and my extended family through her crisp, formal letters. Careful reading between the lines had given the impression of a limp tolerance for mother's little Infidel-fathered bastard.

Honestly, I'd originally considered the flickering lights of the first waves of the blackout a liberation from the British Boys' School, which I thought much like escaping the island in *Lord of the Flies*. Until I actually made my way into Cairo, that was. Then it became obvious the world was so very much uglier than anything I could have imagined.

"Oh," I said, reaching out to touch his hand in apology. "I didn't mean any disrespect, you know, about the flood and... well. Sorry."

Mohammad awkwardly shrugged out from under my gesture. There was something about the shy way he tilted his head away from me that gave me pause. Was he gay or something?

Don't think I have something against being queer. But, unconsciously, I shifted my ass, feeling sharp stabs deep inside. Suffice to say, I was still a little, uh, *sensitive* about that topic having just come from where I had. Which reminded me to be grateful, "Thanks, by the way," I said. "You saved my life. I owe you one. Or maybe a dozen."

We laughed together this time. It was the start of a beautiful friendship, not unlike, say, other famous bosom buddies: Robin Hood and Friar Tuck, King Arthur and Lancelot, and Jesus and Judas.

Jesus and Judas?

Yeah...

But that's getting ahead of things.

Those first few days of my recovery, I was dependent on Mohammad for everything. Too weak to forage for myself, I waited like a baby bird in the nest for him to return in evening with water, and Praise Allah, sometimes, food. Mohammad always came "home" before sundown in time for evening prayers. It had been our routine for the last several days at any rate. He'd show me what bits he'd found, we'd eat any food there was, and then, he'd pray.

I was still too mad at Allah to join him.

"I don't get you," I told him, after one particularly sparse day. We'd eaten dry, weevil-infested flour he'd found in a dumpster. My stomach cramped. "Do you think God is listening? Seriously, dude, look around. He wrecked this place and then packed up and left with the rest of the evacuees."

He sat back on his heels. "If you believe that, why did I find you in the mosque?"

I didn't have a good answer so I picked at the straw, snapping the brittle stems in my fingers. "I needed something, I don't know." I looked at him. "Hope?"

"Exactly," he said, as if that explained something. "That's what I get too."

"You get hope from prayer?"

Mohammad nodded. Shyly he stared at the floor, and rolled up the towel he used as a prayer rug. "Plus, it used to make me feel less alone."

But now we had each other. It was the gift Allah had given us both. But, that was a little too vulnerable and awkward, so I teased, "Yeah, I love you too, man."

Wadding up the towel, he threw it at me. It flapped in my face. "Shut up," he laughed, though I thought there might be a bit of an edge in his tone.

"Just kidding," I reiterated, though I wondered if things were more serious for him. I owed him my life, so I said, "Unless you want to, you know... I mean, I could," Merciful Allah, what was I offering? But it was the only thing I knew I had of any value. And, it wasn't like I hadn't gained the skill set to make it work – for one of us, anyway. "It would be no big deal."

The way he looked at me I knew I'd said the wrong thing. Mohammad stood up and I thought he might leave. Instead, he smoothed the filthy fabric of his pants. His gaze focused on everything in the empty office except me. He shook his head, "That's not why I helped you."

"Why did you?"

He frowned at me for a long time. Then, his stomach growled noisily and he shrugged, "Stupidity? I thought how great it would be to have to have another mouth to feed when I could barely fill my own."

"Good thinking," I said with a sarcastic point at my brains. "Plus you can always eat my corpse when I die."

"Yeah, that was what I was really thinking of – stockpiling for future cannibalism."

"Aren't all great friendships based on cannibalism?"

"Without a doubt," he said, finally looking me in the eye. We spent the rest of the night talking about old holos and games and other inconsequentials from Before. I thought we were cool—

... until he didn't come back the next night.

When the sun went down without him, I struggled to the window. I gripped the sill with white knuckles hoping to catch sight of him coming down the street. The place he'd brought me was an empty office building, much of it still under construction. We were far enough from the mosque's spires that I wondered as I always did, where he'd found the strength to carry me so far.

Now I wondered if I'd die here, alone.

My stomach lurched from more than hunger.

Then, I saw him. In my relief, I almost shouted and waved. But just as I lifted my arm, he stopped and looked around furtively. Was he being pursued? I dropped my hand and held my breath. I watched as he slipped into the alcove of a shop's doorway. He undid his pants, slipped them down to his knees, and crouched.

I knew I should have looked away, but even from this distance it was hard not to notice what was missing – or rather, what had never been there in the first place.

Present Day

"Let me get this straight, we're looking for a guy named Mohammad in Egypt? Needle in a haystack, anyone?" Deidre asks with a laugh, as we stroll down the narrow, crowded marketplace streets. A layer of fine dust covers the pavement, but my mind's eye still sees corridors of impassable sand dunes. How did they dig it all out? Or are we walking over someone's grave?

"Or maybe not," I say, absently, my voice straining to be heard over the callers hawking fresh fruit and dried halal meat. The smell of baking bread rises above the press of humanity.

"Not in Egypt? Or a Mohammad that's not a guy?" She's making a joke, but it's not funny. I give her a grimace because I hadn't meant to say anything out loud. I sucked at keeping secrets. Her eyebrow arches at my silence. "Okay. A girl named Mohammad? Well, at least that narrows it down a bit."

"Mohammad is just... Mohammad, okay. Forget I said that. He...." I falter, feeling the guilt crushing down on me like the heat and humidity of this place. I swat at a mosquito. "Look, I don't even know if he's still alive. It's been, what? Forty years?"

We could go to Mecca and pray for guidance.

"Praying has never once helped me," I snarl to Page. "Anyway, we will get to Mecca. I promise."

Eid Al'aray in less than a week, father.

My heart sinks, and I mutter angrily, "I know. We'll make it."

Deidre eyes me suspiciously. "You know look you old when you talk to people that no one else can see, right?"

Just past the tech and silk stalls, we turn the corner, and it looms over me, literally casting me in the shadow of my own, sordid past. The building looks much as it had when I brought Mohammad here all those years ago.

The tall, forbidding white-washed walls that enclose the compound glow faintly pinkish in the setting sun. Armed men stand in silent sentry at the cardinal points, unnoticed by most of the crowd below. Beyond the walls, brilliant floodlights illuminate an opulent palace with ornately curved, gold-painted window frames and tall, thin turrets. It could be a miniature Egyptian Taj Majhal, but I know it's really hell on earth.

"I always knew you were kinky, but, what, you're into boys now?" She looks at the building I'm staring at and shakes her head. "I can't believe we came all this way just to go to an illegal brothel. Can't you find things like this in New York? And really, is this cool during Ramadan? Before you go on hajj?" Deidre's lips form a thin line of mock disapproval. She's trying to tease, but I'm not there with her. I'm somewhere else entirely. Somewhere far in the past.

"No, there's no place quite like this." My voice is fragile.

It surprises me to realize how scared I am. The chill that snakes up my spine has everything to do with standing in the long shadow of this place. I left here with the clothes on my back in bloody ruins, but now I return as an internationally recognized wire-wizard, LINK-thief extraordinaire. But still my knees threaten to buckle.

Sensing I haven't been listening, Deidre drops her act and considers our plan. "I don't know what you're planning, but I'm not going to be able to get my gun in there."

"Getting *in* is rarely the problem. Trust me, it's getting out that's hard," I say, a cold dread settling deep in my guts.

I'm standing perfectly still in the middle of the sidewalk, causing the flow of foot traffic to ripple and reform around us. A man passing us looks at where I'm staring and clucks his tongue. Women mutter, some in derision, some in prayer.

It's ironic, really. They're disgusted by what they *think* I'm after in this place, but they'd have a bit more sympathy for the plight of the person I left here.

I ignore them all. A multitude of thoughts jitter through my head, none of them terribly helpful, when a familiar — no, exceptionally memorable — red-haired figure strolls up to the front door of my past hell and pulls out a key like he owns the place.

"Morningstar?" Deidre sounds as shocked as I am. "What in God's green earth is he doing here?"

"I suspect if Morningstar is involved, God has nothing to do with it," I say.

Agreed.

A MOUSE THAT ROARED: How Free Access Saved North Africa
By Keela Ryū
Forthcoming from Doubleday Harcourt Penguin, 2111

Excerpted interview of Mouse; footnote commentary by "Page"/Strife

"I'd hoped that the LINK would be the great equalizer. Like the Internet before it, the LINK started out mostly as a military venture. The LINK was envisioned as a way to command vast armies from the comfort of the war room, and for troops to spread important information quickly amongst themselves. I guess it worked like a charm during the Medusa War. Whatever.[1] That was before my time[2]. All I know was that it didn't take long for some enterprising folks to realize how awesome it would be to have all that shit you used to have to carry around to communicate[3] conveniently tucked away in your head, ready to use, literally, at a blink.

And it *is* awesome – if you have it."

---

1. It is unclear why my father seems angry or dismissive here. Perhaps he is thinking about the saying popular in countries occupied by the peacekeeping force during the Medusa War: "Forget battle plans: the fastest thing LINKed between two peaceforcers is the location of the nearest bar."

2. Not really. He was six.

3. Historians say that this may have included any number of external wireless or mobile cellular devices. From what I can uncover, before the LINK many people had a separate phone, Internet-accessing device, electronic calendar, GPS and potentially dozens of other individual methods of coordinating and managing their personal and business communications.

Chapter 2
Morningstar

Cairo, Egypt
Present Day

The blinding brightness of the desert sun reminded me of Them. I suppose, unconsciously, that was what drew me to Cairo in the first place – memories of the celestial city and my former, shining glory at God's left hand.

I slid into the darkened foyer quietly, hoping not to alert the staff. The sudden chill of the air-conditioned interior made my flesh shiver. Despite my attempt at stealth, one of the boys appeared at my side in an instant. My eyes hadn't adjusted so I squinted at him, as he held out his hand for my jacket, "What is your pleasure this evening, master?"

"Turn up the damn heat," I muttered, refusing to relinquishing the linen suit coat I wore. "It's as cold as Hell in here."

He bowed his head, complying with my demands instantly. The hum of the fans dropped a notch as he LINKed his command. "Anything else?"

Truth be told, whenever I thought of God my mood fouled. I wanted nothing more than complete wicked debauchery to take my mind off the past. "Send up dinner and—" Mentally, I tried to run through the list of each of the boys in the house and their special skills, but my brain drew a blank. "—someone very pretty I can hurt terribly."

"Yes, master," he said with another slight bow. "I'll be up as soon as food is ready."

I looked at him intently for the first time and noticed his angelic, nano-enhanced, youthful face. His dark curls and ice-gray eyes reminded me of someone I once loved. "Yes," I snarled. "See that you are."

Blackout

Michael was always beautiful in a way I could never be. His faith shone like a beacon, sharp and fierce, cutting through any darkness – even my own. He looked so much like Them that sometimes the very core of my being ached at the sight of him. Often I think God created him just to taunt me.

I hated Michael.

Yet despite what many would have you believe, it wasn't always so. Once, in this very city, I offered my hand in friendship.

Admittedly, when I first saw him perched among the ruins of downtown Cairo, my intention was to corrupt him. I was pushing a canoe along the narrow tributaries and by-ways of the Nile's new landscape. Gliding through an artificial canyon of half sunken buildings, the boat bumped along rapids caused by debris. The moon blanketed everything in a soft silver, silent light. Pigeons huddled sleepily in muddy, shit-spattered nests wedged into window crevices. In the eddies that formed in the corners, human detritus swirled: plastic cups, cigarette butts, aluminum cans, and a child's toy doll. I smiled. I couldn't help but find the destruction lovely.

Michael squatted like Rodin's famous "Thinker" atop a ragged bit of the remains of the Opera House. Moonlight etched the edges of his finely sculpted body causing his muscles to stand out in sharp relief against the inky darkness.

Though he wore human costume, I recognized him instantly.

"Admiring Mother's handiwork?" I asked.

"So many dead," he said, giving me only a cursory glance before returning to his survey of the necropolis. "What were They thinking?"

The hurt in his tone made my heart flutter. It sounded almost like a loss of faith. Perhaps it was something I could capitalize on. So I had to ask, "Don't *you* know?"

As I came up beside him, the side of my canoe scraped against the edge of the Opera House wall. Gnats congregated in a thick swarm the instant I stopped moving. He watched me as I batted at them uselessly. "I suppose you're here to gloat."

"Why would I dance when Mother's people are drowned? That's your crew's M.O., not mine."

Michael stiffened at my reference though he tried it hide it. His battalion *had* danced when the Israelites escaped captivity in Egypt and Father, that tricky old bastard, had admonished them for it. A small taste of my own shame for loving Allah more than His mud creatures, but that was another story.

Michael shrugged as if I had no power to sting him, "Go away, Morningstar."

I brooded at him silently for a long moment. My neck muscles strained to watch him on his lofty perch a story or more above my boat. Always at his feet, I thought with a snarl. Forget that. I used my oar to push off again. "As you wish, Captain."

Perhaps my use of the honorific changed his attitude or, maybe, he recognized in our little exchange a shared disgust for the mysterious ways of our maker, but before I reached the next turn, he called out. "Wait."

Glancing over my shoulder, I stopped paddling and let the boat drift. He leaped gracefully from the building, spreading his arms, like wings, to slow his descent. Lightly, his booted feet touched the black water's surface. He walked across the glittering wave tops like they were asphalt.

Show-off.

"Let me come with you," my bitter enemy said.

He had no idea where I was going or why I was there, yet he stood beside my canoe with his palm outstretched in friendship. Most times, I would have taken great pleasure in spitting and telling him in excruciating detail how he could fuck himself.

But when I looked up into that face – that beatific, inhumanly beautiful face so much like Hers – I recalled how it felt when we were together, as one. The memory stabbed me like a physical pain. My trembling hand grasped his, and I found myself saying, "Of course, my prince."

Present Day

I'd hardly finished trussing up my boy when the front desk buzzed. Irritated, I tightened a leather strap roughly. "What?" I shouted at the video phone in the wall.

"Someone at the gate."

I swore. There was nothing like being interrupted to make my mood even darker. I didn't spare the screen a second of my attention. Instead, I continued to buckle and clip, delighting in the strangled moans of my captive. "Surely, God gave you free will so you could exercise it, child. Make a decision."

"Yes, master," the voice said contritely. "Normally, I would not allow access by a non-member, but I think you should see who it is."

It had better be Allah himself, I thought. I flicked my glance at the screen near the door. At first I saw nothing but a fist holding up a credit counter, but then, briefly, just beyond, I caught sight of gray-blond curls on a face that made angels fall.

Not God then, but Her mother.

DISASTER IN EGYPT
Dams Fail, Millions Die

Associated Press
February 21, 2059

Aswan, Egypt—At approximately eight o'clock GMT, the main structure of the High Dam at Aswan, Egypt collapsed, sending upwards of 43 million cubic meters of water rushing downriver. The second dam, called the New Dam, failed almost instantly. Though an evacuation order was sent automatically via the LINK, few had time to escape before the flood destroyed Luxor and ravaged Cairo, the largest city in North Africa and home to over nine million people. The dams supplied power to a large section of the Africa and the Middle East, all of which is in a complete blackout.

Little official information is coming from the region at this time, but individual reports on the ground suggest that the disaster has been made worse by the fact that much of the area was undergoing the transition from oil-to-electric powered vehicles. While most countries have made the switch after the Medusa war fifteen years ago, the oil-rich countries have held on until the reservoirs depleted. Due to construction, many of the roads out of the affected areas were impassable.

Also many people did not receive news of the impending disaster. Nearly two-thirds of the population of Egypt is under the age of majority, and many live at a poverty-level that excludes nanobot natal nexus vaccine, sometimes called the 'bot shot, critical to LINK installation.

What caused the dam to fail is not known at this time.

Chapter 3
Mouse

"What are the odds," Deidre keeps repeating, like she can't quite believe in the will of the Almighty even after everything she's been through.

We're standing on the stoop of my past. The shade of the awning is surprisingly deep. I've forgotten about the quality of desert light which, like binary, is either on or off.

The hand that holds the credit counter up to the electronic eye shakes. I try to control the tremors by reminding myself that I'm no longer a child, or a victim, or in desperate need of anything but vengeance.

"Why is Morningstar here, of all places?" Deidre asks again.

I fight the urge to roll my eyes. "It takes a two-by-four to get through to you, doesn't it?"

Those cute, clueless little eyebrows scrunch together. "What does that mean?"

I'm saved from explaining the will of Allah by the door. It swings inward, gracing us with a blast of cool, dry air and the sight of a criminally underage pretty young thing. My guts clench at the sight of his studied glamour and distant demeanor, and I wonder: did I ever carry off that kind of presence or did I always seem like a rabbit ready to bolt?

He gives me a long, measuring look, like he's seen my kind before, but his eyes widen when he takes in Deidre. "Are you at the right place, sister?"

"We're together," she says meaningfully and takes my hand. I'm comforted by her gesture, but I think, *I wish*.

He spaces out for a moment, like he might be LINKing. After a half a second, he blinks. Then the kid shrugs delicately and steps aside. "Enter."

Inside, the lighting is dim. Ornate rugs hung for decoration bring the walls closer, imparting a sense of ducking into a tent. Soft pillows and low chaise lounges scattered across the wide, open floor continue the illusion.

Strains of belly dance music drift through the heavily incensed air.

It was a tourist trap for pervs.

As I glance around the opulently decorated room at the beautiful boys of every size, shape and color, mouse.net hums to life and behind my eyes. As my gaze lights on each lounging guy, prices and erotic specialties flash up in a friendly, inviting, expensive font.

The boy who'd opened the door for Deidre and me deftly separates the credit counter from my hand. The rest of the evening's transactions can be done via the ethereal cloud banks of the LINK/mouse.net, but you have to have "cash" or its portable equivalent to enter. When the boy swipes my counter, I smile.

You spiked the card. Page astutely guesses.

I nod. Already a nasty bit of malware is quietly making its way through the financial byways of this business, rooting out hidden accounts, off-shore investments, and personal nest eggs. By morning the whole of it will be anonymously transferred to charity. I may be a fairly crappy Muslim, but one pillar of Islam I never shirk is almsgiving. Granted, most of the money I give away never belonged to me in the first place, but that seems like a minor technicality. I'm sure God understands.

Unfortunately, the young men of the room are trained to notice even the most casual sign of interest, and one of them decides my smile and slight nod of agreement with Page qualifies. Beside me, Deidre makes a disgusted gagging noise when she reads his particular skill set.

He's black-skinned like Mohammad, and his delicate features remind me a bit of him as well. But he's too tall, too muscular, and his voice far too deep when he asks, "What is your pleasure?"

But before I can wave him off, the door boy does. He looks at us both earnestly, like we've violated some taboo. I start to worry that they've detected my wyrm before it can do its work, then he says, "The master wishes to see you upstairs."

Dee gives me a concerned look, but I shrug. "Morningstar might have the information I'm looking for," I tell her. "We might as well."

She gestures for the boy to lead the way, but he hardly needs to. I remember the way to the master's suite. How could I forget?

Blackout

I never talked to Mohammad about what I'd seen that night. There were other clues, like the scars on his chest, but I kept my questions to myself. I was too afraid he'd leave me again. I no longer needed him for my survival, but I depended on him in new ways now. Besides, whatever he was exactly, it didn't matter; I liked him. He was my friend.

Not to mention the fact that we'd finally landed a gig that had *real* prospects – work that neither of us could do on his own. We'd become warhound poachers.

Night time in the desert, especially during the blackout, was seriously dark. The dams had powered all electricity for much of North Africa, and all that was gone now.

Instead, a glittering galaxy of stars stretched widely overhead and you could watch the battalions of communication satellites drift lazily across the sky. The view above went on forever, while, in the city, you could see less than a few meters ahead, if that.

Despite the poor visibility, Mohammad and I were sure-footed as we made our way along the roof runs. No more than a haphazard collection of old scaffolding and two-by-fours – whatever people could find and lash together, really, even once precious bits of Persian rugs – the crude bridges spanned the streets that the desert had quickly reclaimed after the first of the spring sandstorms. In this neighborhood, the western edge of what was once Islamic Cairo, the streets belonged to the asp and the fennec fox. No human dared tread here, not with the threat of sink holes or cave-ins of unseen, buried structures.

But none of that bothered us; we were giddy with the prospect of another "kill."

Mohammad laughed with unrestrained excitement. "Tonight we're going to bag us a puppy dog."

We were excited because the Americans had recently started sending their warhounds into the city proper. Ostensibly, the dog's job was to sniff out survivors. That, my friends, was bullshit. We found they didn't much respond when one of us pretended to be wounded or even called for help in English. No, to catch these doggies, you had to throw them a "bone." The scent of resources attracted them: credits, oil, or – luckily for us – any working bits of machinery, even memory chips.

Chips, we had in spades.

You see, Mohammad had some kind of second sense when it came to finding salvage. His mad retrieving luck had kept him from the clutches of the beggar kings, Deadboys, golems and parasites. It had kept us in food when I was recovering. Like me, he was small, bone-thin, fast, and agile. He could climb, shimmy, and spelunk with the best of them. Yet, somehow, when others came back empty-handed, Mohammad would find some weird bit of pre-apocalyptic magic that he could sell to Ahmed, the fence.

Mostly Ahmed would simply trade a beating for the goodies. But sometimes, if he was drunk or sentimental or if we were lucky, he'd name a fair price: fresh water bottles, uncontaminated food or, praise Allah, medicine. Antibiotics were the new gold.

Once Mohammad and I teamed up, Ahmed's prices got a whole hell of a lot better. I guess he didn't figure he could take both of us as easily. Plus, we'd started bringing in the good stuff – "learning" memory chips, motherboards, even weaponry. Shit the Russians or the UN or the Americans didn't want "on the street." Shit the black market ran on. We didn't know it, but we were making Ahmed a bloody grand sheik.

Ironic, given that he'd initially turned our trade down. He poo-pooed tech in favor of more obvious goodies, until I explained to him exactly what we had on offer and how valuable this stuff really was.

"You know," I said out loud, as we approached the end of the runs, "If I could get access to the LINK, we wouldn't need Ahmed."

"Yeah, well, good luck with that," Mohammad said, stopping to peer over the edge of the building. A wide boulevard had put an end to our bridge ways. The soft, silvery moonlight revealed a vast shifting dune below. Here and there in the valleys, the half-exposed frame of a car glittered metallically, its paint having long ago been stripped bare by the biting sand winds. French style lamp posts, too, occasionally triumphed timidly over the encroached desert – just tips and bits visible. It was impassible for us, but, to the robots, it was the Champs d'Elysses. And, we figured, the most likely route the Americans would choose.

"I heard a rumor," I said, coming up beside him. "The *zabaaliin* hired some nerds to start cobbling together all that garbage of theirs." The *zabaaliin* were kind of our version of untouchables, they were a sect of Coptic Christians that used to officially collect trash and sort it by hand. The end of the world had made them rich. Their stock piles of crap turned into a mountain of resale when everyone lost everything. "They're trying to build some kind of ancient land-line dial-up to the LINK."

"Dial-up to the LINK? Are they fucking out of their minds? Why not just stand on the roof and sing the 'whale song' and see if you can connect?"

I made a noise. "Why couldn't it work? People used to use hardware to talk to each other all the time."

"I'm just saying, taking a horse and buggy on the autobahn might not work out so well for the horse."

"Why? Your analogy sucks, man," I told him. "The cars would just have to go around the horse, you'd still get where you were going. All roads are good."

"Yeah, but they don't all lead to the LINK. You can't just interface with dial-up. What's your OS? The LINK is a full package. You'd need some kind decoder ring or something, and who understands all the bio-binary that makes up the LINK, anyway?"

I had to shrug. How the LINK worked was still a mystery to me back then. From my point of view it might as well have been magic. Taking apart machines I knew. The rest? Not so much. "I still think it could work," I muttered.

Perhaps if we hadn't been half-heartedly arguing we would have heard the warhound's approach. My eyes should have at least been on the street, and not staring thoughtfully up into the wide, glittering expanse of the universe thinking it was about as far away as LINK access. A shooting star arched into existence in a flash. I'd thought it might be an omen, but for what, I didn't know. Below, the hell hound had trained its sights and the gun had discharged silently. The next thing I became aware of was the floor giving way with a great explosion and we fell.

Like a star.

Like a morning star.

Because he'd readied the rope by securing it to a load-bearing wall, Mohammad's arm got caught by the nylon. Instinct caused him to grab hold when the roof gave way. His shoulder dislocated in a jerk. He was suspended like a marionette and slammed into the interior wall, breaking his nose and crushing his wrist.

At the time, I thanked Allah the rope hadn't twisted around his neck.

Later, I wondered if that fact it hadn't was proof positive that God hated us.

For myself, I had the minor misfortune of having the wind knocked out of me and being the recipient of several nasty cuts and bruises. I was saved from worse damage by having actually fallen onto a corpse wearing a shock-absorbing flak jacket, but, believe it or not, I didn't notice that fact immediately. I laid there, cradled in rat-gnawed dead arms, listening to Mohammad's screams wondering if there were enough datachips in the world to pay for the intensive care he'd need.

I suppose it seems uncharitable to be thinking of how much his injuries would cost us, but try to imagine Cairo after the flood. The closest hospital might as well have been on Mars. The Red Crescent had bugged out after only the first few weeks, even MSF had left us eventually. I'd seen kids die from infections that could have been prevented by a little clean water and the application of a simple skin spray.

Breaking a wrist meant life as a cripple. At best.

To my credit, I began to pull myself upright as soon as I could breathe properly. "Hang on," I shouted to my friend, totally aware of the irony. "I'll be right there."

The weight of my palm crunched through the soft bits of the corpse's ribs. Like rice grains, maggots rained down on my hand. That this was a human body still didn't entirely register, however. A lot of stuff attracted flies and smelled of death and decay in those days. Plus, the falling rubble had flattened what I hadn't. I probably would never have figured it out, if not for the dull-green glowing numbers on the watch strapped to her decimated wrist. The seconds continued to tick around the analog face. The open roof let in a shaft of moonlight. I could make out long, thin fingers and delicate tear-shaped nails. Rats and maggots had made quick work of the soft bits, but the bones had been laced with bio-steel. Adamantium, the soldiers jokingly called it. I jumped to my feet. Merciful Allah, I'd landed on a peaceforcer.

Finding the body was a coup, but the living needed me more than the dead. I left the soldier where she lay and I tried to figure out how to help Mohammad. While I'd been busy catching my breath, he gotten his good hand on the nylon. I might be able to scale the wall, but I had nothing but my teeth to cut the rope. Plus, then Mohammad would fall. He was already pretty messed up. Did he really need a swan dive onto rubble on top of all that?

The room we now occupied was once someone's apartment. A quick survey turned up some useful things. As quickly as I could I hauled a sofa underneath Mohammad's gently swaying form. "Get it upright," he suggested.

I was already on that. A number of angry rats bailed from their nest when I tipped the threadbare couch on its side. The tips of Mohammad's feet nearly reached. "Shit," I commented, looking around for anything taller.

"I think I can loosen the rope," he said through clenched teeth. "Just make sure it's steady."

If he wasn't hurt, what happened next would have been comedic. There was a lot of twisting and swearing but he got the rope loose all right. Landing on the slender edge of the couch was hardly easy, especially given the short drop and the shock of pain when his arm was freed. I held steady, but his feet weren't. He toppled. I lunged to catch him, and both of us bounced hard onto the concrete roof chunks. Two seconds later the couch slammed into us.

I valiantly saved Mohammad from further damage by letting my face take the brunt of the couch's momentum. Heroic, no?

What followed was an unprintable tirade of the choicest words in both English and Arabic, and a lot of inspecting various injuries and more ear-scorching expletives. In the end, I righted the couch and we sat on it deject-edly and debated the finer points of limb dislocation. Mohammad tried to assure me that popping his shoulder back into place was easy. He'd seen people do it in the holos all the time. Yet, when I actually gave it a try, he had nothing but criticism for my technique.

"I think maybe holo magic isn't easily repeatable in real life," I suggested after our last attempt ended in more swearing and a few tears. Not that I noticed the tears. That would violate the man code. "We need, you know, an expert."

"Like a doctor?" Mohammad sniffed.

"No, an actor," I said with a smile, but neither of us laughed. Instead, we stared at the floor again because we both knew how unlikely it was to find help of any kind any time soon. Except, I'd momentarily forgotten about the corpse. I hopped up excitedly, nearly tripping on some stray bit of roof.

"What are you doing?" Mohammad asked, as I shuffled through the debris like a frantic dog.

When I found the glow-in-the-dark watch. I held up the mummified arm triumphantly. "Tah-dah!"

Mohammad failed to share my excitement. "Wow, an antique. Thank Allah, we're saved."

I had to admire someone who could muster that amount of dripping sar-casm while in screaming agony, but his uncustomary lack of vision frustrat-ed me. To be fair, he probably literally lacked the ability to see the entirety of my find. The moon had moved. I should be impressed he could make out the watch from that distance. "This antique is attached to a dead peaceforcer, my friend."

His breath sucked in an excited hiss. It was several seconds before he could distill his thoughts, "Fully-loaded?"

That was a good question, and one I hadn't had the opportunity to inves-tigate. Mohammad shouted helpful suggestions while I ransacked what remained of Officer Dead. She offered up one analog watch, a mostly uneat-en combat-model flack jacket, boots, an UN-issued credit counter, and a

Lawgiver. I flinched away from the gun because, well, I'm a sworn pacifist, but also because of rumors that, like their comic book namesakes, they were DNA-triggered. If someone else tried to use the Lawgiver besides its owner, the gun blew up.

Greed briefly overwhelmed Mohammad's pain. "Can you imagine what the peaceforce will pay to get that back?"

I wasn't nearly as comfortable at the idea of haggling with the United Nations Peacekeeping Force over a dead captain's service weapon. I could far too easily imagine a scenario where we ended up in one of their ubiquitous "interrogation" cells. "Uh, we should sell it to Ahmed."

"He is going to rip us off. Again."

Well, there was that. "Maybe there's another middle-man we could use. Someone with a lot of experience with peaceforcers."

"You know one of those?"

Actually, I did. Granted, I had only just recently escaped his employ with my life, but I thought I was too smart to end up fucked over again. With Mohammad at my side and an ace of a Lawgiver up my sleeve, I figured we were damn near invincible. So, with a smug tone, I said, "He has a private doctor, too."

And so it was agreed.

But before we left, Mohammad insisted I let him look for something in the apartment. The way he instantly headed for the bathroom, I was certain he was looking for some linen to fashion into a sling. I found a sheet in a closet, while he was still rooting in the toilet. "Hey," I shouted. "I got one!"

He came rushing out, but said, "What the hell is that?"

"For your arm," I said. At his frown, I added, "A sling? That's what you're looking for, right?"

"No, I—" he stopped, and his mouth as worked around something he must have decided he couldn't say. "Forget it."

With Mohammad's injuries we had to be careful crossing back into the city. It was hard enough for the able-bodied to run the gauntlet of Deadboys, rat kings, golems, Gorgons, and ghosts. In less than a kilometer, we'd already had to avoid the notice of three zombies.

Like their namesakes, zombies weren't terribly clever. You had to be quick, but they made so much racket moaning and groaning that you were usually well aware of them before they even got a whiff of you. The best defense against zombies was to run away. Fast. Hunger had wasted them into mindless, easily exhausted skeletons wrapped in rotting, filthy rags.

Luckily, fast was a relative term when it came to zombies. Mohammad wasn't up for a hundred yard dash, but with a few quick turns and twists, we kept our distance from their mindless slobbering hunger.

There, but for the grace of God and the mercy of Allah, go I.

Although the ones that freaked me out even more were the ghosts. Women in long black shrouds of abbya, their faces invisible, drifted like shades from shadow to shadow. Silent as the grave, they never begged or jabbered mindlessly. They hardly seemed human any more.

I caught sight of one just before she ducked into a narrow alley. *Another bad omen*, I thought, with a shiver. Anxiously, I tugged at Mohammad's good arm.

Apparently having also caught sight of the ghost stopped Mohammad dead in his tracks. His barely-there Adam's apple trembled underneath wisps of beard. "Was she looking at us?"

Who could tell with all that fabric? Yet I'd had the sense of being observed, too. "Maybe," I said, but ghosts were usually harmless. "Why?"

I watched his face as he struggled to find an answer. I saw a myriad of emotions twitch into existence before disappearing: pity, fear, and something I didn't understand or perhaps misinterpreted that might have been longing. Finally, he shrugged, "No reason."

Liar. This was the stuff I wouldn't touch, so I bit my lip.

"We should go," I reminded him. We picked our way along the street carefully. The sun was starting to rise, and the city, broken though it was, began to wake.

Truthfully, it never slept, but in daylight Cairo made its shabby attempt at normalcy. Broken, electronic muezzins warbled a call to prayer. I glanced at Mohammad wondering if he'd heed it, but he had a grim expression on his face that stopped all questions. Anyway, this far in into the city where we didn't know the lay of the land, it would be dangerous to stop.

We'd reached the first of the high watermarks. Brown stained the walls to the second-story windows. The river smell, an oddly compelling scent of death, fish and green, hung in the humid air.

We were nearly there. I propped Mohammad up against the wall of a nearby mosque. "We need to hide this stuff."

"Why?" he asked. "I thought it was our bargaining chip."

"Yeah, well, you know Ahmed? Franklin is much worse. He'd just as soon kill us for the stuff." I found a loose cobblestone in the mosque's wall and began pulling.

Mohammad watched my progress with a dubious look. "Are you sure this is a good idea? I mean, going to this guy?"

Of course it wasn't, but sometimes a deal with the devil was better than nothing at all – at least, that was how it seemed at the time.

After most sane people evacuated, certain enterprising citizens took up residence in formerly public spaces. One such person was Franklin del Rosa, the guy we were here to see, who took a shine to *Beit El Suhaymi*. The building that was now Franklin's house had been built by a wealthy merchant in the mid-sixteen hundreds and preserved for centuries as a museum of domestic life.

Even if the building itself weren't already famous, the armed guards that surrounded it made Franklin's place stand out. Dark, serious-faced men in bright white *galabiyaya* paced the rooftop with automatic rifles. They protected the solar generator that powered Franklin's electricity and running water. Franklin, rumor had it, had friends everywhere, even among the scientist underground, the sort that could design and build a working generator out of the decimated scraps of Cairo in a matter of months.

The guards watched us, but didn't impede our progress. They were used to scraggly, desperate boys making their way to this place.

"Where are we?" Mohammad's eyes scanned the men on the roof nervously.

"Franklin's place," I said. "Pretty much hell on earth, if you ask me."

Mohammad's eyes went wide. "What are we doing here, then?"

Lightly, I tapped him on the arm, which sent him into near-convulsion. "Do you want a pain pill for that arm of yours or not?"

"Yeah," he managed to say through gritted teeth. "Fuck yeah, I do."

"Then we have to walk through hell."

So resolved, I knocked at the heavy teak door. I chewed my lip nervously as we waited on the doorstep for an answer.

Down the road, a Bedouin market set up not far from the spot where we'd stopped to stow most of the peaceforcers' gear. The sharp cries of sellers hawking their wares echoed on along the wall. The scent of baking flat bread wafted through the air, making my mouth water. For the desert people, the disaster seemed to have meant nothing. Their lives remained mostly unchanged.

Just as I raised my hand to knock again, the door opened. Franklin himself glared sleepily over the threshold at us. Tall and lithe, and like many Nubians, his skin was the color of cinder. His hair hung in gnarled dreads past his shoulders, interwoven with sparkling mini-LEDs that glittered beneath the thick ropes like stars in fog. In the corner of his right temple sat the tell-tale almond-shaped lump of the LINK. He wore cut-off shorts and an orange, silk, short-sleeved shirt that showed off a bicep tattoo of the Goddess Bast, surrounded by hieroglyphics. Her yellow-cat eyes, sparkled with holo-ink, and seemed to blink lazily at me.

At first I thought he might shoo us away, but then he seemed to recognize me. "Ah, it's the little rat I thought I'd lost," he cooed delightedly. His eyes lit on Mohammad and took him in appraisingly. "Oh, and look, you finally brought someone home to mama."

Present Day

Satan sits casually, like a prince, in an overstuffed chair, his hand resting on the naked ass of a boy, bound and straining. I would have been shocked, but the tableau has so obviously staged to provoke the exact reaction Deidre gives him.

"Oh for the love of God," she continues the rant that started from the moment we walked in.

Ooooh. Probably a bad choice of words, since Morningstar's eyes narrow threateningly. "What brings you to my humble abode, Deidre McMannus?"

"Actually," I clear my throat. "Coming here was my idea."

Morningstar turns his gaze to me for the first time. It's a strange thing. We've met several times, but each meeting is like our first. The years haven't aged him, but his hair is now close-cropped, though still the brilliant red I remember. "I know you," he says, but he's not certain.

I'm not sure if I should remind him of our last meeting. It had to do with his antichrist girlfriend and the rogue AI named "Victory" they wanted me to contain. I struggle to keep my eyes on his face instead of the shivering, tormented flesh beside him. "Look, it doesn't matter. I think it's significant that we're all here at the same time. Insh'allah and all that crap. You're going to help me find Mohammad," I insist.

Tipping his head back, Satan laughs. "The prophet, like so many before him, is gone, I assure you."

Crappy Muslim or not, his blasphemy momentarily stuns me speechless. In my head, I hear Page take in a breath.

"You need to let that boy go," Deidre says to no one in particular. She can't appear to do anything but stare, open-mouthed at the skin and bondage gear that I desperately try not to see. "That cannot be comfortable."

"It's not meant to be," Morningstar assures her offhandedly. He swings his gaze back to me and seems to study me, open curiosity on his cruelly handsome face. "Why are you looking for the prophet now, during Ramadan?"

"Because I betrayed him and I need to apologize," I say, not bothering to correct Morningstar's assumption.

"Oh? How very interesting," Morningstar's fingers absently stroke the bare bottom beside him, eliciting a tortured moan. "And you think God wants me to help you?"

"Why else would Allah bring us all together?"

A MOUSE THAT ROARED: How Free Access Saved North Africa
By Keela Ryū
Forthcoming from Doubleday Harcourt Penguin, 2111

Excerpted interview of Mouse; footnote commentary by "Page"/Strife

"It is my contention that if everyone had equal access to the LINK regardless of age or ability to pay before the dams broke, Cairo would have been spared much of the ugliness that festered during the Blackout Years. That's easy to say now, in retrospect, of course, given that my hypothesis all but proved itself when mouse.net took off[4].

But back then, my opinion, provided had anyone been able to hear it, would have been mocked as naively simple.

Maybe it was.

Certainly, Cairo had other issues[5], but from my perspective they only got worse in the intervening years before I birthed the shadow-LINK of mouse.net.

Infrastructure crashed when the dams broke. Roads heaved and shattered, bridges got swept away, and anyone with a working vehicle left as soon as they could. Remember, too, the last war for oil[6] had glassed our petrol supply, and so Egypt, like the rest of the world, had been in the

---

4. Many historians do, in fact, allow that mouse.net may have played a major role in the earliest reconstruction efforts in Egypt, particularly in its role as a clearinghouse for barter notes which bolstered the failed economy. Also, as mouse.net's reputation grew, Cairo attracted a new tourist trade of crackers, hackers, and other digitati who made pilgrimages to its birthplace. One should also not discount the mass appeals to the Muslim world sent out via mouse.net by my father himself for alms to be sent to Egypt, not to mention his own donations once his information brokering business boomed. Currently, my father's income, the taxes on it as well as donations he gives, makes up over two percent of Egypt's gross national product.

5. Mouse.net, for instance, could not solve the food shortage problem. Before the Blackout Years, Egypt imported over fifty percent of its food. Now, of course, that percentage is much lower due the vast farms run on the floodplain managed by the cult of Osirus (popularly referred to as the "Deadboys").

6. The Medusa War, World War III. Referring to WWIII as "the last war for oil" is seen as akin to those in the American South who refer to the Civil War as "the war of Northern aggression."

process replacing its roads with electric rails... all of which were powered by the Aswan Dams[7].

Officially, the only way in or out was military transport. Otherwise, money talked. Barter, less so. There wasn't a lot inside Cairo that people wanted outside... except things that quickly ended up being controlled by the beggar kings, pimps, mob bosses, and other greedy, unethical, LINKed sorts.

See how everything comes right back to that business of access?"

---

7. This is known as the great irony of the Blackout Years. Near-instantaneous communication is possible with the LINK, and thus many in Cairo knew that the dams had broken, but the power went out immediately taking with it most people's ability to escape. The flood itself came very quickly, perhaps too fast for an organized evacuation plan, but, based on the survival rate of the monsoon in Bangladesh two years prior to India's switch to rail, many historians suggest the death toll might have been significantly lower in Cairo as well had it not been transitioning.

Chapter 4
Morningstar

Cairo, Egypt
Present Day

The fierce intensity of the little Arab and his strange proposition intrigued me. Had the prophet returned? And why come to me? Surely, Michael was a better choice for such a hunt. Unless...

On the last day you shall be reprieved.

Was it time already?

I stood up and gave the boy's butt a hard slap, mostly for Dee's benefit, "All right," I said. "Why not?"

The noise my captive made caused Deidre to pale most exquisitely. I allowed myself a small, evil smile. Her companion frowned and asked, "So where do you think he is?"

"The prophet? Have you checked Medina or maybe Mecca?"

"Don't be an ass," the little man said with a surprising amount of pluck, though at least he had the wisdom to nervously check my response. I merely watched him impassively, trying to place his face. I was more than certain we'd met before. Those ears of his stuck out so familiarly.

"Mouse," I said, with sudden memory. "Or was it Christian? Yes, that was it. Christian in search of the prophet? Indeed."

"Yeah, can we just get on with it?" Despite his best efforts, I could see that he was unnerved by my little plaything's discomfort.

"No hurry, and anyway, I have things—" I ran my hand along the quivering, exposed body "—to finish first. We'll meet in an hour. You two can... amuse yourself downstairs?" Deidre made a comment about my heritage that was surprisingly accurate. "Then at the cafe across the street?"

Mouse nodded, and they left.

"They didn't even say good-bye," I remarked to my shuddering prisoner, as the door latched behind their retreating forms. "How rude. Let's see now, where were we?"

He groaned in anticipation.

Except now I was far too distracted to enjoy the diversion, thus, in little less than a half hour I found myself at the restaurant. Garish tin Ramadan lanterns sparkled where they hung along the awning. With the sun down, it was time for *iftar*, the first meal after the fast. The cafe was near capacity and filled with the laughter and chatter of late night revelers. Festive streamers had been strung along the ceiling and danced among clouds of tobacco smoke. Through the press, I spotted Deidre's tousle of blond hair near the window.

She looked up at me with pure disgust, "What would your mother say?"

I chuckled. "Mother is surprisingly tolerant of sexual diversity. You should see what Her bonobos do."

Dee snorted.

Mouse, at least, offered me a seat.

From the smears on the plates in front of them, it was clear they'd nearly finished their dinners. So I used the touch pad at the table to order myself a cup of *karkaday*, a strong hibiscus tea, and dessert.

Deidre continued to cluck her tongue at me. Mouse and I watched each other warily. Finally, I asked him the question that had been on my mind for a while, "When was the last time you saw Mohammad?"

"During the Blackout Years here, in Cairo," he said.

I nodded. It made sense. "Yes," I told him. "I met a prophet then, too."

Blackout

I never trusted Father. He always had a plan. If God destroyed Egypt – a favorite target for holy wrath – again, I suspected it was because He was sending yet another prophet into the wilderness.

Originally, I'd come to Egypt to find that person and stop them, but now I had Michael as a tag-along. Of course, his presence here seemed to confirm my suspicions that Mother was up to something.

He'd positioned himself in the back of the canoe. This meant I couldn't see him, and my back felt rather exposed. He was the one with the flaming sword, after all. It also meant that he was steering. Michael always did have a thing about being in charge.

We followed the current northward around the island. The waterway narrowed to trickle and the river became impassable. We were forced to portage over algae-slick ruins of the Egyptian Museum, keeping a watch out for the darkly glittering eyes of Nile crocodile. The wreckage formed a waterfall.

The river softly trickled over the stone and steel, but the spray that misted our faces smelled slightly of sewage.

"You never said why you were here," Michael noted, as we set the canoe down on the other side. He kept his voice low. Nearby, the Deadboys had their headquarters – Cairo Tower, which had somehow withstood the onslaught of the flood. The structure loomed over us, a darker shadow against the blackness of the night.

"No, I didn't," I agreed, wondering if I should investigate the Deadboys for a prophet. Would Father be that ironic and place one of His messengers among the Goddess worshipers? "What do you make of them, anyway?" I asked, jerking my thumb in the direction of the listing, decidedly phallic structure. "Kind of sloppy, don't you think, letting a new religion rise up like that?"

Using his oar, Michael shoved us into the widening river. He remained silent for so long that I twisted to see if I could gauge his expression. Noticing my curiosity, he shrugged, "It's hardly *new*."

"Indeed," I said, though I was impressed to hear Michael admit so. I often wondered if God hated Egypt in particular for the pyramids, an indestructible testimony to older, powerful Others. "Osiris hasn't had this many followers in several millennia, though. Despite the whole castration thing, He seems to be gaining quite a foothold here."

We drifted past sprouts growing in orderly rows which the Deadboys had planted any place the Nile had deposited rich, fecund loam. Squash vines climbed rebar and crumbled walls. Wheat shafts rose in alleys and on rooftops. The fragile seedlings made a compelling argument for the Deadboys' belief that life could rise from the dead and that the Nile would nurture us all, if allowed to return to ancient flood patterns.

Michael had no comment.

Perhaps he and I had a similar goal, after all. Maybe Michael had come as the sword of Allah. The more I considered the possibility, the more I became convinced of it. For one, it explained his brooding mood.

"You've been sent to add to the death toll, and it bothers you," I said with sincere sympathy. It sucked being used as a tool. I should know. But I was often, at least, allowed the dignity of cleverness; God used Michael like a blunt instrument. "I'm sorry. What are you going to do?"

If his face hadn't been hidden from me, I would have known to expect the righteous anger in his voice. "What I have always done: my duty."

"How predictably boring," I said. But, before Michael could strangle me, I put my oar down and swung my feet around to face him. The boat rocked with my movement, and the water sloshed noisily against the sides. Thing was, I could hardly stand the pain in his voice that he tried so hard to mask with bravado. "I'll make you a proposition, my brother. Let *me* take the fall. I came here with the same agenda, after all, and my hands are already bloody."

Michael's body stiffened with resistance. "I was the one that was sent."

"And? You're here now. Mission accomplished."

The darkness could hardly hide the frown on his face. The reason I stayed here was the same that Michael avoided it. On earth, the experiment of free will reigned supreme – even angels were infected by it the moment left the safe confines of God's presence. The mere idea of free will seemed to give Michael a migraine.

"You can do as you wish here. You don't have to be a slave."

"Better to rule in Hell, is it?"

"It's better not to be played, is what it is." I shot back, but even though I could see the stony resolve in Michael's eyes. I tried to smile, but it came out a tired grimace. "Just let me do this for you. It would hardly the first time I inadvertently did God's bidding. At least this time I'd be doing it on purpose."

The canoe bumped along with the current. In the open areas, bats darted and dipped near the water's surface snatching up mosquitoes.

Michael crossed his arms in front of his chest. "You want to take up the sword for me. Why? To what do I owe this sudden show of altruism?"

Love?

But Michael could never understand that I would gladly dirty my own hands to keep his clean. I hated to see him forced toward darkness even the tiniest bit. It wasn't fair. But, he would mock me if I told him the truth, so I lied, "Be the Almighty's bitch then, see if I fucking care."

I turned my back to him and picked up my oar. The crack of a rifle bounced through the steel canyons. Automatic fire responded. Instinctively, I ducked, though the skirmish sounded several blocks away.

Pirates. No doubt after Russian or peaceforcer property – food and water.

I put my shoulder into my next stroke. Behind me, I could feel Michael doing the same. Honestly, I was surprised he was still with me. I'd have thought for sure he'd have poofed back to Heaven for a shot of righteous focus.

Once we'd gone some distance, I relaxed my pace a bit. I remained on high alert, however, since we neared the Sixth of October Bridge. It, like the tower, had survived the deluge mostly intact. Unfortunately, that meant crossing under it came with the risk of being snagged by rat packs. As bold fires burned brightly at each end, it seemed that a relatively strong group currently occupied the bridge. Golden light danced on the dark waves below. Curtains of billowing nets glistened like dew-speckled spider webs in the moonlight.

Though we pulled our paddles from the water almost simultaneously, the heads of shadowy figures popped up over the rails at the sound of our approach.

We'd been spotted.

I held my breath until I saw the glint of the lens of binoculars or telescope. I sighed in relief because, if they got a good look at us, I doubted they'd be interested in what they saw: two angels in a boat with no food, no supplies.

Rats, like their namesakes, weren't known for their bravery. No doubt, there was some whispered risk assessment taking place on the bridge. We had nothing visible worth taking. Perhaps we had tech or weapons hidden, but we were healthy and strong looking, probably even unnaturally so by Cairo standards, which might cause the rats to consider the possibility that we were rogue peaceforcers.

As if on cue, the nets rolled up.

I put my oar back into the water with a splash that sounded loud after the tense silence. Where else was there to go but forward? Michael offered no contrary opinion, as we skimmed the boat into the light. We were close enough that I could see eyes peering through the battered stonework, watching our progress. The bridge dominated the skyline, blocking out the sky.

Too late I noticed the trolls hiding in the understructure. They leaped down the moment we passed underneath, bringing the nets with them. I could have brought my .45 out from its holster and shot both trolls dead before either hit the water, had Michael not put a restraining hand on my shoulder just as quickly.

"Insh'allah, brother," his breath tickled my ear.

So I feigned a reaction of human slowness and allowed them to capture us and take my gun. Up close, the trolls were hideous. Their faces swelled and blistered from repeated dives into the cesspool of the Nile. Despite their outward appearance, however, they were strong enough to tow the canoe to the shore where the other rats waited to take us to their leader.

"Let us go. We have nothing you want," I kept telling them, because I thought it seemed plausible that I act afraid or at least indignant. "Get your fucking hands off me."

Having less practice, Michael didn't play human very well. As they lugged him along, he stared at them with a haughty indifference to their pokes and jabs.

They'd twisted the nets around us as makeshift manacles, but we could easily have overpowered them had Michael not implied this was some part of some damn plan. I made my captors drag me up the muddy hill, at least, slipping and sliding in the recently deposited silt.

Most of the rats were little more than boys. I noticed a few ragged ghosts drifting among them as we reached the bridge proper. Tents and lean-tos made of bits of discarded clothing and bed sheets were setup along the sidewalks. Goats bleated in improvised pens. Cooking pots steamed over small fires. A fleet of bicycles leaned against lamp posts, many outfitted with trailers.

Our arrival caused a stir. Whispers swelled and fingers pointed as we were yanked along. It appeared we were being herded toward one of the larger bonfires near the center of the bridge, and, I could only hope, to the presence of the rat king. If I had to endure much more of this bouncing about, I was going to blow our cover with a show of angelic force.

Finally, the pushing stopped. I glanced around trying to determine who might be in charge. My eyes landed on an older man in Western dress. He had frizzled curls and clouded, blind eyes. "Let us go," I demanded. "You have my gun. We have nothing more you could possibly want."

"As it happens, we need able bodies." To my surprise, it was a woman in a black shroud that answered me. I had not noticed her standing behind the old man, her robes blended so perfectly with the shadows. She moved forward into the light and seemed to examine Michael and me. A ghost rat queen? This was new and quite interesting. She came up to stand in front of me. "Are you deserters?"

"I am," I said, with a little smile. Jerking my chin at Michael, I quickly added, "He's not."

"What army?"

"Allah's," I said.

Not surprisingly, she laughed. "Well, Allah will have to go without. You've been conscripted into mine now."

I glanced over at Michael. He lifted a shoulder to my implied question and returned his regard to the ghost queen.

Though her burqa was shabby, it had been repaired with carefully sewn patches. So much was hidden behind the straight column of fabric that I could tell very few details, except that she was moderately tall for a woman, maybe five foot seven or eight. I thought she seemed more than a little flat-chested, but, honestly, it was hard to tell.

What was obvious was that she carried herself with a regal sort of confidence that was very attractive. Without exposing her face or one shred of her body, she commanded quite a following.

I could see how God might like a woman such as this. She was the outsider's outsider. At best, the rats were seen as parasites, and women had always had a tenuous position in society – despite their exalted place in most scriptures.

"Very well," I said. "We are at your service."

She tilted her head like someone else might arch an eyebrow. "Just like that? No demands, no arguing, no bargaining?"

I decided to try something out: "Your reputation precedes you."

"They call you a prophet," Michael spoke his first words since entering the rat camp. His voice resonated in that spooky way of angels speaking for the Lord. The crowd noticed. Whispers rippled outward.

The ghost queen noticed her people's reaction. She straightened. "Hush! That's blasphemy. There is no Prophet but Mohammad, peace be upon his name. No, I'm no one special," the ghost queen shook her head, her robes undulating furiously. "I'm a simply trying to survive."

Her faith and vehement denial cinched it.

I was going to have to kill her.

Present Day

A waiter deposited the fragrant tea and a large square of baklava without much ceremony. Barely acknowledging my gratitude, he quickly disappeared into the growing crowd.

Mouse was staring intently at me, chewing his lower lip with an expression that made it seem as though he found it distasteful. "Are you shitting me? You knew Mohammad during the blackout?"

"I had the pleasure of serving *under* her," I said with a fond smile, and a waggle of my eyebrows. "As it were."

"Hey, 'her'!" Deidre said happily, giving Mouse a poke in the ribs.

Mouse seemed less ecstatic. "Are you trying to imply you slept with Mohammad? Because then I'd know you were a liar."

EGYPTIAN RESCUE EFFORTS DELAYED
Sandstorms Defeat Peaceforce

Associated Press
April 2, 2059

Cairo, Egypt—Rescue efforts screeched to a halt today when the United Nations' Peacekeeping Force was forced to retreat from the region affected by the Aswan Dam flood as sandstorm season in Egypt began. The khamsin, as the windstorms are called, can reach speeds of 140 km/87 miles per hour and cause reduced visibility. Sand and dust threaten to bury already debris-clogged streets. Planes and military air support have been grounded.

The Secretary General issued a statement that until the storms subside the rescue operations will be conducted by remote, using robot soldiers popularly called "warhounds." "They are simply more sturdy and maneuverable than their human counterparts," insisted the Secretary General. Food and water drops are stopped until weather permits. The Secretary General made no mention as to whether or not the new elite cyborg unit would be deployed to assist the robots.

Already unhappy with the response of the UN PKF to the disaster, president-in-exile Amsi Mubarak called the withdrawal an "absolute failure" and questioned whether the deployment of wardogs was appropriate given the controversy surrounding the Bangladesh hurricane recovery efforts two years ago. Resolution of three civil suits against the United Nations' robotics team is still pending.

Doctors Without Borders/Medecins Sans Frontiäres (MSF) vowed to stay as long as the supply chains remain open.

Chapter 5
Mouse

Cairo, Egypt
Present Day

Leaning back, I cross my arms in front of my chest. I hate it when Satan fucks with me.

I know he smiles like that just to get under my skin, but I already feel so guilty about Mohammad that I'm easy to unnerve. Thank Allah my wyrm is stealing Morningstar's stuff even as we speak.

While I fume incoherently, Deidre actually says something helpful, "Maybe we should focus on where she might be now."

Morningstar picks up his fork. Stabbing the baklava, he cuts off a large section. I suspect he enjoys our rapt attention, and so try to resist the urge to jump out of my seat and shake him until he tells us everything he knows. I'm beginning to think we may have known the same person after all, but it's hard for me to think of Mohammad as a 'her,' despite what I know. "Just tell me Mohammad was alive when you left," I say.

"She was," he sounds... disappointed? Morningstar uses his fork to push a string of honey around his plate for a moment, lost in a memory. He looks up at me, and, without his customary pride, says, "But I destroyed her reputation and drove her from the path of righteousness. She was not spared the wrath of God, not one bit."

"You are such a fucking bastard," I all but spit.

"I am." His brown eyes snap up at me, and hellfire dances around his pupils. "But where was Mohammad when you left her, I wonder?"

Blackout

The lights in Franklin's hair danced hypnotically. But it wasn't their mesmerizing pattern that enchanted me the most; it was the luxurious scent of fresh, cool air wafting in from the house. Beside me, Mohammad stifled a groan of pain.

"My friend's hurt. Can we come in?"

"Of course, darling. 'Me casa, su casa' and all that." Franklin stepped out of the way to let us pass.

Walking through the door was like traveling back into a better time. Air conditioning cooled and dried the interior. Lights flickered on tables, and computers hummed on desks. It even smelled good – no hint of decay, rot, or Nile.

Unlike me.

Franklin crinkled his nose and made a disapproving noise when I came near. "Oh, good God, what have you been rolling in? Stop right there." We had just entered an alcove of carved lattice screens, when Franklin put a hand on my shoulder to stop me. "I'll get Pierre to help your friend. You go upstairs and take a shower, little rat." Franklin snapped his fingers impatiently. "Pierre!"

Pierre appeared – a sullen, half-naked French kid with muscles and styled-hair right out of some fashion magazine – and looked completely put out by our very presence.

"Take this poor injured dove over to the couch and fetch him some tea and sandwiches. Little rat and I and will join you in a moment." Franklin told Pierre.

"Uh," I didn't really expect to be separated from Mohammad quite so soon, but Pierre swept him out from under me.

"Your lover's in good hands. Now go upstairs. Venti. Pronto."

I started to protest that Mohammad and I weren't lovers and that he'd be particularly horrified to hear someone suggest that we were, but, as with so many of my dealings with Franklin, I found myself obeying his good-natured orders unthinkingly.

Evil was seductive like that.

I swore Bast winked at me again as I headed upstairs. The calluses on my feet slapped noisily against the marble stairs as I skipped quickly toward the awaiting fresh, hot, running water.

The bathroom at the end of the palatial, arched-ceiling hall was more than a toilet; it had a full-sized tub for soaking and a separate walk-in shower – and hidden LINKcams in every nook and cranny. A little live-feed video indecent exposure was the price of a hot bath at Franklin's. I checked to make sure the soldier's credit counter stayed secreted inside the pocket of my jeans, and then tried not to think about who might be watching as I stripped off my filthy clothes and stepped into the shower.

It'd been weeks since I washed every part of my body, and the water felt so good that I soon forgot about all the cameras. There were scented body washes and expensive soaps, and I lathered every inch of myself – even scrubbing the bottom of my feet. I stayed under the spray until the water no longer ran black.

Once finished, I dried off with a decadently fluffy terry cloth towel. I looked at my stained and rotting clothes. I decided it was an injustice to put them back on, so I palmed the credit counter and slipped it between my skin and the tightly wrapped towel around my waist. In some ways, though I felt a bit vulnerable and silly, being mostly naked would probably help my bargaining position with Franklin.

Right, as if anything would.

Before heading downstairs, I stopped and took a steadying breath. The boy in the mirror looked back at me with dark, worried eyes. I raked my fingers through my curls, trying to make myself look more alpha than I felt. It was an exercise in frustration. The more I messed with my hair, the more I appeared like the sort easily taken advantage of. I blamed it on my particularly youthful face. I had a lot of baby fat still, and, unlike Mohammad ironically, I couldn't grow much of a beard no matter how hard I tried. My brown eyes were wide and lined with the kind of thick, black lashes that women loved to coo and fuss over. My skin was sort of fawn-brown, though only thanks to constant exposure to wind and sun. Where my shirt protected me, the color was more of a barely-there olive.

We were so screwed. What was I thinking coming back here?

I'd have to watch myself, and not let myself get swept away by Franklin's charisma. I did have some advantages to bring to the table after all, and some to keep hidden. The peacekeeper's jacket was worth its weight in gold, and thanks to the interwoven Kevlar armor, it was heavy. Plus, she'd had the watch, a pair of simple earrings hidden in the inside pocket, and a few Egyptian pounds in change. It was something.

With more hope in my heart than was wise, I headed downstairs.

The instant I reached the living room, however, I realized I'd made a tactical error coming here at all. Pressed between Pierre and Franklin on the couch, Mohammad looked trapped. Each one had a hand on him. Franklin twirled a bit of curls above Mohammad's shoulder, and Pierre stroked his thigh. Then they gave each other a look of pure joy, like they'd just won the lottery.

I supposed they thought they had.

Meanwhile, Mohammad's secret slowly seeped onto the white fabric of his sweats. I finally understood what Mohammad had been so desperate to get back at the apartment. When he shifted to get away from Franklin, I could see a tiny dark stain between his legs. At first I thought maybe it was just a random spattering of blood, but then it hit me.

He was getting his period.

"Merciful Allah," I said, though I didn't mean for it to come out .

Franklin's gaze caught mine and held it just long enough to let me know he'd noticed, too. "God is great," Franklin agreed with a creepy smirk that made my ass twinge.

At least they'd taken care of Mohammad's most pressing concern. His eyes glazed over from some happy pill, probably an opiate, to mask the pain. The arm itself was tightly wrapped against his chest in a splint. "Hey, Chris, guess what? My arm probably isn't that bad." His words slurred; my heart sank.

"Yeah, great," I tried to muster genuine enthusiasm, but all I could do was try not to stare at the betraying blood. I looked behind me to the door. No guards, at least. "Since you're all better, maybe we should go," I suggested.

"You'd cause quite a stir on the streets dressed like that," Franklin noted, letting his gaze roam my body appreciatively. Then, he put a restraining hand on Mohammad who struggled to get up. "The little dove, however, is mistaken. All I said was that the bone wasn't sticking out at least. His wrist may be broken. I've called for my doctor."

His doctor. His *private* doctor. That was going to cost me. Cost us both.

Franklin leaned back against the couch with a smile of a man who's called "checkmate." His arm rested loosely, yet possessively around Mohammad's narrow shoulders. "I thought maybe my physician could bring some other things the little dove might need."

I frowned, trying to imagine what he was talking about.

Mohammad perked up, but his face paled. His eyes darted around, as though trapped. Once again his mouth opened like there was something he wanted to say, but couldn't. Did Franklin mean hormone therapy for Mohammad? Was a lack of testosterone what caused him to start? Franklin watched my face for understanding, and then nodded.

"Why would you do that?" I asked. Not that I understood anything about Franklin or his world, but I thought the "market" for such things would be higher if Mohammad was more of a girl, not less.

"We want our little dove to be comfortable, now don't we?" Franklin crossed his arms in front of his chest and his cat tat winked languidly.

"Uh, *comfort* is really important," Mohammad said. The fingers of his uninjured hand dug into the fabric his thighs as he stared down, momentarily, at his lap. His face twisted in a kind of pain that had nothing to do with his arm. He didn't to look up for me to see the desperation in his eyes.

"Comfort is expensive," Franklin reminded me. "Very expensive without a valid prescription."

I wished Mohammad and I had been able to talk about this earlier. There was so much I didn't understand and this talking in code was giving me a headache. "Is comfort entirely necessary?"

Mohammad couldn't meet my eyes and his jaw was doing that trying to talk thing.

It *was*.

I ran a hand through my hair, desperately trying to think. There'd been a scenario skittering around my head that involved a cut-and-run. I might have convinced Franklin I'd already given him plenty of pings from my little shower scene to cover the painkiller and the sling. I would have even willingly surrendered the counter just to get us out.

But watching Mohammad struggle to ask without giving himself away meant everything had changed.

"Just let us – let *him* go." Sadly, my voice chose that moment to break into a squeak. I cleared my throat. "I'll work for what he needs."

Franklin put his hand to his heart as though touched by my words. "Such a brave little rat," he sneered. "But as lovely as you are, you're... used, and not worth half what's sitting next to me and you know it."

Mohammad's head snapped up. He looked at me, and it was clear he suddenly realized the full extent of where we were. "Holy fuck. This is the... 'accident,' isn't it?"

It was my turn to be unable to answer, though the shame that flushed my cheek probably told him everything he needed to know.

I stared hard at Franklin, "Let's make a deal," I said, though I had no idea any more what I could really offer.

"My favorite words," Franklin purred. Turning to Pierre, he commanded, "Where are my sandwiches? Didn't I tell you to get us some tea and bread?" He clapped his hands, indicating that Pierre should snap to. "Food makes for better negotiations."

Well, that was one thing we could agree on.

I pulled up a chair, and, still wrapped in my towel, awkwardly lowered myself onto it.

"Look," I said, trying to sound a lot more casual than I felt, especially with the credit counter jabbing me sharply in the abdomen. I shifted slightly, pretending to stretch my leg. "I'm about to come into a lot of money."

Over the bridge of his nose, Franklin shot me a disbelieving stare. "Oh?"

"I found this body in this apartment, right? Well, she still had some stuff on her. Like this," I pulled out the counter. I'd intended to wave it under Franklin's nose in a "ha, ha, look what I have" gesture, but I managed to loosen the towel enough that I had to make a grab for dignity instead.

Franklin straightened, looking interested, though not wildly so. "Okay," he drawled, with a lot less enthusiasm than I'd hoped.

Pierre came back into the room with a silver tray holding cups of tea, a pot, and a pile of steaming hot flatbread. Franklin offered a cup to Mohammad, who looked to me as if to ask if it's okay. *Dude*, I thought, *you're already drugged, even if you're too addled to know it.* So I nodded, and he accepted. I picked up my own cup and a piece of bread.

I hesitated before taking a sip. After all, this little tea party was almost a perfect copy of the scenario that ended with me thrown into the pits of hell. I put the cup down. "Here's how it's going to go," I started, taking, instead, a big bite of the chewy bread. It had a nutty flavor, like sesame.

"No," Franklin interrupted, taking a dainty sip of tea. "Here's the deal. You give me that card as a down payment for today and the physician. And two-thirds of whatever else you fence, and I'll leave the *boy* alone." He emphasized "boy" totally unnecessarily, I thought. "The treatment will be extra."

Mohammad swallowed his tea noisily.

I wished that part didn't matter so much, but it was clear it did. I wanted to do what was right by him, but so much of this was wrong. Worse, I couldn't see any other options.

"Half," I said, but it was a crappy counteroffer. But, in my culture, if I didn't barter, it wasn't a real transaction.

We went back and forth for a while like this, while Mohammad munched on bread and shot angry looks, well aware that I haggled over the price of his soul.

Eventually, we settled exactly where I knew we would, back at Franklin's original terms. Mohammad nearly spit out his tea when we returned to where we started. "You can't..." he stammered, when I shook on it. "My friend," he said to me, reproachfully. "You negotiate for crap."

I shrugged. Honestly, any deal with the devil was a bad one. I was just pleased Franklin agreed to leave Mohammad alone. It seemed too good to be true, in fact. I started to place the soldier's credit counter into Franklin's open palm, when I hesitated. "You promise, right?"

"Promise what, little rat?" Franklin drawled.

I jerked my chin in the direction of Mohammad. "You'll take care of him? Treat him right?"

"Count on it."

You might think I was a complete naif or maybe even a blathering idiot, but I believed him. I had to. The problem with being taken for a fool was that sometimes it was the only choice.

Before handing the thin plastic over, I tossed out one more valiant volley. "How about some new clothes for me and it's a deal?"

"Done," Franklin agreed, and we shook hands again like any of it really meant anything.

"Go fetch the little rat something from your wardrobe," Franklin ordered Pierre.

Pierre sniffed contemptuously. "Why should I give up my stuff?"

"Because it's not yours," Franklin reminded him. "It's mine. Just like you are. Now go."

Pierre pouted sullenly for a moment, and then with a heavy sigh stomped off toward the stairs.

With a wink at Mohammad, Franklin said: "He's a bit high maintenance, but the pretty ones always are, don't you agree, dove?"

It took Mohammad a few moments to realize he was being spoken to. Though jealousy of Frankin's attention wasn't something I normally experienced, I ruefully wondered how it was that Mohammad got to be the "dove" and I was a "rat."

"Uh, yeah, I guess." Mohammad crooked his eyebrows at me, as if wondering if I knew what Franklin was talking about. "So, uh, Chris," Mohammad leaned closer to me and away from Franklin. "What the fuck did you just give up, exactly?"

I opened my mouth to explain, but Franklin cut in. "You, my dear dove. In exchange for the profits of whatever caper it is the little rat has planned, I will have your medical needs – all of them – taken care of. You, my sweet dove, will lounge on silk pillows and Pierre will feed you bon-bons until your arm is well enough for you to run away from me."

"Bon-bons?" Mohammad looked at me as if hoping for a translation from English into something that made more sense.

"I'm sure he's exaggerating about the bon-bons." I told him, "Though you never can tell with Franklin."

"The point is you will be in the lap of luxury – very expensive luxury," Franklin added, massaging his palm along the edges of Mohammad's shoulder blades. "You'll love it."

Watching Mohammad cringe away from Franklin's touch, I doubted he'd enjoy a moment of it. So, really, even if Franklin kept his word, it was a lose/lose proposition that would end up costing us everything we might have gained from the soldier's gear and more.

Fan-fucking-tastic.

I sipped the tea finally. It tasted mostly of boiled muddy water with a hint of an overused bag of English Breakfast. A lifetime ago, before the dams broke, I'd have made a face at this pitiful excuse for a beverage, but today I thought it was the best thing I'd ever tasted. The bread was even more exquisite. I suspected Pierre bartered it off the Bedouins who'd set up down the street, because its flaky crust had the tang of goat butter. I ate and drank while Mohammad edged further away from Franklin.

I looked at him over a mouthful of bread and tried to will him the strength to get through these next few hours or days or however long it took me to rescue him. His wounded arm might would spare him some, and, despite all of it, this was still a safer place than out there. And then there was Franklin's promise. He might hold to it. For a minute or two.

I wanted to say something useful, but no words came. I wished I could make some kind of impassioned speech to Franklin about decency and honor that would cause him to have an epiphany that changed his wicked ways forever. And to Mohammad – well, to Mohammad mostly I just wanted to apologize.

"I'll come back as soon as ever I can," I said to Mohammad. "I swear."

"You're going to leave me here?" He panicked now – his eyes darting between Franklin and me in horror.

He never left my side when I was in pain, even with all the awkward.

I swallowed and tried to remember to breathe. "I have to. Your arm, it needs attention. Antibiotics, pain killers, and all that *stuff*," I tried to remind him how much he's wanted that unnamed "stuff" with my eyes. "We'd die out there."

"I'm going to die here," he whispered.

"No," I told him from experience, "it's just going to feel like it."

Present Day

Morningstar's accusation still rings in my ear, and I'm on my feet, fists swinging, before I consider the consequences of punching Satan in the mouth. My knuckles connect with bruising force, but his head barely shifts.

I'm ready to hit him with my left when he catches my hand mid-pummel.

"Enough," Morningstar's grip is light, but I sense he could crush my bones with a thought.

Be careful, father, Page advises, a little late to the party.

Likewise, Deidre finally reacts. Pushing her chair back, she stands up. Her hand slowly moves toward the gun she has hidden under her coat. "Stand down, Morningstar."

With a mocking quirk of his eyebrow, he releases me.

I can't stand the look he gives me, like somehow he knows all the sins of my past. "He's not going to tell us anything useful," I shout, well aware of the eyes on us. At least no calls have LINKed to the police yet. "Let's go."

Without waiting for Deidre's response, I stomp out the door like it's that easy to walk away from my guilt.

A MOUSE THAT ROARED: How Free Access Saved North Africa
By Keela Ryū
Forthcoming from Doubleday Harcourt Penguin, 2111

Excerpted interview of Mouse; footnote commentary by "Page"/Strife

"What? Yes, I'm well aware that Page shifts gender.

You do realize that, technically, Page is a collection of electrons – or a string of binary? On and off. If you want to go all Pythagoras[8] on it, you could think of 'on' as male, and 'off' as female, positive and negative, white and black, or some other simplistic duality. So a person could make the case that he is either on or off, male or female, at any given time.

Yes, I just said 'he.' Wow, I am so totally busted. Thank you for pointing that out. Listen, lady, would you like to be called 'it'? I didn't think so. Page mostly looks like me, so I usually call him 'him.'

Oh, is *that* the real question? You're trying to figure out if Page's multiple gender has something to do with me? Huh. Okay.

Why are you wasting your interview time on this? Aren't people over this already? We're more than a decade into the twenty-second century. Can't you just admit we're all a little mix of everything? It seems to me like maybe you're the one with the issues. Do you need to talk about why it matters so much *to you?*"

---

8. A sixth century Greek philosopher/mathematician, who was very keen on numerology and postulated that maleness was first, a one (which he equated with intellect and purity), and femaleness was two (which he saw as muddied and base). As my father might say: dude has a lot to answer for.

Chapter 6
Morningstar

Deidre rested her hands on her hips and regarded me with loathing and, God help me, *pity*. Impatiently, I waited for her to say something pithy I could scorn mercilessly. Instead, she shook her head sadly and silently followed her friend out the door.

I rubbed my cheek where Mouse hit me. A few of the cafe customers stared curiously, but when I noticed their attention they quickly turned it elsewhere. My flesh wouldn't bruise, but the blow stung nonetheless.

Seems we both had loved the prophet.

From his reaction, I guessed Mouse's betrayal was probably at least as ugly as my own.

Blackout

It was easy to see why God feared the prophet. Her hospitality was practically Biblical. Knowing nothing of us, she took in a pair of wandering angels, fed us, and offered us a place to sleep.

The plate she handed me had once been a dog-gnawed Frisbee, but it held a deliciously steaming pile of stewed goat meat, canned corn, and rice. With a broken credit counter for a spoon, I joined the crowd gathered around the fire. Some people sat on ratty lawn chairs, others on folding metal ones. Not finding a free seat, I sat tailor-fashion on the cobblestone with a group of small children near the prophet's feet. Michael, perched on a nearby crate stamped with the UN flag, had already begun to engage her in philosophy.

"Is everything not the will of Allah?" he was asking. The firelight danced along the hard planes of his face. "Why then should we not blame Him for the flood?"

Turning her shrouded face toward where I sat, she seemed to look at me when she asked, a smile in her voice, "Which one of you was the deserter again?"

"My brother is ever the faithful sword of Allah," I said, as though offering an excuse for his bad manners. "He tests your faith, prophet."

"I see," she said, and I wished I could read her expression then because her tone sounded light, almost playful. She turned back to Michael. "Well, I'm sorry to disappoint you then, my man. I don't know any answers. What matters isn't why all this happened, but what we do now. We can live like animals or we can live like people – decently, kindly."

Oh, she was good. As she continued on about the virtue of helping others, heads nodded in agreement around the fire. A child no more than six clambered into my lap and helped herself to the choicer pieces of meat on my plate. She snuggled against me in full trust, her tiny bony body warm against my own. Instantly, I knew this was a special place, one we should fight to protect, not destroy.

No wonder Michael resisted this assignment. It should have been mine from the beginning. This was a True Prophet, and only I could corrupt her. I was the one who came to messiahs in the desert and offered to make them kings of earth if they would but surrender heaven. It was *my* apple to offer.

When I looked for him, I discovered Michael had been watching me. Ah, now I understood. God had never intended Michael to dirty himself with this job. God knew me so well that She played on my affection easily. I gave Michael an angry glance that said: *message received.* I could see the concern in Michael's eyes as he continued scanning my face. Would I do it now that I knew I'd been set up? Would I play serpent in Eden again?

Surrendering my plate to the adorable little beggar with a tousle of her matted hair, I stalked away from the light towards the comfort and familiarity of darkness.

The prophet had offered us a tent on the outskirts of the camp in exchange for sentry duty. I retreated to its meager privacy now. It was really little more than a child's fort, a dozen or so towels stitched together and tied so that they draped between the bridge's railing and a bent stop sign. Our beds were cardboard boxes, flattened out to provide a bit of protection from the cold stone road. Bags of rice doubled as pillows.

Too cramped to even sit up properly, I stretched out on the cardboard and listened to the noises of the camp. The murmuring, the shuffling, the clanks, and the clatters were the ancient sound of people making do. Yet it was more. Nearby, a couple quietly made love, as a bright, hopeful burst of laughter drifted above the misery.

"You want me to destroy all this," I said to the anxious presence crouching just beyond the thin curtain of towels. "And people think I'm the evil bastard."

"If she's true, she'll prevail."

I snorted. "Or the *memory* of her will." I was surprised at him. "You would extinguish this oasis – for all these people – just to prove her mettle?"

Michael yanked aside the partition nearly undoing its flimsy construction. "You almost sound like you care about them."

I shouldn't. They were just mortals, after all. I shrugged off the uncomfortable roiling in my gut. "*You* care. And if you care, I can hurt you."

"Of course," he said with a clenched jaw. "I should have known you'd be this petty."

How little you really understand, brother. I shook my head at him. "You want me to do it, and I won't. It's that simple. Go home. Tell Father you failed."

Despite himself, I saw him swallow uncomfortably at the thought. I smiled, enjoying my brief victory.

"Or," I added, "Go fuck the prophet over yourself, if you have the balls."

"I will if I must," he said with an unsteady hitch in his breath.

I laughed cruelly. "You couldn't even if you wanted to. You have so little guile."

"I know. That's why I need you. That's why We need you."

He leaned in, and his lips lightly touched my cheek. My breath caught in surprise. Inches from my face, his eyes locked on mine. For a second, They were Present. God's grace filled me. The sensation was unbearably beautiful. It burned too brilliant, too searingly painfully. I had to break away. With all my willpower, I gave Michael a shove. He stumbled backward, nearly collapsing the tent on top of us. "Fuck you," I whispered, my voice raw and shaking. "I hate you for this."

Michael nodded. Dusting himself off, he readjusted the tent's supports and crawled inside to sit beside me. His back rested against the railing, his leg against my arm. We lingered like that, in silence, for a long moment. Finally, he spoke, "I'm going on patrol. I'll leave you to it."

I wanted to remind him I hadn't agreed to anything, but it would have been a futile gesture. I couldn't remember the last time Mother had come to me quite like that, so personally. I would kill all of humanity for such a tiny taste of love and They knew it.

With a sigh, I got up. I crawled out just as the loving couple next door kissed goodbye. With an apology, I quickly ducked out of their way, pretending not to see the brief flash of the woman's uncovered hair. As I moved away, I wondered what the prophet looked like under her robes, and whether or not she might take me as a lover so that I might discredit her.

I found the prophet, along with a bevy of other women, tending the children. Plastic garbage pails filled with water heated over the fire acted as washtubs. Children splashed and giggled as she tried to scrub faces and behind ears. The sleeves of her robes had been rolled up. Blunt, square hands with a surprising mass of black hair above the wrists pressed washcloth to squiggling bodies. Muscles jumped along powerful forearms. Her size belied surprising physical strength. Was she a rogue soldier herself?

A tot playfully grabbed at the hood that hid her face. It tumbled sideways for no more than a second. As busy as the others were with their work, I doubt anyone but me had time to see the patch of beard on the prophet's chin.

She was either a man masquerading as a woman, or a woman who was once a man.

No wonder the hand that carefully replaced the fabric trembled in naked fear. Dear God, for such a secret, the prophet would be utterly crucified.

Present Day

I set aside my fork. My stomach soured at the memory of things done in God's name. A dark blush colored my cheeks.

My fingertips brushed my face, shocked to feel the heat rising there. What's this? Shame?

Embarrassment and regret were not feelings I was accustomed to. I found myself standing up, anxious. I threw a credit counter worth ten times the price of my order at the waiter in my hurry to escape this place, this decidedly human emotion.

Outside, the crowd and the cool evening air enveloped me. Electric lights transformed the night into an artificial daylight. A street band hammered a techno-pop rhythm, while whirling dervishes spun ruby red skirts in ecstasy. The smell of *koshary*, a bubbling oniony mixture of lentils, pasta and tomatoes, wafted from a nearby charity stall set up to feed the poor during Ramadan.

Rubbing my face, I tried to erase my growing unease. A bustle of black-robed women, laughing, passed me by. I turned to watch them weave through the joyous, Carnival-like atmosphere.

I felt a deep a pang again, haunting me.

Was Mouse right? Was the prophet still alive somewhere?

God had been wrong about her. Her goodness had not survived the evil I'd wrought. The message of kindness had been curtailed by human cruelty. No scriptures rose up. No well-placed converts spread her ideas of love. She had been disposed of and forgotten by humanity.

Though not by me.

Nor, it seemed, by a mouse.

Would the two of us be enough to resurrect her?

QUEER ISRAEL?
Transgender Conference Scheduled in Jerusalem

[Ramadan date, 2110]
Agnostic Press

Jerusalem, Israel—An international conference highlighting transgender/queer issues is scheduled to take place this week at Mount Sinai Hotel in Jerusalem.

The local authorities are expecting protesters. The military is on high alert for potential terrorist attacks. Family First, the American group considered largely responsible for Congress passing the "Leviticus Laws" in the United States, plans a large presence outside the conference. "Cross dressing is against God's law," said Family First founder Herman Byrne. The Biblical verse Family Firsters reference is actually in Deuteronomy (22:5) and reads, "The woman shall not wear that which pertaineth unto a man, neither shall a man put on a woman's garment: for all that do so are abomination unto the Lord thy God."

Zoe Santiago, one of the conference organizers and president of Aguda, The Association of Gays, Lesbians, Bisexuals and Transgendered in Israel, says this kind of misunderstanding is exactly why the conference is necessary. "Many transgendered people don't consider themselves violating Leviticus Laws. They're not cross-dressers; they are dressing their true gender. It's just not what you perceive on the outside."

Even though America, once considered very liberal on these issues, has since embraced religious orthodoxy, several countries in the Middle East, particularly Iran, Egypt, and Israel have shown surprising tolerance of transgendered people. Iran carries out more sex change operations than any other place in the world outside of Thailand. "We see gender dysphoria as a disease to be cured," said Dr. Mirrim Fieldman of Jerusalem.

Dr. Fieldman went on to explain that the procedures involved in correcting gender dysphoria have changed dramatically since nanotechnology has become widespread. "We can do amazing things now on the microsurgical level," she said. She went on to caution that the process is still slow and difficult, and, often prohibitively expensive for many people, but, she added, "Even simple hormone delivery technology has advanced dramatically in twenty years."

Dr. Fieldman will be one of the many guest speakers at the conference. She said that she was a bit nervous about attending the conference, but was grateful for the promise of security. Israel's Prime Minister has stated that violent demonstration will not be tolerated. Border security is expected to be tight.

Chapter 7
Mouse

Cairo, Egypt
Present Day

Deidre catches my arm before I get to the corner. A steady stream of electric cars flows through the intersection in front of me. Handcrafted steam-powered scooters skim through any opening, sending a barrage of honking rippling through the tangle.

"You're being unreasonable, you know," she says gently, without reproach.

"I know."

You've come all this way, father.

"Do you think he really knows anything?" I ask. Slumping dejectedly against a stoplight, I let my gaze follow the organized chaos of the traffic.

Tucking her arm into the crook of mine, Deidre leans against me. "There's some kind of history there. If it's with the same girl, I don't know."

"Guy," I correct. "He *wanted* to be a guy."

"Whatever," she says as if the distinction doesn't matter. "Where do you want to go now?"

A plane leaves for Mecca in six hours. We could be on it.

On the window ledge above us, a white cat stretched and blinked at me lazily. I considered booking the flight, even calling up the details on mouse.net. After all, this would hardly be the first time I turned my back on Mohammad.

Blackout

As I walked away from Franklin's place, I felt a bit like Judas – if he'd had to pay Caiaphas for the pleasure of nailing his best friend to a tree.

Merciful Allah, not even thirty *piasters* to show for it. Worse, Pierre's sleezy purple silk shirt smelled nauseatingly of cheap aftershave. Between the odor and the brilliant white sun beating down on my uncovered head, I was developing a serious migraine.

What was I going to do now? Somehow and completely accidentally, I managed to convince Franklin I had a plan for off-loading the soldier's gear. Hell, I'd just cut him into my profits. Only, I had no fucking idea what to do with any of it, or even how much it might be worth. I could go back to Ahmed, but he'd give me a pittance. I needed solid gold to buy back Mohammad.

Or, I could just bail.

I could tell myself I'd done what I could for Mohammad. He'd live.

I stopped at the end of the street. Ingrained habit had me checking both directions for traffic. Across the street, few scrubby date palms decorated both sides of a metro stop a half-block up. Coarse alfalfa grass sprouted in the cracks between the sidewalk stones. A lizard sunned itself on the median. The street was otherwise devoid of life.

The only noise was the rustle of wind through dry leaves, and a sharp, harsh, masculine cough.

I froze.

My instincts cried out for me to bolt like a jackrabbit, but where? The metro station seemed like a good bet, except that even from this distance I smelled sewage seeping from its maw. If it was flooded, I could find myself easily cornered.

When a fist closed around the nape of my neck, I realized I'd hesitated for a fraction of a second too long. My face slammed into the nearest wall. Intense close inspection revealed a cracked advertisement for a popular pre-apocalypse carbonated beverage.

"Ouch," I managed to say, despite the angle of my lips and the pressure on my teeth.

"Where'd you hide the stuff?" A male voice growled in my ear.

Who was this guy and how did he know about the soldier's things? Immediately, I considered the possibility that Franklin had double-crossed me, except it would have been much more convenient for him to simply beat the information out of me in the comfort of his own home. Franklin was nothing if not pragmatic like that. Plus, then Pierre wouldn't have had to part with his lovely, stinky cast-offs.

Over my shoulder I glimpsed a bit of the man who held me against the wall. His face was a gnarl of sun-baked wrinkles and missing teeth. His robes reminded me of those I'd seen on the men who guarded Franklin's power generator, but I was sure that was contrived.

A rival gang with spyware stashed in Franklin's place?

"Who wants to know?" I asked.

My face left the advertisement long enough to slam back into it. My teeth cut the inside of my cheek. I tasted blood.

"Shut up. I ask the questions," he snarled. "Where's the stuff?"

First the guy tells me to shut up, and then he wanted information? Okay, I figured I could safely rule out that he was from the welcoming committee of MENSA.

"What's your counteroffer? How much are you going to give me for it?"

"Your life." He shoved me into the wall again. "Give over, little rat."

"No, my life isn't worth it," I said, my lips still contorted by the pressure of my face against the wall. The paper of the ad melted with my bloody drool.

He hit me. Hard. In the kidney. I wasn't usually this brave, but I could still see Mohammad's expression in my mind, and I knew it would haunt me forever if I abandoned my promise to him.

Anyway, Judas committed suicide, so why shouldn't I?

"Uh," I said. "You know? I believe you can fuck yourself."

When his fists found all the tender parts of my body with vicious accuracy, my convictions wavered. Luckily, the pain was so intense I really couldn't formulate any coherent thought – much less one of surrender. All I could say was: "Gah, muh" or something equivalent.

All of a sudden, the pain stopped. The pressure on my neck vaporized, and I heard my assailant gasp, as if someone had grabbed him.

Praise Allah.

I turned to thank my rescuer, only my breath caught when I saw the Eye of Horus tattoo surrounding his left eye. My savior was a Deadboy. My mouth hung open in horror as my gaze traced the black lines around his lids that extended past his eyebrow in a thin, squared line.

Before I could run, the Deadboy snagged my elbow in a vice-like grip. He pulled me close and I smelled sewage and the distinct sourness of human sweat. The sun reflected off his shaved head and beardless chin. "What's your name?" he asked rather politely, considering that I was literally caught between a rock wall and... well, him.

Somewhere beyond the Deadboy's shoulders, I heard my assailant putting up a good fight, though it didn't sound like he was winning. "Uh, El-Aref," I said. "Christian."

"Uh El-Aref Christian," he repeated, his tattooed eyebrow arched sarcastically. "Really?"

I nodded stupidly.

I'd never seen a Deadboy this close, and I was impressed by how much he looked like those pyramid paintings of scribes we had to study in school, even down to a bony, naked upper body and a funky skirt. Though closer inspection revealed the latter to be a black-leather, studded... kilt?

"Christian? Is that your denomination or your name?"

I searched the Deadboy's eyes, wondering which answer was better. Would he go easier on me if he thought I was a Copt? The truth seemed safest. "My name," I said. "I'm Sunni."

"I see," he said, as if my answer solved some dilemma for him. To the others, he shouted, "We'll take this one. The other you can kill."

I threw up on his shoes.

The Deadboy seemed neither surprised nor disgusted as I continued to spew watery bits of tea and bread. Stepping out of the trajectory, he lightly pressed my shoulders to the wall as I continued to gag. Very ugly sounds pushed me into dry heaves.

When I recovered enough to make a break for it, all I got for my efforts was a more bruised chin and handcuffs. Handcuffs? Steel and chain seemed like advanced alien technology in this wasteland. I even checked to see if they weren't the trick ones with a quick release. When I discovered they weren't, I hoped to hell the Deadboys had a key. As they hauled me toward the metro entrance, I asked, "Where'd you get handcuffs?"

My rescuer-turned-captor, the Scribe, as I'd started calling him in my head, laughed. "Majeed was a cop," he jerked his chin in the direction of another bald, beardless guy in a skirt – although his was a tutu, complete with gauzy ruffles.

Majeed waved and gave me a crooked-toothed grin. I tried not to notice his face was splattered with blood from the goon as I nodded and smiled back.

Things had definitely gone from worse to surreal.

Story of my life.

"Why would a cop become..." I started, but swallowed the rest because it occurred to me that what I was about to say might constitute an insult. "I mean, why not evacuate?"

"Because the Nile called to us all, little brother." Scribe indicated his companions with a broad, sweeping gesture. His other hand still held tightly to my elbow, and he propelled me down the stairs into the metro station. His hold became a crutch as I slipped. Sand made the descent perilous. Suddenly, shadow swallowed us completely. Panic seized me in the utter blackness and I tried to back up the stairs. The Scribe's hand tightened. His voice sounded too close in my ear. "The Nile calls you, too."

Actually, the only thing I could hear was the thudding of my heart against my eardrum. I could smell the Nile, however. Dank, fishy rot choked the air from my lung in gasps.

Someone struck a match, and lit one of those tiki torches with orange mosquito repellent candles in them. Thankfully, the smell of citronella overwhelmed the stench of the Nile.

In the flickering light I could make out the old station. Damp, drooping advertisements for Cairo University and some long-past Bollywood movie clung stubbornly to stained pillars. Rotting, wet garbage slicked the mosaic tile floor all the way to the platform where now, instead of trains, black water ran along the track.

The Deadboys jumped the turnstile. As they hauled me over awkwardly, I got a strangely guilty sensation, like, despite the obvious ruin, I'd dodged the fare.

Looking at the water, a hysterical laugh bubbled in my throat. I didn't expect it to be so close. I'd hoped to have a few more moments to plan my escape before my man-parts, or maybe all of me, was sacrificed to the gods.

The Scribe seemed a bit startled by my reaction. But then he nodded, like we had something in common. "Yes," he said slowly, happily. "You see."

His voice echoed in the cavernous space, bouncing around the pylons and off the curved walls in strange, eerie ways. The reverberations faded into the sound of water lapping gently under the lip of the concrete platform.

They led me to the edge, and I shrunk back against the naked chest of the Scribe. If he hadn't grasped my shoulders, I'd have considered throwing myself in to drown rather than suffer castration.

But then there was a light at the end of the tunnel.

No, literally.

Something bright shone around the corner, glinting off the dark waves of the canal, illuminating twists of cable and rusted duct work.

"What's that?" I asked before I could censor myself.

"The ferryman," the Scribe explained. "Anupu. Anbuis."

Fabulous.

"Do not be afraid," The Scribe said solemnly, almost comfortingly. "It is he who shall weigh your heart and judge it worthy or not."

"That's Ma'at," my nerd brain corrected before consulting my better sense. "She's got the ostrich plume of truth. Your heart had to be lighter than the feather to pass into the underworld...?" My voice finally came to a stop with a crack at the Scribe's deepening frown. "But you knew all that already," I guessed stupidly. "Shutting up now," I said, because, really, I couldn't. Terror had brought out the idiot in me.

Waves lapped softly, as the ferryman's light grew closer. A kerosene lamp swung from a pole attached to a flat raft. "Anubis" himself scored a much higher quality costume, no ratty tutu for him. Golden cuffs probably looted directly from the Egyptian Museum glinted at his biceps. Turquoise beads filled a wide, flat necklace that lay across his broad, brown chest. The skirt wasn't entirely authentic, but it had been expertly tailored to better resemble the ones shown on the pyramid carvings. The mask – at least, I hoped that's what it was – cast a sharp-nosed jackal's profile in the shadowy light of the tunnel.

A desire to babble incoherently rose in my throat. A strange thought stuck me: maybe sacrilege was a way out. Maybe if I annoyed them enough, the Scribe and his colleagues would just kill me quickly and be done with it.

Even though cuffed together, I held up my fist, except with my pinkie and pointer fingers extended. I made the doggie shadow-puppet on the opposite wall. Pumping my fingers together, I mimicked a mouth opening and closing. "Anubis loves you!"

Apparently not the greeting he was used to, Anubis nearly fumbled the staff he'd been using as an oar.

The Scribe bopped me on the head. "Are you insane?"

"Would it help?"

Somebody, maybe Majeed, snickered. The Scribe flashed a disapproving sneer behind him. "Who dares insult the gods?" Shaking my shoulder a bit, he spun me around in order to remind me face-to-face: "You're supposed to be scared. No cracking jokes, asshole. You hear me? This is serious business. The gods demand serious sacrifice."

That sounded hopeful. Maybe silly sacrifices *were* unacceptable. "You expect me to be serious? You're the guy in a kilt."

Oh, he did not like that at all, although someone in the crowd sure thought I was funny.

"Oh! Oh!" The Scribe was incoherent with rage. "Insolence!"

"Good comeback," I muttered with much, much more bravado than I felt.

"Silence!" Anubis shouted in a commanding voice that boomed theatrically in the yawning, hollow space. Not only did everyone instinctively shut up, but they dropped to their knees, dragging me down with them. Roughly, the Scribe turned me to face the god.

Though I'd rallied a bit having given in to my desire to gibber insanely, my courage evaporated at what I saw. Anubis' mask seemed so realistic because the upper part of it once *had* belonged to a living dog. Though, instead of a jackal, it was a German Shepard whose fur had been spray-painted black to match the stiff fabric helmet it had been haphazardly sewn to. Yellowed fangs obscured the features of the man behind the mask, who peered out at us from the dog's hollow, empty eye sockets.

There was something deeply disturbing about the tattered fur that made it appear freshly killed. Worse, I suspected it took a certain amount of grue-some taxidermy skillz to preserve skin and bone so well. I didn't really want to piss off the guy who knew how to do *that*, all of a sudden.

Anubis must have notice my horrified expression, because he smiled. "Ah, I see you've found the appropriate attitude."

Something about his smug, sadistic superiority that reminded me of Franklin, plus my knees started to ache from kneeling on the floor for so long. I broke: "Fuck off. Fuck all of you. Just fucking kill me and get it the fuck over with, you fucking assholes."

Unfortunately, at times like this I tended to revert to English because, frankly, the Brits own expletives. They have so many varied and fun sounds to say. "Fuck" has truly awe-inspiring guttural punch that really is unsur-passed in any language, in my humble opinion.

Most Egyptians understood some English, especially the more colorful expressions, thanks to the legacy of colonization and the evils of modern capitalism, but these guys all stared at me like I'd started speaking in tongues.

Anubis cocked his head at me, all the world looking like a curious dog. "You speak English. Do you read it?"

"Fluently," I said without any pride.

I mean, it was kind of a requirement at the British boarding school. I was-n't precisely a whiz in languages by any means, but logical patterns were kind of my thing and, you know, total immersion tended to do the trick. That, and passion. Before the flood, I'd been learning Japanese to try to impress a girl. She was the cousin of the biggest bully in school, a kid named Sullivan. Hated him, but she was quite fine and very into anime.

I wondered where she was right now.

"Are you lying?" the Scribe said from behind me, his voice filled with contempt for my character.

"Huh?" I asked, my mind having returned to happier days of kisses and comic books.

Anubis didn't seem as concerned because, in his booming god voice, he declared, "We are in need of a translator. You will be he."

"And, in exchange," I got up off my knees. "I leave your company unaltered."

I'd been negotiating in a lot of crap situations lately, but, you know, a boy had to try.

Anubis looked me over from head to toe. He stared pointedly at my crotch until I felt my face heat and my cuffed hands automatically moved to shield my privates. He sniffed. "The gods are not in need of such a tiny offering. Your services shall suffice."

I bit my tongue. I wanted to state that for the record, my manly attributes were perfectly proportioned to my body size, thank you very much. Instead, I focused on the fact that I appeared to have won a small victory.

Most of the afternoon was spent on arduous, smelly, sea sickness-inducing travel via raft through the metro's flooded passageways. We glided past dreamlike ruins of Art Deco inspired stations littered with scores of crocodile nests. Water snakes hung from that symbol of industrial efficiency, the clock, its elegant hands pointing to the moment of its own doom. An elaborate, entirely manpowered, lock and dam system shunted the raft upward until we merged, like a tributary, into the great Nile itself. After the cold, gloom of the metro system, the bright, white of the sun nearly blinded me, as Anubis paddled us to the half-submerged remains of the Hilton.

Now I found myself sitting on the balcony of the presidential suite, looking into the faces of gods. As far as I could fathom from their costumes, they were: Anubis, Ra, and Osiris himself.

The shade of a plastic umbrella kept the sun from our eyes. On the shores of the nearby Gezira Island, the sun sparkled off the white stone ruins of the Opera House and Museum of Modern Art. A large flock of egrets fished canals that were once roads, and seagulls filled the air with their harsh cries.

By doomsday standards, it was a nice day.

Ra, a regal, athletic man in his mid-thirties, nodded his shaved head. Like the Scribe, the eye of Horus surrounded one eye, but he also sported a very intricate holo-tat on his bare chest. It showed the classic image of Ra: a sun with rays ending in extended hands offering an ankh to a female, goddess figure – Isis? The tattoo shimmered and shifted, like sun on the water. It was very well done and made me wonder: who out there was making a killing as a post-apocalyptic tattoo artist?

Ra's eyes flashed intelligently under wiry, tangled eyebrows. Of all the gods assembled on patio chairs, his skirt was the most authentic, being a simple white, knee-length sheath. Very stylish, though a bit "bridesmaid," if you asked me.

"Yes," Ra said in response to the implicit question of my tone. "It's an oil rig. Now you need to tell us how to get into it and how to operate it."

Osiris took a drag on a cigarette. The chief god reminded me of an uncle of mine, honestly – if you skipped the eye tattoo and the half-nakedness, of course. His black hair, which he'd cut short but not shaved, was streaked with gray and he had a proud, hawkish nose. I knew he was supposed to be the pharaoh because of the deference the others showed him, and, well, the tiara. Of course, it said "Happy Birthday, Princess!" in pink glitter, but I wasn't going to quibble.

"We plan to seize the means of production as a first step of returning Egypt to the Egyptians," he said, alternating a sip of his coffee with another puff. Like Anubis, Osiris wore wrist cuffs and a heavy, beaded necklace that, frankly, clashed with the cheap, paper tiara and the knotted, terry-cloth towel wrapped around his waist that he wore in lieu of a skirt.

The others grunted in agreement and saluted their leader with a tip of coffee mugs.

A mug had been placed in front of me, as well as a plate full of fresh fruits and fish. I nibbled a bit at the orange and mango slices, but avoided the fish. Before setting it on the table, they'd thanked the bounty of the Nile, and, even before the flood, eating things caught in the river was a very, very bad idea. The coffee, however, was divine. I happily joined in the toast to Osiris.

I worried about the Deadboys' ability to carry out this little nationalist plan of theirs, however. Clearly, they were much more organized that I ever imagined, and, frankly, more sane.

But not *entirely* sane.

Funky fashion choices and a penchant for eye tats and self-mutilation aside, this little tableau was a perfect example. They had fresh coffee and the kind of supply-line savvy that could score cigarettes, but their headquarters, the hotel, was clearly sinking into silt and stank of human waste. It had no electricity or running water. When they first brought me inside, the stench of piss made my throat sting; it was like walking into a sewer. When the breeze shifted the smell brought tears to my eyes.

And these were the guys who were going to rescue Egypt from the flood and foreign devils?

I had my doubts.

Yes, okay, I could see their cultivated farms from this vantage point.

They'd cleared much of the rubble along the banks and planted seeds they'd imported somehow... but it was a strange sort of insanity to plant a garden in a cesspool of thieves and whoremongers.

Anubis had pushed his dog mask further up on his head so it perched slightly askew, like a really weird ball cap. Underneath, his face was dark black. Acid scars marred the right side of handsome, broad features. "Are there other languages you know? Do you read Israeli?"

"Hebrew? A little, I guess," I said, as he handed me a manual for a rocket launcher.

Oh boy.

Despite my protests, they'd decided I was their resident language expert.

"Write down everything," Osiris instructed, putting a spiral bound notebook and ballpoint pen sporting the Hilton logo on the table in front of me. "And make it legible."

After adding a few more manuals – including a warranty pamphlet for a refrigerator, a Chinese take-out menu in English, and a humorous instruction booklet for an archaic computer language – onto my stack of materials, the gods left me to continue about whatever business it was Deadboy gods did.

I convinced them that my lettering would be neater if my hands were uncuffed, but the gods posted the Scribe and Majeed in his tutu on guard at the doorway.

My Arabic handwriting skills weren't the greatest, so it was slow going. My fingers cramped by the time I heard the call to prayers. One of the electronic muezzins on the island's mosque must have had one seriously powerful battery, because the song rang out clear and strong... and totally in the wrong key. It was too high, like it was being sung by a woman, which seemed alien on so many levels. First of all, even when the city was intact, loudspeakers and recorded songs were the norm. Secondly, even in the most liberal sections of Cairo, no mosque would allow a woman to sing the holy call to prayers.

Which, of course, made me think of Mohammad, and so I stood up and faced Mecca without so much as a second thought.

"What are you doing?" snarled the Scribe.

"I can't believe they haven't caught her yet," muttered Majeed, as he peered over the balcony.

I looked, too. Below, on the nearby waterfront, Shirtless Deadboys swarmed out of various buildings and headed off in organized pairs, some carrying what seem from this distance like spears.

The Scribe's arm grasped mine. "Get back to work."

"It's sunset," I pointed to the west where the sun quickly disappeared below the jumble of buildings. The desert was funny that way. With so few clouds and a flat landscape, one minute there was light, the next: dark. "I'm praying. Remember the five pillars of Islam?"

"You're a Deadboy now," the Scribe insisted.

"No he isn't," Majeed said before I could. However, I managed to emphasize Majeed's point, by jerking my arm from the Scribe's grasp and turning back in the approximate direction of Mecca, across the Nile. "Let him pray," Majeed cajoled. "What difference does it make?"

"What difference? That's our Nile out there he's praying over. This is what angered the gods to begin with, this new religion that took over our country."

Islam a new religion? That derailed me, and I totally forget what I was supposed to be doing. I quickly picked up the rhythm of touching my head to the ground and back up into a kneeling position. It surprised me how much I remembered. Like riding a bicycle, I guessed. The physical act brought forth words I swore I'd forgotten. Interspersed, I added: "Allah, please protect Mohammad, if it's your will and all that."

And that was when the first bullet hit the concrete railing.

Strangely, my first thought was, "Oh no, I haven't finished my translating." I leaped up and threw my body protectively over the papers. Bullets slammed into the walls with deafening cracks. Majeed and the Scribe yelled something, but it was garbled in the all the chaos. I scooped the manuals tight against me, refusing to move without my work.

See, the thing was: I made some promises today, and I'd damned if I wouldn't keep them.

The hail of bullets abruptly stopped. The umbrella, which had been shading my table from the afternoon sun, creaked on its wooden pole, whacked me in the back, and then tumbled over the balcony to splash in the Nile.

Miraculously, this appeared to be the only injury any of us sustained.

The Scribe and Majeed stood over me, shouting about what an idiot I was for not making a break for cover. Keeping one hand on my papers, I straightened up slowly. "I won't leave this undone. It was our deal."

Majeed shook his head sadly, like he thought I should have run further than just away from the bullets. The Scribe muttered something about his growing conviction regarding the instability of my mental state.

"Look at this," Majeed pointed to the size of the hole in the wall. "I don't

think this was our crazy muezzin woman this time. This looks like a 30.06
– professional, sniper rifle stuff. The most she's ever used is a .45 pistol."
Then, as an afterthought, he added, "And the crazy lady is much better shot.
She'd have killed us. Easy."

"A sniper? We should go inside," the Scribe glanced nervously out over
at the nearby island. I followed his gaze, though my eyes drifted to where a
crocodile hefted its weight onto the shoreline, scattering concerned sea gulls
in its path. "Do you think it could be the UN?" The Scribe asked. "Do you
think they're on to our plans?"

I began to gather up my things into deliberate piles, but I shook my head
at the men. Not only did I not what to go any closer to the stink of the interior of the building than I had to, but what they're saying made no sense.
"Riddle me this, Batman: if your sniper is a well-armed, professional soldier,
why did he miss? None of us were exactly moving targets."

"Good point." Majeed considered this, rubbing the five o'clock stubble on
his head. "I suppose our crazy lady harasser could have gotten hold of a bigger weapon." But he didn't sound like that was his favorite theory, and he
looked at me with a considering glance. "Or maybe this sniper wasn't trying
to kill us, just make us bolt."

"Why would he do that?" I asked, loving this kind of puzzle.

"Provide cover for your escape perhaps?" Majeed offered. "Only when it
was clear you weren't going to take advantage of it, he quit."

"Which means he might try again," the Scribe suggested.

"Yeah, we should get you somewhere safer."

"Wait, wait," I said, as the Scribe grabbed hold of me again. "Your theory has one huge problem. Nobody knows I'm here, right? And, anyway, it's
not like I have a lot of friends with access to high-powered weaponry."

Majeed flashed me that patented cop expression that said he thought I
was lying, which was made only slightly ridiculous thanks to his frilly, tattered tutu.

"What?" I asked, wrestling away from the Scribe long enough to tuck all
my papers under my arm. "What's that look supposed to mean?"

"You're one of Franklin's boys, aren't you?" Majeed said. Then, when the
Scribe glanced at him severely, he added with a nod at my silky purple shirt,
"It was obvious where you'd come from."

"And you think Franklin would send someone after me even if I were?
Obviously, you don't know Franklin Del Rosa very well."

"Oh, we do," the Scribe said. "Some of our best converts were once in Del
Rosa's employ."

Okay, I could sort of see the twisted logic there. Cut off the part that offends thee, and all that. "Yeah, sure, but I'm just not that important," I reminded them.

"And yet," Majeed said, taking my other arm to help the Scribe propel me into the presidential suite, as my feet dragged, "You're enough of a favorite that he'd sent someone to haul you back home, didn't he? Or were you just randomly being mugged when we came across you?"

Trust a former cop to jump to all the wrong conclusions. I decided not to dissuade him of them, however, since the truth just complicated things.

"Whatever," I muttered.

The two men shoved me somewhat unceremoniously onto a battered hotel couch. I nearly bounced onto the floor, the springs were so stiff. The rest of the room looked much like what you'd expect from a Hilton, except with a certain after-the-fall decor. Muddy boot prints tracked across the faux Persian rug at my feet. Water stains from burst pipes grayed the plaster walls in streaks. The Scribe and Majeed struck matches to light the candles scattered throughout the room, and something scuttled furiously in the wall behind me.

But outside of the smell of urine and sewage that permeated the place, it was a more comfortable and spacious place than many of holes Mohammad and I'd found to sleep in over the months. Majeed sat down beside me and offered a fresh coffee. I took it gratefully and resumed my work.

"You don't have to go back to him, you know," Majeed said kindly, and conspicuously not touching me in any way. "You could stay with us. If you go through the ritual, no one would ever molest you again."

"Yeah, but not for the right reasons," I said. Suddenly, I understood my "rescue" a lot more clearly. "You stake out Franklin's place, don't you? This argument works pretty well for a lot of kids, I bet."

"It does," The Scribe agreed from where he leaned against the archway separating the lounge from the kitchenette. "We offer a better life. You could have a place here with us. We always need strong, young men to tend the crops."

"What about young women? I mean, Deadboys. Where are all the girls? I mean, Isis gathered up Osiris' missing bits in the story, right? So they wouldn't have to cut anything off. You'd think that'd make your religion pretty appealing to women, wouldn't it?"

Majeed and the Scribe looked at each other like no one had ever asked them this question before. The Scribe shrugged, then answers: "The sacrifice is an important part of the novice's commitment to the gods."

"Besides," added Majeed. "Most of the women and girls have fled. My wife and daughter are somewhere in Syria."

We all sort of just left that hanging there. I wasn't quite sure what to say except that I could only imagine how crushed his wife must have been to learn which cult he'd joined.

So I put my head down and went back to translating.

Somewhere after midnight, I looked up. The Scribe's head lolled against the back of the overstuffed chair. Snores whistled softly through his nose. Majeed, on the other hand, was nowhere to be seen.

Setting my pen down, I stood up. My shoulders ached from their hunched position, and my brain swam with half-remembered Hebrew and mechanical terms. My bladder was full thanks to all the coffee I'd been swilling. I needed to pee.

I really didn't want to go anywhere near whatever passed for toilet facilities here, and I was thinking about leaving anyway because I'd completed everything except the computer manual. Even so, I did summarize its general scope in a paragraph (though what DOS was exactly, I couldn't quite fathom). It was a huge book, which would take me days to translate, and, besides, I didn't know what they'd need it for. No one used box computers any more, and these guys didn't even LINK as far as I could tell. Though they could; I noticed the Scribe had the tell-tale almond-shaped lump at his temple.

"Are you hungry?"

Majeed's voice startled me. He held a butcher knife as he stepped out of the kitchenette. Blood, or something equally reddish and drippy, spattered the blade. The image of my assailant's violent death sprang into my mind. I took a nervous step backward and nearly fell back onto the couch.

"No," I said, my voice breaking. "I've finished. And I have to pee."

"You translated all of that?"

"Yeah," I said, pointing to the pile of paper filled with my careful Arabic script.

He casually wiped the edge of his blade on the ruffles of his tutu. "You've been working hard. I'm surprised; you kept your word." He nodded approvingly, but then added. "Still, Osiris will be back soon. He can decide what to do with you then."

Uh-huh. I should have known.

Just once, I'd like someone to live up to their end of the bargain. "I still have to pee," I said, like I was perfectly cool with being their prisoner for the rest of my miserable life. "Can you tell me where should I go?"

"Anywhere is fine," he said, confirming my worst nightmare. "Balcony is probably best, though."

He turned his back and returned to his work in the kitchen. I glanced down at the Scribe, who looked back at me with annoyingly alert eyes. I pointed to the balcony. "Got to pee," I told him.

He nodded like he could care less, and propped his feet up on a nearby footstool. I walked out to the balcony, completely deflated. I knew they had no intention of letting me go. Ever.

Out on the balcony, the air smelled fresher. Dozens of fire pits dotted the island. The listing, twisted form of Cairo Tower flickered in the wavering light. Laughter drifted in the breeze, and somewhere nearby a man sang "Baladi," the Egyptian national anthem.

It wouldn't be difficult to like these people and their cause. But the bright, white moon stared down at me with an androgynous face that always looked to me like its mouth gaped wide open and screamed.

I couldn't stay here. Mohammad had been in that horrible place already too long.

Undoing my pants, I pissed into the potted palm at the corner of the balcony. Once I've finished, I hauled myself onto the balcony railing. I didn't let myself think about the fact that the Nile was no longer actually that deep, and a seven-story drop could easily kill me.

Instead, I focused on Mohammad and what I owed him.

And I jumped.

Present Day

"No," I say, mostly to myself, but, no doubt, Page notices as I close down the airline information. "I need to see this thing through."

The light changes and we start across the street, mindlessly following the herd of pedestrians. Deidre chews on her lip, clearly wanted to say something.

"What?" I prompt.

"Why is this so important *now*? Sounds like the last time anyone saw this Mohammad woman was the Blackout. What makes you think she's here in Egypt or... even alive?"

Tell her what Dragon found.

"He left me a message," I say, though can I barely stand to squeak it out. "I only discovered it a few months ago and even then I didn't understand it, actually, until Dragon decoded it for me."

"What kind of message?"

We pass a group of people sitting in tables and chairs set up as overflow for a crowded restaurant. I smell the tempting odor of *sahlib*, a hot, creamy drink made with nuts and raisins.

"Horse and buggy on the autobaun. I should have seen it, but I zoomed right around it." Dee frowns at me in confusion. I shake my head, too embarrassed to explain my lapse to a former LINK vice-cop who would mock my incompetence. "It doesn't really matter. Dragon was able to pinpoint the message's origin. Mohammad was in Egypt, alive, at least as of this time last year."

Maybe he's gone on hajj, Page says. *Perhaps we could meet Mohammad in Mecca.*

I sigh. *You're like a broken record, Page. Anyway, why are you so anxious? Haven't you already gone in a cool suit with Rebeckah?*

I have, Page admits. *But I wish to go with* you. *I think it's time to admit that this is a fool's errand, father.*

Shock by his words, I stop short. "What? What makes you say that?"

"What did he say?" Deidre asks, searching my face as if to read Page's thought's there.

"Well?" I demand.

It is impossible to rescue Mohammad now. You left him to his fate forty years ago, father. It's too late.

"I know," my voice is quiet. "But it's not too late to apologize."

Are you sure?

A MOUSE THAT ROARED: How Free Access Saved North Africa
By Keela Ryū
Forthcoming from Doubleday Harcourt Penguin, 2111

Excerpted interview of Mouse; footnote commentary by "Page"/Strife

"The Russians freak me out. Something very weird happened to Russia after the Medusa War. The blast that glassed huge sections of the Siberian petrol fields was last bit of non-government regulated news to leak out of Russia, and after that, everything went silent. The great bear retreated behind its silent curtain...

... and came out another gender.

I think something very bad happened to Russian men[9], but hardly anyone has been allowed in or out of the country in the intervening years...

---

9. Conjecture, of course, but my father lays out an interesting theory.

besides me, of course.[10]

I have a theory. It's based on nothing concrete or substantial, just guesses I made during my brief stint as the Minister of Economy, after escaping imprisonment in the United States. My hypothesis is that the Americans changed the Medusa bomb at some point, ala some Manhattan Project mad-scientist deal gone wrong, and instead of making Gorgons, their new version fucked up the male chromosome. Only they didn't know what was going to happen until they dropped it. Once they did, they unleashed this new and improved Medusa on the Russians and whammo: no more dudes. Or, at least a plague of some kind of whacked-out radiation which spread like the glass and mutated the boy gene.

Maybe that's why all the ladies all seemed pretty interested in, shall we say, spreading my genetic material around. I've never been luckier than I was in Russia.

What a great country.

But, I digress.

Point is, Russian soldiers are all women. You didn't see many during the Blackout Years, but they always stood out. The peaceforcers had a few female volunteers, but they'd all been hybridized into things that were more weapon than woman.

Uhm, when I say it like that, it sounds pretty hot. Too bad the reality was up in your face with a bulletproof shield and a shock stick. Not sexy at all, unless you're into the whole beat-up thing, which I can't really say that I am. You can talk me into handcuffs any day, but anything that needs a safe word or a blackmarket painkiller in the morning stops being fun for me."[11]

---

10. And me. After all, I am the entirety of the Russian operating system.

11. This falls, for me, at least, into the category of far too much information.

Chapter 8
Morningstar

Cairo, Egypt
Present Day

When I spotted the angel on the boulevard, I ducked into a nearby news-stand to avoid detection. But, as I watched her over an English-language edition of *Al-Ahram Weekly*, I grew angry. Of all the angels in heaven, God sends this one?

Ariel moved slowly down the street toward me, window shopping with friends. An over six-foot frame was a bit too square for the tasteful gray skirt she wore, and strangely incongruous with the Asian cast to her features. Her straight, black hair was demurely covered with a brightly patterned head-scarf, the kind favored by female tourists making an effort not to offend.

The gaggle of young men who traveled with her, however, don't even attempt to disguise their exuberant fabulousness.

"God has some nerve sending *you*, Ariel," I said, stepping out from my hiding place.

A number of her escorts gasped in surprise at my sudden appearance. "Who the hell are you?", one of them demanded. I ignored the irony of the question, and the mortals in general.

"Morningstar, darling," Ariel smiled as if we were long-lost friends chancing to meet on some Egyptian byway. Her voice was deep and masculine, and I found the sound of it set my teeth on edge. Was Father mocking the prophet's sacrifice?

"I'm so glad I ran into you," she continued. "I have some news."

"Of course you do," I said dismissively. You'd think the four would tire of being God's personal messengers. "Why don't I invite you and your friends back to my place? I'm sure they could find some diversion there and we could talk privately."

"Lovely! Where are you staying?"

Ariel pursed her lips in disapproval when I showed her my establishment. Some of her friends, at least, seemed moderately impressed. "Yes," I assured them. "Whatever you want is on the house."

"Still peddling sin, I see," she said. Though I thought she sounded more disappointed than she needed to, given that at least half her friends chose to decline my generous offer.

I shrugged. "Sin hardly needs me for an advocate, but I might as well profit from it."

She followed me upstairs without further comment. As we passed through the antechamber, I was pleased to hear her choke a little at the toys I hadn't bothered to put away in my haste to meet up with Dee and Mouse. Inside my private room, I offered her a choice of chairs. She picked my favorite leather recliner near the window. She primly placed her handbag onto the nearby end table.

I stood by the door, my arms crossed. "House," I said, addressing the voice-activated butler system. Since I didn't have the LINK, I'd revived the ancient, nearly decrepit program when I took over the business. "Have one of the boys bring up tea for two."

"By your command," it replied in a tinny, robotic voice.

"Quaint," Ariel noted, as she adjusted her skirt.

"It's all part of the whole 'old-world charm' for sale at Franklin's Place," I said, but I was impatient with this pretense of friendly banter. "I will not be stopped, Ariel. *Especially* not by you."

"What makes you think that anyone wants to get in your way?" she said with a Mona Lisa smirk.

"I'm not playing *that* game either," I said with a warning shake of my head. "You aren't going to convince me that there was a plan from the beginning. I know the truth. Mom fucked up. She sent me to do the devil's work, but she didn't consider how vile and disgusting her pet mortal creatures really are. Now that I'm considering fixing Her mess, you flutter down to take credit. No. No fucking way. You can kiss my ass, you—"

My rant was interrupted by a polite knock on the door. "Master, your tea," said a hesitant voice on the other side.

Irritated, I stepped aside and whipped the door open. Apparently thinking my appetite insatiable, my young servant had brought tea and himself – the silver tray the only thing shielding his privates from full view.

"Just the tea this evening," I said, relieving him of the service in more ways than one. Reaching into my pocket, I pulled out a credit counter and handed over a substantial tip.

Sketching a quick bow, he left.

"You were about to call *me* a name, brother?" Ariel prompted.

"It still applies," I said, setting the tray down on my desk. I made no move to offer her a cup, but I poured myself one. I wished it were something much, much stronger, but alcohol was harder to come by during Ramadan. "How can you stand to sit there so smugly? Look what you have to do to get around God's rigidity."

She scratched her chin with polished nails, composing her thoughts. After a moment, she said, "Flesh, clothes – it's all a costume, Morningstar."

"But it's a decision He makes for you," I said. Every time God sent an angel from heaven they came down in a precast form. God had made all the archangels male. Interestingly, that meant that the moment Ariel hit the wall of free will, she consciously made the decision to dress as a woman – and there would always be things she could not hide or change. "And it bothers you, sister, or you wouldn't transform the way you look."

"The way I look doesn't change who I am."

"Lovely words, Ariel, but they belie God's hypocrisy on this subject."

"The hypocrisy is not God's, but humankind's. When you remove man from the equation, it is obvious God's opinion on the subject. Nature is abundant with gender diversity. Oysters change gender. Reed frogs easily switch at will. Clown fish will alter their sex with environmental pressure."

"Nice, and I should say, a bit ironic, for the lower creatures to be more God-like than precious 'adam'."

She shrugged. "God leads by example. If people can't see the connections, that's a by-product of free choice."

"That's a cop out, Ariel, and you know it. Look around; God stacked the deck. Day and night, sun and moon, living and dead, the list goes on – they seem inordinately fond of dualities. It's no wonder Their people are confused."

"Actually, I think it's beetles He's inordinately fond of, some of which have three genders, *and* I disagree. The point is that duality is a very human concept, and not even every culture even ascribes to it. The Hindu philosophers have a third sex."

I stared at my tea cup, trying to will its contents to become a nice, peaty Scotch. A sip disappointed, and I frowned darkly at it. "It doesn't change the fact that Father knowingly sent His lamb to the slaughter. *Again.* Only this time His little kindness meme didn't replicate, did it?"

"There's still time."

I glared at Ariel over the rim of my cup. Honestly, I didn't like the sound of that. Father tended to think the best way to spread a message was to create a martyr.

Ariel got up and walked over to the desk. She used the tongs to put two cubes of sugar into her cup before pouring. Casually, as she stirred the tea with a spoon, she noted: "You didn't actually *finish* the job We asked of you, did you, Morningstar?"

Blackout

After learning the prophet's secret, I couldn't sleep. Instead, I volunteered for a double-shift on patrol. I paced the camp's boundaries, my mind churning. It was a surprisingly familiar story. Father certainly seemed to relish putting his favorites into no-win situations. He hardly needed me to heft a sword, one slip and there would be no mercy shown the prophet by the people to whom she had given nothing but love.

I supposed I might as well assume my role in this doomed morality play. What should I tempt with, I wondered? A softly-made bed? Clean water? A pain-free, perfect sex change?

I was near the women's compound when the first rays of sunlight broke on the mangled remains of the National Museum. The prophet sang out the call to prayers in a hauntingly beautiful voice, though I thought I detected a slight American accent in her otherwise perfect Arabic.

Curiouser and curiouser.

With the others, I turned to face Mecca. Bodies bent in supplication, but not mine. Belligerently, I stared in God's direction, while the words of worship reverberated through the multitudes. I was still contemplating how to get close to the prophet when, after prayers had finished, a hand gently touched my sleeve.

There was no reproach, only curiosity in the question: "You don't pray, soldier?"

The prophet stood at my side, her head barely reaching my shoulder. The morning revealed dust and grime stubbornly clinging to the tattered fabric of her robes. I gave Mecca one last look before turning my back to it. "I kneel only to Allah Himself, never to any creature of mud and clay."

The breath she took in sounded horrified. "You would *mock* the holy Quran? You would pretend to mouth the words of Iblis?"

"I pretend nothing," I said, letting just a hint of my true nature show.

"Merciful Allah," her voice revealed the affect my small disclosure had had. Whatever she had seen, it made her entire body quake. "It can't be."

I simply nodded. Michael and the others were always better at this part than I was. I knew I was supposed to say something awe-inspiring or at least Scripture worthy, but, well, you'll notice my last conversation in the desert had been paraphrased too.

"I don't believe it," she said. "You... It can't be."

I smiled. "Nice try, but I wouldn't be here if your faith was truly so weak."

Around us, the camp began packing up. Even as breakfast was being prepared, tents were dismantled and belongings stowed into bicycle trailers. The prophet reached up as though to chew thoughtfully on a fingernail, but the veil stopped her.

"Still not entirely used to it, are you?"

Her denial was entirely unconvincing. "I don't know what you're talking about."

"Are you seriously going to lie to me?"

"I don't suppose that's advisable, eh?"

Her ability to find the humor at this moment utterly charmed me, and I laughed.

"Should we walk?" she asked, turning her head as though to glance around for a fruit tree or a desert.

"We should have breakfast," I smiled. "I'm starving."

A long buffet table had been fashioned from concrete blocks and a piece of a broken door. Breakfast options were simple: beans, rice, or beans *and* rice. I went for the latter.

"I sometimes pray that the peaceforcers might drop more interesting manna from the sky," the woman who ladled my breakfast into a chipped coffee cup said with a smile. "Insh'allah."

"Insh'allah," I agreed.

After taking chopsticks from the pile of "utensils," the prophet and I found a shaded spot on the sidewalk far removed from the camp where we would be undisturbed. We put our backs to the railing so we could watch the decamping process. The Nile gurgled through its restricted pathway beneath us. Seagulls drifted lazily overhead.

"Different food would be nice," the prophet agreed, lifting her veil only enough to slip the jar lid she used as a spoon underneath. Her arm moved awkwardly, like it had been injured and never quite properly healed. "But I pray we continue to stay ahead of the pirates and rat kings."

"You should lead your people out of the wilderness," I suggested. "You could take them to the promised land. Israel isn't that far from here."

"Is that what Allah wants me to do?" she sounded surprised.

"How would I know?" I asked with a snort. "We're not that close."

Tilting her head, she regarded me. "Oh? So why are you here, then?"

I gave her a look that let her know how little I appreciated smartasses. "Typically it's my job in these kinds of stories to see what it is I can tempt you with. You deny me, yada, yada."

The rice seemed to catch in her throat. "These kinds of stories?"

"I'm sure you've heard one or two. They tend to happen in this part of the world, angels show up and make all sorts of pronouncements, and things end badly for our hero... or heroine, as the case may be."

She set her bowl of rice on the ground. Wiping her hands lightly on her robe, she stood up and said in English, "This is fucking crazy. You're not Iblis, and I'm no al-Mahdi."

Shoveling beans and rice into my mouth, I gave her a long considering glance as I chewed. "I can make everything normal if that's what you *want*."

Of course, it was a lie. I had no more power over the affairs of mortals than anyone else. But that fact never stopped people from believing that I could grant them fame or fortune or whatever they thought their ridiculous human soul was worth. The contracts I negotiated were complete shams. People forged their own fate and caused their own downfall, while the only thing I ever got out of the deal was the blame. Well, and an entertaining spectacle now and then.

The prophet contemplated my words as the sun rose higher in the cloudless sky. Through the thick soles of my boots, I felt the concrete beginning to bake in the heat.

"Could you end the suffering of the people here?"

"I'm not that kind of angel," I said. "Besides, it's that kind of altruistic attitude that gets you nailed to a tree. This isn't about them, it's about you."

"Me?" her voice broke strangely, almost like a boy's. "What does Allah see in me, anyway?"

Seagulls wheeled overhead, crying out plaintively. I watched their lazy circles, as I tried to guess God's mind. "In my experience, it's surprisingly simple messages that prophets impart. Be nice to other people. Everyone is important. Try to do more good than harm." I shrugged. "Basic stuff that your mortal colleagues never seem to really 'get' unless someone dies trying to tell them about it."

There's a slight quiver in her voice. "I don't want to die."

"You won't. Your soul is immortal. That was an early message, and a very dramatic death, I might add," I wave the chopsticks her chest pointedly. "You're supposed to be more advanced than the others. Get with the program."

She laughed. "I guess I can't be a prophet, I'm too stupid."

I'd met many of these sorts before, but none of them charmed me quite as easily. The prophet had a way of bringing out a genuine smile in me, so I teased, "I could grant you greater intelligence. Is that what you want?"

She shook her head, "There isn't anything I want."

I leaned back and stretched my legs out. Now it was time to pull out the ultimate temptation. Tilting my head up, I asked, "Nothing?"

"No," she said, and I thought I detected a little righteousness in her tone.

"Not even to be fully a woman?"

To my surprise, she scoffed. "Definitely not that."

Had I been wrong? No, I know what I saw. I pulled at my lip, considering. The way she so quickly rejected "that" offer made me suggest the other, "A man, then?"

This option gave her pause. She looked around to see if anyone was listening. When she found her voice, it was all breath and hope, "You could do that?"

I couldn't. Miracles cost a lot of energy. Though I had the ability and the will to perform them, I'd been selfishly saving a massive one for the final day.

Still, a better angel would have stayed silent and allowed the prophet to think her wish was well within my power. But at that moment for some reason, I found myself unable to lie. "No," I said, looking at the dust swirling at my feet. "That's one thing I can't do."

"What? Why not?"

"I don't have a good answer for that," I looked directly at the lighter weave of the hood that concealed her eyes. "Despite the very nature of God, such things are predetermined for angel and adam. I'm honestly very sorry."

The prophet stood in silence for a long time. I ate my breakfast and waited. I was scraping the last of the food from the mug, when she finally asked, "How am I supposed to feel about the devil's sympathy?"

My jaw flexed angrily. I pulled myself up to my full height and glared down at the prophet. "I was once the greatest of them all. I stood closest and burned brightest."

Other people would have taken a step back, but the prophet put her hands on narrow hips. "Alright," she said. "If you once knew Allah's heart so well, tell me this: why did he put me in the wrong body? Is it his will I suffer?"

"It is," I said without hesitation. This was a question I had more practice answering. "But your pain is part of what you are, and what you are is part of the divine All."

"What the hell does that mean?"

"Work it out," I said with a shrug. Thing was, I didn't want the prophet to doubt the truth, and she might, if the Adversary told her it meant that God might treat her like shit, but He loved her.

While I spoke with the prophet on the bridge, I felt watchful eyes on me. A woman with a baby in her arms passed close, trying to catch the prophet's attention. But the prophet was still trying to work out the eternal theological conundrum of how it was that Allah could be such an ass and love her at the same time. I tried to smile at the prophet's friend with her bright pink hijab and her happily gurgling child, but she shot me a dark look and turned her infant's face away from my influence.

Smart woman.

In my experience, women often protected their prophets the most fiercely. Friends might become betrayers or deniers or doubters, but not mothers, sisters, wives or girlfriends. They never got much credit for their loyalty, but there it was.

"They know, don't they?" I asked the prophet. To her startled posture, I explained, "The women. You share your tent with them. They all know what you are – or are not, as the case may be."

"What of it?" she asked, nervously belligerent.

"It's just – interesting," I lied smoothly. "How do you convince them not to betray you?"

The prophet seemed to be staring over the river at the rising sun, Mecca, or both. "My sister... she recognized me on the street and followed me... here. She was a ghost, wearing this." Her hands swept the length of black robes. "I didn't even know she was alive. We'd been separated when the dams broke. She was with my parents at Mugamma, trying to straighten out my visa. I'd been arrested and detained at the airport – for fraud."

"Fraud?" I raised my eyebrows. "Like this one?"

"No," she said sharply, turning back to face me. "This is the fraud. What I was then is what I am."

I'd always thought Egypt was more tolerant than a lot of other Middle East countries. I told the prophet so.

"After the Medusa, things have been harder. Fundamentalism is taking hold all over the place in weird ways," she said. "The customs officer was particularly upset because of, well, my name and where we'd just come from."

"America?" I guessed from her accent.

"Well, yes, but, Mecca," the prophet said. "I had been on hajj."

I suddenly thought I understood. I laid out my theory for the prophet, "Let me guess. You changed your name after hajj to Mohammad, as is your right. But, your legal name, the one on the passport, belonged to a woman. The customs officer found that particularly sacrilegious."

She nodded.

"But why the burqa now? Why not just live as a rat king?"

Her fists clenched, and she turned her head as if to spit. "Because that fucking bastard lied to us. He never planned to pay for any testosterone. He just gave me a tampon and told me to cowboy-up."

"Oh. You're not..." I found I didn't know the right word, so I said, "... finished."

"It's an incredibly long physical process, okay? Mentally, spiritually, I've always known, but I only just started transitioning my body. They make us wait until we're at least fifteen. I was lucky. My parents are..." she hesitated here, then corrected the tense regretfully, "*were* supportive. They let me do what I could, but the testosterone is prescription. I had a six-month supply implanted, but, well – the fucking dams broke, didn't they?"

I nodded that I understood. The prophet was stuck somewhere in-between. I guessed I should start thinking of the prophet as "him," but first impressions were hard to shake. Besides, the burqa hid so much that my imagination had forever invented an image with no bearing on reality. "So you need the women. They're helping you with your—" slang had changed so much in my lifetime, I settled on, "monthly feminine issues. So they *do* know."

The prophet seemed to consider the prudence of confirming my suspicions. Finally, she said, "Some do. Others think what they want."

I nodded. Her secret would still kill her. Even if the women didn't feel lied to, the men would. There's little people hated more than thinking they'd been duped. And some of these boys probably had a crush on her... and if they thought she was a he or wanted to be one-

To banish the image that sprung far too easily to mind, I shook my head, not at all certain I wanted to see this thing through to the end.

A man came by pulling a bicycle trailer full of gear. "Tell me, prophet, where are your people headed?"

"The bridge is too exposed in the daylight. We have too few weapons. We can't defend it from those who would take our goods. We wander during the day, sometimes taking to the tunnels."

I supposed that made sense. "May I travel with you?"

"What of your brother?"

"Honestly? I'm hoping to ditch him."

She laughed at my choice of words. "Considering who I think he is, I'm not sure that's a good thing."

"Oh, it most certainly is. Michael was sent here to kill you."

Present Day

Ariel delicately replaced the spoon on silver tray, as though she hadn't just reminded me that I'd failed to assassinate the prophet. She took a sip and nodded appreciatively, guessing, "Jasmine?"

"Mother is stickler for detail," I said, ignoring the discussion of tea. "I discharged my duty."

"You incited a riot you thought would kill Mohammad, but you didn't hang around to make sure things played out."

"I fell for her. I probably loved her. Excuse me if I recused myself from the horror of watching her body torn limb from limb." I set my cup down, and turned to stare out the window. Fireworks burst in the sky.

"You were meant to be Our sword. You broke your promise to Us."

I snarled at the crowd below. "You asked too much."

A soft touch brushed my shoulder. I stiffened under the obvious show of pity. Wisely, she dropped her hand. I heard her pick up her tea and settle back into the chair. "You're so unpredictable, so chaotic. They should never have trusted you with such an important assignment."

"True," I said sharply. I turned to face Ariel. Fury burned, shredding the earthly disguise I wore like a flimsy burqa. "They should have sent *you*. The irony would have been lovely, and you could have buried your sword in the prophet's tender heart and given it a twist."

Watching me carefully, she set the cup down slowly. Standing up, she held herself at the ready. "Your wings are showing, brother."

"Damn straight," I hissed, wondering if I looked to her as I did on heaven's battlefield when I stormed the citadel with two-thirds of the host at my side. A dark, challenging smile slid across my lips. "Now let's see what you've got."

"I didn't come here to fight," she said, though the crackles of fireworks flashed the shadow of the long, thin wings of a crane onto the wall behind her.

"With your insults and accusations, what did you come for, exactly?"

"To make things right."

I laughed. "Right? Are you sure His plan is the right one? What about justice? Is what He's asking really fair?"

She frowned, as if the thought that God might be wrong about something had never occurred to her. "The will of Allah is not for us to judge, brother."

"I disagree. But then, I always have. If you plan to harm the prophet, you will have to get through me."

"If you won't finish this, We will."

"The hell you will," I said as I rushed across the room and grabbed her by the blouse. Where my hands touched her, the flame of my rage burned the flesh from her skin. We tumbled to the floor.

The ground shook as angels fought.

ABANDONED!
Six Months after Dams Break, Boys Discovered at School

June 7, 2059
Associated Press

Maadi, Egypt—Seven survivors were found still living in the ruins of the British International School located in Maadi, a wealthy suburb south of Cairo. Though the sandstorm season has slowed efforts elsewhere, the British government pressured rescue crews from the United Nations Peacekeeping Force to investigate the school after the British Prime Minister's office received what they are calling a "distress signal." The exact nature of the message, however, is unclear. Though the spokesperson for the Prime Minster's office referred to their source as "electronic," none of the survivors are old enough to be LINKed, which has led to concerns regarding a possible hack.

When asked whether or not security could be breached, LINK expert Brian Wang emphatically stated, "It's impossible. The only access to the LINK is through the proprietary operating system of a triggered nexus." However, the British government has agreed to turn over the message for study to the Advanced Lymphatic Kernel Research team in Calcutta, India.

The survivors claim no knowledge of how their plight was uncovered. Most were severely malnourished and have been airlifted to Israel, where they are expected to make a full recovery.

Chapter 9
Mouse

Cairo, Egypt
Present Day

A firecracker explodes overhead followed by the phantom sensation of the ground shifting slightly beneath my feet. Deidre senses it as well. She gives me a curious look. "An earthquake?" she asks.

Unlikely.

I shake my head. Other people felt it too. A shopkeeper coming out to look around catches my eye. I smile and shrug as if to say there's nothing to worry about, but I understand his concern. Though the traces of it have been erased from the architecture, the Blackout made its indelible mark on memory.

It wasn't so long ago.

Some things make a lasting impression.

Mohammad will not have forgotten either.

Blackout

Jumping wasn't my smartest decision. I'd fallen a lot lately, and I couldn't say that the sensation improved with repetition.

This go-round, at least, I had time to desperately try to remember if it was smarter to hit the water feet-first or pointed head-down like a diver. I opted for the former, though less due to conscious thought then by accident. I kept my heels together tightly and hugged my chest as hard as I could.

The tepid water shocked like a slap. Curling myself into a ball, I prayed I stop moving before I slammed into the debris-laden bottom. Instead, I sunk deeply into silt and mud – a possibility that hadn't occurred to me.

My hands groped blindly in a direction I hoped was upward. Suddenly, my hand hit something solid and rough, like rebar – amazing that I hadn't skewered myself on it. I used the debris to lever my body out of the muck that dragged at me like a weight. Each pull sapped precious strength. Finally, the mud released me from its death-grip.

The water was black as the night above. My brain recalled something about bubbles and labored to follow them. My lungs burned, but I mechanically stroked and kicked. Thank Allah I'd suffered through Mr. Smythe's swimming lessons, which I'd snarkily thought fairly useless living in a desert.

The blackness disoriented me. A strong undercurrent threatened to shove me further under. It occurred to me at that moment that, despite my noble intentions, I was going to drown.

My muscles spasmed from fighting the undertow. Strength ebbed from my exhausted body. It was ironic, really, that I escaped the Deadboys, only to die in the clutches of their holy Nile.

I clung to the ragged edges of consciousness, as something took hold of me and lifted me up. My first thought was, "Oh, crap. Crocodile," but I was too weak to protest. Suddenly, solidness supported my back. Before I could be grateful for that, someone hit my solar plexus so hard that I heaved out great, huge quantities of water I hadn't even realized I'd swallowed.

"Oh, this is bad," I thought, as I continued to struggle for breath. Water poured out my mouth and nose. The whole river was "toxic soup" even before the bodies began to decompose and raw sewage bled into the Nile.

When I finally stopped coughing, I looked up into a face back-lit by a halo of moonlight. I honestly couldn't tell if my rescuer was a man or a woman because all I saw were wings.

Feathers, like sharp shards of moonlight, blinded me. With the blood-curdled screams of the damned, a thousand voices trumpeted through the silence of the night. My voice joined theirs.

Then my ears popped.

"I said, are you okay?"

A gurgling noise died in my throat, as I shielded my eyes from the flashlight shining in my face. My movement rocked the boat. Waves splashed against the wooden sides. Water dribbled from my nose, and I sneezed.

A hand helped me upright, and I leaned against the hard metal seat of a canoe. I stared at the face looking with deep concern into my own. I finally registered features: a rather delicately heart-shaped face belonging to a white woman with short-cropped, dark-brown hair. A slight dusting of freckles spotted her nose. A high-powered rifle slung over her shoulder.

My rescuer used the flashlight to dig through a military-issue, olive-green bag. After rummaging around for a moment, she handed me a medicine bottle. I blinked at her askance.

"Antibiotics," she said, her English betraying an Eastern European accent of some kind. "Given how much water you managed to drink, you should probably start taking those right away."

"Uh, okay," my eyes stayed riveted to the rifle, thinking of the sniper who attacked the Deadboys' compound earlier. She retrieved the paddle from where she'd tucked it and began to steer us along the river. She wore a black muscle shirt that showed off a hard body, a silver chain disappeared into the swell of her chest. Dog tags? That assumption made sense given the combat boots, camouflage pants, and the Sam Brown belt that held a pistol, a hand-cuffs case, and other military bits of some kind. Only, I didn't see any insignia. No display of rank was visible anywhere, though I thought one of her biceps had a tattoo of some kind.

What was it with everybody and tattoos?

"Are you going to stare at me or take your pills?" she asked.

I struggled with the child-safety lock top for a few minutes and then shook a couple of huge pills into my hand. "How many?" I managed to croak.

"I have no idea. How about two?"

That ruled out the medical corps, I thought as I reached for the flashlight rolling around in the bottom of the canoe. My arms felt heavy and sore as I shone the light on the bottle, hoping for instructions.

They were there, only in Greek... or maybe Russian. Neither of which language I could read terribly well. I wondered if my rescuer did, though like with everything lately, I got the feeling I didn't want to know the answer. It would lead to too many questions, like: why would a Russian soldier with-out any identifying insignia just happen to be floating in a boat close enough to the Deadboys' headquarters to rescue me, of all people, from nearly drowning? Or, perhaps the more nagging one: does anything in my life hap-pen by coincidence? Was I going to have to start believing in God and fate and angels?

I couldn't deal with any of that right now, so I swallowed the pills dry. Sticking the bottle in my pocket for later use, I shivered. The temperature didn't drop as hard near the river as in the desert, but the chill was notice-able.

"You need dry clothes," my rescuer informed me in that accent I was more and more convinced was Russian. She kicked her duffle at me. "Find something."

I resisted the urge to respond, "yes, ma'am." Instead, as I used the flash light to inspect the contents of the bag, I said, "So, like, thanks for saving my life, uh – what should I call you?"

"Katarina," she replied. "You?"

Oh, I see, first name basis only: "Christian."

She laughed. "What, not Mohammad?"

I would have sneered, but the woman carried more ammunition than clothes in her duffle, so I decided on diplomacy. "My mother, the comedian, I guess."

I managed to find a sweater and a pair of black drawstring pants that might fit. In the interest of modesty, I switched off the flashlight. My shirt stuck to my skin. But the pants, which never fit well to begin with, oozed off easily, though I rocked the canoe enough that Katarina shouted for me to be careful. The new clothes smelled of gun oil and dust, but they were dry and snug. I sat on the seat, and looked out over the Nile. We navigated through narrow passages of toppled buildings. Moonlight reflected on the glass of windows.

"I guess I was, uh, lucky you were hanging around when I decided to swan-dive off the building back there, eh?"

"Yes," Katarina agreed without offering the further explanation I'd hoped for. "And, as you seem intact, my presumption is that you're running away from the Deadboys?"

"I like to think of it as contract renegotiation," I said, not wanting to consider how it was that she got a chance to inspect my intactness. "Which I need to do a bit more of. Tonight." A glanced up at the moon which still showed that accusing face. "Soon."

The bottom of the canoe scraped on something below the water, and Katarina used the oar like a pole to push us over it.

"Where are we going?" I finally realized I should have asked some time ago.

"To Franklin Dela Rosa's," she said. "I believe you left something of mine there. I want it back."

I scratched my hair and felt kernels of sand wedged in my scalp. "Uh, okay. I guess I left something important there, too."

"Good, then we are agreed. We will retrieve it together."

While I liked the idea of having a little firepower at my side for once, I had a strong sense we aren't talking about the same thing.

The oars splashed rhythmically as the canoe sailed swiftly through a canyon of tumbled buildings.

We glided past a sideways wall of glass-plated windows. A white, marble spire of a submerged mosque rose gracefully in the center of watery court-yard. The moon blanketed everything in a soft, silver, silent light. "It's love-ly, isn't it?" Katarina said.

"If my people weren't buried under it all, it might be," I agreed.

"Come now," she chided. "Even graveyards can be beautiful."

"Depends if you're living or dead."

"So which are you, Christian?"

For I moment I remembered the image of the angel, and wondered if I should consider her question literally. But my body ached too much for this to be the afterlife, and, though Katarina had a certain butch hotness, she did-n't really look like all those virgins I was promised. "Death would be nicer than this."

She laughed. "Yes, I suppose it would."

Katarina steered the canoe through an artificial rapids caused by tumbled debris. We swung around a tight corner and then were pushed out into a more open section of the Nile. The wave tops glittered darkly. Continuing downriver, we slid though swirling swarms of gnats.

With the slap of the oars, Katarina propelled us toward a shoreline of crumbled concrete. "We will walk from here," she informed me, as the boat thumped against the rubble.

With an expert leap, Katrina was out and on land.

I was a bit more wobbly on my feet still so I let her help me onto the rocks. My bare feet struggled for a grip on the slimy, algae covered stones, but somehow I scrambled up the pile. Katarina pushed the canoe into a wedge of rocks, and secured it with a rope. From the back of the boat, she removed a tarp. Once spread over the canoe, she made one final flick of an adjustment and it disappeared.

I blinked.

I couldn't see the canoe. It wasn't terribly visible before in the dark, but now it was gone. The only thing I could make out was rock and water. I wondered how she'd ever find it again, though it occurred to me that if Katarina had access to holographic tech, there was probably some secret GPS unit that would help her relocate the hidden boat.

I whistled lowly in appreciation: this chick had access to some serious firepower.

As if I hadn't already guessed.

No, the real mystery was why she fished little old me out of the black water. Except that was beginning to seem pretty obvious too. "So this impor-tant thing you left at Franklin's place, it doesn't happen to involve a dead soldier does it?"

Katarina strolled over casually to where I stood. Her eyes stayed on me while her hands automatically checked the status of her weapons. She, of course, towered several centimeters over me. Ropy, stone-hard muscles bulged like those of some aging American rock star. The tattoo on her bicep showed a red star some Cyrillic lettering formed an arch over the point. My luck, it probably stood for KGB or whatever their secret assassin corps was called these days.

"Why do you ask questions you know the answer to?"

Why did I, indeed?

Katarina took me by the arm, like we were lovers going to a ball. I looked up into cold, sea-green eyes, and had an epiphany. "You know, if we're going in to Franklin's, we're going to need a plan."

"Ah," she said with a delighted smile. "You sound like you might have one."

"It involves deceit. Do you have the stomach for trickery?"

Katarina's grin was as soulless as sin. "Darling, I invented it."

So I laid it out for her, and it went like this. She pretended to be a wealthy customer and asked for my guy inside, Mohammad.

"You have a guy inside? And, Mohammad, really? Is that a joke?"

"Do you want your stuff back or not?"

She did, so I explained that, "The thing is that you've got to convince Franklin to let you have your way with Mohammad off-campus, as it were. Tell him, maybe, you're into the whole after-the-fall fuck, I don't know. We've just got to get him out of there."

"And this Mohammad guy, he has my stuff?"

No, but I wasn't going to tell her that. "Yeah, yeah, he's got it."

She gave me a sidelong look that seemed very considering and skeptical. "I thought you offered it to Franklin directly."

What, was she in the room? Franklin's place must be riddled with spyware. I waved my hand like I wasn't worried about such a small detail. "Mohammad can get it off him. I'm sure of it."

"How will Mohammad know he's supposed to get the device out? Do you have some kind of signal worked out?"

Oh, if only. "Of course we do," I tried to sound like I was deeply insulted that she took me for such a fool. And "device?" That was new information.

"So what is it?"

"What?"

"Your password." Katarina got that look in her eye again, like she was on the verge figuring out my entire deception.

We passed a house covered in scaffolding, as so many building had been before the flood since no property taxes were required for structures under construction.

Out from under the planking scooted a little brown rodent. It dashed into the relative light of the moonlit street, and then back into the safety of the shadows.

"You do have a password or some other code, yes?" She asked again.

Don't hesitate, Chris. Say anything, say anything fast: "Mouse. Tell Mohammad a mouse sent you."

Katarina laughed, not a sound I hoped to hear. "So, is this your street handle? I thought Franklin called you his little rat."

Merciful Allah, she'd somehow heard every word between us. I wasn't sure where all this chutzpah is coming from, but I rolled with it. "Yeah, that's Franklin's attempt at a joke," I snorted derisively, like this was common knowledge. "*Every*body calls me Mouse."

"Well, it's a sight better than Christian," she shrugged. "And with those ears, you do sort of look like a rodent."

Oh, nice. At least it would never stick.

Present Day

"Mouse?" Deidre looks up into my eyes, concern bringing out deep wrinkles. "What did the message from Mohammad say, Mouse?"

"Oh, um." Apparently, I'd stopped moving, but then everyone had come to a halt to make way for a donkey-driven wagon. "It was really more like an anomaly in mouse.net more than a specific message." Her mouth opens, and I anticipate what she's about to say. "I know it was him because of the nature of the thing. Mohammad and I had this conversation about how we could access the LINK without being connected that, well, inspired me."

"Mohammad helped you create mouse.net?" She cranes her neck to see if the road is clear yet. "Doesn't that kind of destroy your loner wire-wizard genius cred?"

"Shut up," I say teasingly. "It was a conversation. It's not like he coded it."

Actually, the Russians did that.

Not exactly, I remind Page. *They just provided a blueprint, and a crappy one at that. It would never have worked the way they wrote it. It didn't sing.*

"And Dragon's sure Mohammad is here?" Deidre asks, when I nod she continues. "Well, you knew him. Where would he hang out? What would he be doing tonight?"

I snort. "I knew him during the apocalypse. Trust me, that don't translate."

Deidre looks doubtful. "Just humor an old lady. Tell me what you used to do together."

We'd come to the wheat fields near Al-Gaza bridge. Though much of Cairo had reverted to its pre-flood appearance, the Deadboys still controlled Gizera Island. The sidewalk ended, and we leaned on the levee wall and looked out over the bundles of harvested wheat. There was no electricity on the island at all, but fires burned in the palms of modern scrap-metal sculptures of Anubis and Horus that ringed the boundaries of their territory.

"We scrabbled for food, avoided pimps and pirates, and captured war dogs to sell their parts back to the peaceforce."

"War dogs?" Deidre muses. "So she might be working in tech. Maybe doing reverse-engineering or building robots or something like that. Makes sense, you know," she adds when sees me looking at her. "How better to get your message out?"

She has a point. I guess Deidre wasn't a detective back in her day for nothing. I'm nodding, getting into it. "Maybe somehow connected with Islam. He was always much more devout than me."

"Okay," Deidre says smiling. "We have some leads."

Page?

Already on it.

A MOUSE THAT ROARED: How Free Access Saved North Africa
By Keela Ryū
Forthcoming from Doubleday Harcourt Penguin, 2111

Excerpted interview of Mouse; footnote commentary by "Page"/Strife

"It may come as a huge surprise to you, but I never served in anyone's military. I have hacked the systems of several divisions from a multitude of nations[12], however – including the infamous boy.net,[13] the Peaceforce's vulgar social-platform.

Boy.net! There's an awesome idea turned stupid. Imagine the LINK populated only by cyborg soldiers who think no one is watching, not even their commanders. Of course, they're wrong about that last part. I didn't say they were smart. This is the reason boy.net got raided and closed down on a regular basis in its infancy. What a peaceforcer thinks is hot nudie footage of his lover right from his very own camera-eyeballs, other people call a prosecutable offense. Go figure.

The deeply amusing part is that the government that created boy.net can't control it. As long as there are peacforcers with operating systems in their brains[14], boy.net finds a way to reconfigure and continue. A boy's just got to share his porn and kill count, you know?

And, on the surface, that's pretty much all boy.net is.

Of course, it's really command central. If the United Nations ever decided to flex its cybernetically-enhanced muscles and use the peacekeeping force to do a bit more of the force than the peace, well, boy.net could control the largest cyborg and robot[15] army in the world."

---

12. Twenty-seven, precisely.

13. "Boy.net" is officially "pkf-e.gov" but no one calls it by its proper name.

14. The operating system of a UN peacekeeping force soldier is, more accurately, located in his or her nexus. The nexus is a small shield-shaped device implanted into the bone tissue of the skull at infancy. Micro-wires extend into various points in the brain, not unlike the LINK's technology. With a PKF soldier the infiltration is much more intense, of course, as their nexus must facilitate communication among enhanced muscles, laser sights, eye-cams, sub-vocal routines, etc., and the combat computer. The combat computer, despite popular belief, is not located in the brain, either. Its exact whereabouts in the schematics of a peaceforcer's body is a highly guarded secret.

15. Yes. Most people forget that there are several hundred robot soldiers serving in the UN. Like newsbots, they are entirely non-human, mechanical, and, of course, non-sentient. Though, that last handicap apparently doesn't bar them from receiving commissions, commendations, promotions, or being granted military funerals. A mindless hunk of metal can rise to sergeant and be so beloved by its comrades-in-arms that, if damaged, it is rescued by those braving firefights to do so, while I have to pass the Turing Test and no one considers me human. An actual body is critical for android-oporhism, apparently. Jealous much? Hardly. Okay, completely.

Chapter 10
Morningstar

Cairo, Egypt
Present Day

No single angel on earth can defeat me. Though they would claim the victory, heaven was shattered after I stormed the gates. It took the combined strength of four archangels to break my wings and, even then, I was not banished easily.

Here, they were a mere shadow of what they were there.

I thought this fight with Ariel would be no contest.

Except, despite our conversation, I'd forgotten.

I shoved Ariel hard against the wall. Her left hook caught me squarely on the chin. My head snapped to the side, and the force of the blow knocked me back a step.

Me?

I, who had broken heaven with the force of my will?

Stunned, I stared at Them, my eyes wide. I rubbed my chin, the resonance of Their power still smarting. Slowly, I began to understand. Ariel was different. Unlike the others, she was two in one. S/he wore the very face of God – man and woman and all that lay between and beyond – and with it carried she carried twice, or perhaps a multitude, of strength.

She looked ready to continue what I had started, but I kept my distance. "Okay, I think I get it now." I said. "This whole affair isn't about teaching Your clay creatures to be nice to each other this time, is it?"

"It's time for a paradigm shift," Ariel said in a tone neither female nor male. It was as if several people spoke at once in a singular voice.

God had come to the table.

I let my heat cool, though not entirely. "I still think it's a shitty way to go about it. It never works the way You plan. Look at the take-away lesson they got from last couple messiah experiments. It's all Christian soldiers and jihadists. You can't even get them to agree on what it all means."

I watched for God's reaction in Ariel's eyes, and was disappointed that God had already departed. Ariel, who had dropped her wings in favor of that lovely silk skirt, shrugged. "Times are different. More people will be watching."

"So this time the crucifixion will be televised?" I had to laugh, my anger now completely dissipated.

Ariel went back to her tea. Sitting, she inspected the toes of her high heels as if our confrontation might have scuffed the leather. "The LINK angels showed Father the potential of this era."

"Really? Then why did I find the prophet in the wilderness?"

Ariel stopped staring at her toe to look up at me. "Because prophets are *made* in the wilderness. There's something about desperate times that distills either the best or the worst in humanity."

"That last is certainly true," I agreed.

Blackout

Michael didn't trust me.

I found the Prince of Heaven frightening the livestock. A donkey brayed miserably at the sight of an angel leaning against the hulk of an abandoned car at the edge of the encampment.

"Still scaring asses, I see," I said when I came up beside him.

"Better than being one," he said. His toe kicked at the sand and dust that filled the cobblestones.

"Ah," I smiled dryly. "More than heaven itself, I miss your witty repartee, my brother."

He shot me a dark look. The donkey kicked at its stall of hastily cobbled boards and old electric cords knotted together. I pressed my back into the hood of the car, trying to see what it was that captured Michael's attention. I saw nothing beyond the camp disassembling with surprising efficiency. They would easily be on the move before the sun was midway in the sky. Say what you might about the prophet, but she took care of her followers. They would be sheltered somewhere before the day became oppressive with heat.

Since Michael didn't seem forthcoming about whatever was bothering him, I said, "You can go home. The prophet is easily ruined."

"Oh? How do you have that figured?"

He hadn't guessed, and I didn't feel particularly inclined to enlighten him. "Trust me," I said.

The snort he uttered was far from complimentary, "Right."

I shrugged. "Father made it easy this time. Not unlike that brave girl in France who heard your voice on the battlefield." Okay, so I didn't mind dropping broad hints. "It didn't take long before people were brandishing torches and shouting witchcraft then, either."

"I liked Joan," Michael reflected. He flicked imaginary dust from the shoulder of his leather jacket.

Crossing my arms, I glanced at him sidelong. What the fuck was this sadness in his voice?

"The other prophet lived a long and quiet life for the most part," Michael said with his storm-grey eyes focused on the toe of his booted foot. "Islam is the fastest growing religion in the world today."

So why does this prophet have to die, is that it?

I shrugged, "Mysterious ways."

He grimaced uncomfortably at my answer. "I should see this through. I was sent. I can't let you do my duty for me."

"What are you talking about? You know this is what Mother wants. She moved mightily through you, Michael. Anyway, I'm better suited in so many ways."

"That's what bothers me," he said angrily.

Someone had finally come for the donkey, which, when freed, galloped wildly away from us. A cacophony of shouts followed after its retreating form. I watched the chaos with amusement.

"You want to be me all of a sudden?" I smiled and shook my head at the irony.

"You seem to have more faith in the plan," Michael said.

"The only thing I have faith in is that human beings are evil, repugnant snakes who devour their own with a relish that is unmatched in the animal kingdom. I have no idea what God is thinking with this prophet, but I have no doubt his 'people' will once again prove that, given the opportunity to be decent, they'll fail."

Michael stared at me for a moment, his mouth working. Finally, a small smile spread across his face. "Okay, you're right. I don't want to be you."

"See," I said, grinning back, though it occurred to me that I rarely heard Michael complain of a lack of vision. Had he been sent as a test of his faith? Had he already failed?

The donkey had been calmed with a soothing voice and offering of a cooked rice ball. I watched as a boy in a ratty school uniform carefully captured the animal with a lasso made of telephone wire.

Michael's smile faded when he asked, "So, you're going to do it?"

I took in a long, measuring breath. "You know I think it sucks."

"We are in agreement," he said. Without meeting my eyes, he quietly reminded me, "You *are* the first rebel."

Sedition from Michael? I scoffed, "No wonder Mother tests your faith."

Michael tried to look shocked and failed. With a lift of his shoulder, he once again found something more interesting downriver. "Unlike you, I'm fond of mortals, and I grow weary of this story's conclusion."

God *could* use a new script. But, as Michael pointed out, He had used others before. "Are you sure of your orders?"

He ran his fingers through short-cropped curls. "You know how it is, I *was*. Then I left."

Nice of him to think I still remembered. But the only time I'd been hurled from heaven, I was cast out. "All right, then, let's do nothing," I said with enthusiasm. "We'll make a solemn pack not to lift a finger to advance the plan. If God wants this done, She'll throw more angels at the problem. Then we can decide."

I could tell Michael didn't like the idea of doing nothing. It wasn't in his nature. Neither was decision-making, honestly. "I don't know."

Of course he didn't.

"You could still go home," I suggested kindly. "Mother will know what to do. Then you will, too."

Though I could tell he still didn't trust me entirely, he could hardly resist the temptation I offered. In a flash that nearly blinded me with its brilliance, Michael was gone.

The donkey shrieked.

But now I was left wondering what to do myself. I wiped my hands on my jeans and squinted up at the sky. Perhaps I *would* wait to see if more angels appeared.

When one did, it wasn't at all who I expected.

The prophet and I grew closer as I established my place among her followers. Using tactics perfected skirmishing in heaven, I soon had an army of scavengers under my command. Instead of running from pirates and the like, my rag-tag battalion began to challenge claims on clean water, food, and medicine.

"Why are you still here?" the prophet asked one morning after prayers. We'd fallen into a habit of meeting for breakfast. The camp had taken up residence in a car park on the border of the City of the Dead, still occupied by the *zabaaliin*. The *zabaaliin* had once been the "untouchables" of Egypt – dirty, unwashed trash collectors. Now they were trading sheiks, and we had come to the edges of their territory to barter for replacement bicycle parts.

"I'm still here because I rather enjoy playing Robin Hood," I said, relishing the tang of fresh peppers in my cup of beans and rice. My raiding party had stolen them from the Deadboys' gardens the night before. "Why do you ask?"

"I keep expecting... trouble."

We sat side by side, our backs resting on a pillar. In front of us, a bright slash of sunlight spotlighted a stall that had once been reserved for a dentist. After a mouthful of rice, I said, "And I suppose it makes you nervous to know you're keeping company with the devil."

Now familiar enough with her habits, I recognized that she glanced at me when she spoke, "You once told me you'd come to tempt me."

"I still could," I said with a wolfish grin. "But you never let me into your tent."

"I've told you already. I'm not gay."

"Pity," I shrugged.

My response seemed to have stymied her momentarily, because we ate for a minute in silence. "You also told me that Michael or maybe Allah had come here to kill me. If he left, does that mean...." she trailed off, as if embarrassed. Clearing her throat, she then offered: "Have things changed? With me, I mean?"

"You're wondering if you've lost your holiness?"

She used a credit counter to push her food around the saucer balanced on her lap. "Kind of."

"I don't know," I admitted honestly. "Try to remember that Jesus – Isa, got in a good thirty years before the shit hit the fan. Angels didn't show up every day. And he only got scary to the powers that be when he got popular. If we're following the same storyline, the peaceforce is going have to feel a lot more threatened by you."

"If we're following the same story...?" The prophet's head shook violently. "We're clearly not. I don't remember anything about Isa hanging out with the devil."

"The temptation in the desert?"

"Yeah, but we're just... I don't know, palling around."

"Well, there were those missing years."

"Now you're just messing with me."

"Am I?"

"Argh! You make my head hurt," the prophet said, though not entirely unkindly. She handed me her plate and smoothed out her burqa. "We should get ready to meet with the matriarch. Did your men secure what she asked for?"

"We did," I set both our vessels on the concrete. One of the many women that I hardly noticed any more scooped them up. I stood. "It was difficult, but we located the Coptic cross. I should warn you. It's not intact."

The prophet nodded. We were lucky to have found it at all, given all that the thieves and looters had absconded with during the first few months after the flood. "We'll have to hope it will do."

With that, I was dismissed. A woman who was always nearby took the prophet's elbow. The sister, perhaps? Their heads dipped toward each other and whispered words exchanged.

A lover?

"General?"

I turned, expecting one of my motley crew – perhaps with news that they'd discovered the whereabouts of the missing arm of the cross.

Instead, I saw an angel. She wore the uniform of a Russian deserter, identification patches and insignia torn from the smart fabric. Her hair looked just grown out from a regulation military cut. By her gender, I knew she was once one of mine. As they fell, the two-thirds decided for themselves what form they would take on earth.

But I had no idea who she was. Had she been a Throne? Someone I once trusted or despised? I hoped she'd tell me her name, so I stretched out a "Yes...?"

She snapped a salute. "I am at your service, as always."

Okay, given her continued devotion she was probably from a lesser order of angels. Who was she? What should I do with her? Clearly, this was not the sign from God that I'd been hoping for. Why hadn't He sent anyone? It had been weeks.

The angel waited on my word.

I wished I could remember what her rank had been in heaven. "What are you doing here?" I asked.

"I came to offer my services, General. I've been with the *zabaaliin* and I sensed your nearness."

A scout! "Well done," I clapped her on the shoulder affectionately. Scouts were invaluable for their ability to intuit the proximity of others of our kind. It was their own strange nature that they'd managed to keep despite the banishment. "I have a job for you, as it happens."

Present Day

I was just about to ask Ariel where Michael was at this moment, when the house interrupted. "Breach," it announced with the same excitement as it might place an order for more tea. "Intruder."

"Visual," I said, and obediently an image crackled to life on the small screen near the door. The cameras were as old as the butler system itself, so the picture was grainy. I could make out a figure on the roof. The person wore a combat cool-suit with the camouflage turned off. So their intention was not surprise. The butler system scrolled an impressive list of both visible and concealed weaponry the visitor carried. I was suspicious about why anyone would feel the need to so overtly break into my establishment, at all, but most especially via the roof.

I glanced over at Ariel, who had come up beside me to check out the image as well. "A friend of yours?"

"Mine? More likely yours, carrying all that."

I peered at the picture trying to place the face. Truth was, while I may have been a great battlefield commander, I'd abandoned the fallen the second the fight ended. The intruder reached the roof access door. With the flick of a toggle switch, I turned the live feed off. "We'll see in a moment."

As soon as the invader was spotted inside, several of the boys LINKed the house to let me know what I'd already seen. "Yes, I'm aware," I explained. "Let us see what it is he wants before we panic."

"She," one of my boys corrected. "And she's asking for you."

"What's her name?"

"Pyriel," was the answer.

Ariel flashed me an "I told you so" look, and went back to her seat by the window as though she intended sit back and enjoy whatever infernal drama Pyriel represented.

"Tell my little soldier I'm busy with one of her superiors," I said. "She can come back another day. Through the front door."

There was a touch of panic in the voice that replied, "She's, uh, pretty insistent." It was not difficult to imagine the micro-blade knife pressed to his tender throat. "She says it's important."

It was always so damn urgent with the fallen, but I didn't want to have to clean up the carnage she was no doubt willing to inflict. "Very well, send her through."

Ariel chuckled softly into her tea.

Repressing the desire to respond to the archangel, I opened the door. Pyriel was only just releasing my boy, who wisely dashed through the antechamber to where the security guards stood at the top of the stairs, guns drawn. I waved them off. As she sheathed her knife, Pyriel gave me a nod of acknowledgement. "General," she said.

"Brigadier," I said, though after reading the Russian insignia on the lapel of her uniform, I corrected, "Colonel."

Pyriel wasted no time getting to the point. "I sensed an enemy in the area," she stepped past me into the room. She took in a breath of surprise when she saw Ariel, and, without hesitation, pulled a gun.

I'd hardly begun to form the order for Pyriel to stand down, when she pulled the trigger.

The bullet hit Ariel right between the eyes. Her body exploded into a burst of searingly brilliant light. The china cup shattered on the floor.

I rubbed the spot between my own eyes, "I was talking to her, you know."

"Ariel was a distraction, General. It's time to recall your army. The host gathers at Megiddo."

Megiddo? *Armageddon.*

PEACEFORCE TO SET UP BASE IN EYPTIAN RUINS
Egyptian President Incensed, Nearly Declares it an Act of War

April 15, 2059
Associated Press

Cairo, Egypt—Though warhounds have assumed the bulk of the remaining rescue effort in Egypt, the Secretary General of the United Nations' Peacekeeping Force announced plans today to set up a military base on the eastern edge of Cairo. The peaceforce is expected spend over 2.5 million credits to convert an historic structure known as "The Citadel" into a modern military base.

President-in-exile Amsi Mubarak could hardly contain his anger at a press conference early this morning in Syria. "It is insane. They won't send their precious elite soldiers to help the starving women and children left behind, but they will spend millions on an unauthorized military presence. On the site of three holy mosques." He went on to state that though his nation might be broken, its sovereignty should not be in question. He fell just short, however, of declaring the move an act of war.

"With all due respect to President Mubarak," said Colonel Lars Heinrick, the likely candidate for base commander and spokesperson for the Secretary General's office, "Egypt is in anarchy. If the president has any hope of returning to his country, he must understand that our presence there is an absolute necessity for establishing order."

The peaceforce also insisted they had no plans to occupy any of the three mosques on the site, though they do plan to invest in restoration of the damage the flood and looting caused to the Mosque of Mohamed Ali.

Many pundits contend that the peaceforce, while likely correct that it is a necessary measure, has an ulterior motive for establishing a base in Cairo proper. "They could put it anywhere in Egypt," claimed LINK columnist Eugene Mintz, "but they're going into Cairo because the Deadboys."

The cult of Osiris, as the Deadboys are properly called, do seem to be a flash point for regional nationalistic sentiment. Though official information on the Deadboys is difficult to obtain, rumor has it that they have begun planting gardens in the streets of several towns along the Nile with seed imported, possibly even donated, from Saudi Arabia and other neighboring Islamic countries. It is believed that if they can provide food to a starving country, their popularity will grow and with it, political clout.

"It is ridiculous to think we're concerned about a bunch of castrated crazies," replied Colonel Heinrick when directly questioned about the peaceforce's interest in the Deadboys' operations in Cairo. "We are going in there to keep the peace; it's our only mission."

Chapter 11
Mouse

Deidre and I relax on a bench overlooking the Deadboys' "park" as we await the results of Page's search. I bought us each a cup of *umm ali*, a sort of bread pudding, from a street vendor, which we enjoy with the requisite "hmmm, ahhs."

Absently, I stare at the people passing. A group of kids – gear twinks from looks of the steam-powered toys darting around their heads – keep glancing in our direction. Finally, a girl sporting neon-green dreadlocks saunters over to me, a metallic origami crane no bigger than my hand sputtering behind, billowing white puffs of exhaust in its wake.

"You're Mouse," she says. The crane swoops in to land on the backrest next to my shoulder.

LINK controlled. *Impressive*. I inspect the mechanical creature. Its gears are tiny. She must be a master. I wonder if I'm looking at my future replacement. "What are you? Sixteen?"

"No, uh, actually, they call me Scooter June. Or sometimes just Scoot." She glances around as if looking for someone. Her delicate eyebrows knit together, "Are you expecting Sixteen?"

"No, Mohammad," but at her confusion, I offer a gentle smile. "Never mind. It's nice to meet you, Scooter- June-Sometimes-Just-Scoot," I offer my hand, which she pumps enthusiastically when I add, "I am, indeed, Mouse."

With what can only be called a squee, she waves her friends over. Soon, Dee and I are surrounded by a happy gaggle of mechheads and their flying circus. In fact, one of the mechanical wonders is a perfect, miniature replica of Baron Von Richtofen's biplane.

Deidre takes the words from me, "This stuff is amazing. You kids have some serious talent."

Uncomfortable laughter ripples through them, like they're not quite sure what to do with a compliment from someone old enough to be their grand-mother.

"Yeah, it's cool mech," I agree, repressing the impulse to flick off a multi-legged, antenna-waving thing that chugs its way onto my shoulder. They treat me like I'm part of their tribe even though I haven't played with heavy hardware in a long, long time. I touch Scoot's sleeve to divert her attention from the lanky, shy boy with dancing LED polka-dot hair and a Victorian opera coat. "But why steam?"

She scoops up her bird and tucks it in her dreads like a queer hairpiece, and then hops up on the backrest. I marvel that she can breathe in that corset with its clockwork fasteners. As she arranges the pleats of her leather dress, I can see that she's clearly settling in to lecture on her favorite subject. "Steam represents, like the difference engine for you, unexploited potential. An alternative direction we could have gone."

"Yeah, but, see, the difference engine was never made because it was clunky as all hell. As for steam, there are so many easier energy sources to exploit, like, a battery."

"No poetry," she insists with a sniff.

"Poetry?"

Scooter Jane misunderstands the expression of surprise on my face. "Don't give me that. I know you understand," she shakes her multi-ringed finger teasingly. "Mouse.net is extreme art."

Dancing dot hair boy, who's been listening in, raises his thumb in approval, "Subversive."

Beside me, Deidre helps a wildly-tattooed, red-haired girl re-braid her hair. The girl sits between Deidre's knees and Dee tucks and twists like a pro. Do girls get some kind of hair handbook when they're born?

"There *is* magic in poetry," I agree.

The magic that made me, Page says. *Sihr halal.*

Blackout

Somehow Franklin's place looked even more ominous at night.

Floodlights, powered by ridiculously expensive electricity, illuminated the front of the building. The generator growled and ground its gears, but louder was the crowd milling around on the sidewalk and spilling into the dusty street. My stomach flip-flopped slowly at the sheer number of "appli-cants" waiting for the pleasures and perversions of Franklin's place.

"We're too late."

Katarina snatched at my arm. "What do you mean? Is the equipment gone? Has someone else gotten to it first?"

I shook my head. Of course, I was thinking of Mohammad. She looked relieved, but my eyes stayed focused on all those people pacing in front of Franklin's like caged jaguars.

Merciful Allah, how I hated them all.

I shook off the thought with some effort. And, continuing to play smarter than I actually was, I asked, "Who else is looking for it?"

"The peaceforce, of course."

"Of course." Great, now I had at least two armies after me or after the stuff I boosted off a dead body. "How about the Egyptians? Are they after it?"

She snorted a derisive laughter. "Darling Mouse, they wouldn't know what they were looking at it even if it fell into the palm of their hands."

Apparently, neither would I. Though at least I now suspected it might be something small enough to fit in my hand – if she was being literal, of course.

"Now, the Americans... they might want it."

I shrugged. "The Americans want everything."

She smiled; her lips curled warmly, like she appreciated the way I thought. "That is why I suggest the possibility. And besides, they have decided they want to be Russia's enemy again. It's a game they can't resist."

I wondered if by that, I could assume the whatever-it-was might be Russian made. I just scratched my head absently; I was completely out of my league. "Let's focus on the problem at hand," I said. "The first step is to get Mohammad out of that snake pit."

Katarina surveyed the crowd from where we're crouched in the shadow of an alleyway. "So, I go in. Ask for Mohammad. Seems simple enough. Will Franklin part with him? What's his specialty?"

I made a face to show my disgust. "Mohammad doesn't have a goddamn specialty."

"No need to get angry, Mouse. I need an angle here."

I bit my lip. There was, after all, one sure way to make sure she saw Mohammad. I started to open my mouth to tell the secret I'd never shared out loud in so many words, and found that what came out instead was, "His arm is probably in a cast."

"He's wounded?"

"So? Say you're into pain porn or something. I don't know."

Katarina glanced at me out of the corner of her eye, like she was trying to decide something about me. I glared back daring her to ask. Instead, she lifted the bandoleer over her head and handed it to me, Uzi and all.

I held it gingerly, like it might explode any second. "What am I supposed to do with this?" My voice squeaked.

"Ah," she laughed, patting me on the head as she stood up. "Now I know why they call you Mouse."

"No you don't," I snapped, but she was already walking toward Franklin's front door. Quieter, to myself, I added, "Anyway, no one but you does."

Katarina's relaxed stroll betrayed none of the anxiousness I felt. She moved easily into the clot of foreign men, many dressed as she was in army fatigues. Waving to someone, she moved closer as though to exchange a few casual words. In a second, I lost sight of her as she blended into the crowd.

I stayed in the shadows, clutching the gun, trying not to hyperventilate. After a few minutes, there was some commotion at the door. Franklin stepped out surrounded by a cadre of armed guards. He greeted the assembled throng of perverts with a broad, welcoming smile and began taking bids. From experience I'd rather not remember, I knew that seconds earlier a satisfied customer slipped out the back door and now all the boys in the upper rooms waited fearfully for the next one to come through that door. Hopefully, with any luck, this time it would be Katarina, and Mohammad could escape with her.

A cockroach scuttled away from the light down the alley, and I batted at it with my toe. I dropped the gun with a clank that sounded loud to my ears. Scrambling to pick up the weapon, I hastily checked the crowd to see if anyone spotted me. The alley was far enough away that no one seemed to have noticed. I rested the barrel of the gun awkwardly against my knees.

The weapon gleamed dully in the shadows, a deadly thing. An insane part of my mind toyed with the idea of taking the thing into my hands and shooting my way into Franklin's place. Except I couldn't imagine a scenario where I didn't end up dead – nailed by forty-thousand bullets from the expertly trained soldiers in the crowd.

Turning my attention back to the scene in front of Franklin's place, I heard offers shouted in a babble of tongues. I strained to hear Katarina's sharp feminine bark above the all the others. Franklin pointed and gestured like a professional auctioneer. Finally, the bidding war finished, and, miraculously, I saw Katarina step to the doorway and take Franklin's proffered arm with a smile. She turned and gave the crowd a rude gesture which was greeted with hoots, catcalls and a few boos.

It was almost like she knew what to do.

The door shut.

Now, unfortunately, I had to run.

If I didn't return with the soldier's stash by the time Katarina uncovered my deception she might just kill us both. Given what happened last time, I decided to bring Katarina's gun with me on my little foray up the road. Besides, she'd kill me twice if I lost it.

As I passed the metro stop where the Deadboys grabbed me without incident, I felt kind of lucky. Just another corner to turn and I was home free. I smiled. Maybe my luck was finally turning. I might even be back at Franklin's with time to spare.

"You there," a voice shouted in English. "Freeze."

With a sinking heart, I turned to see two UN soldiers approaching. Both wear the black "Military Police" armband and their hands hovered distressingly close to the quick released of their side arms.

I put my hands up in surrender. I should have known things wouldn't go well.

Peaceforcers always traveled in pairs. These two could be clones, not that I could see many distinguishing features under the riot helmets. They stood broad and tall and looked just like cybernetically-enhanced perfect killing machines they were. Black as the night, their smart-fabric uniforms camouflaged them so well they seemed to step right out of the shadows. One of them brandished a flashlight, nearly blinding me.

The confidence I had earlier shriveled up and died at the steely gaze that glared into my face.

"You're out past curfew," one of them informed me in English. The other one circled behind, slowly, his eyes on Katrina's Uzi, hanging heavily across my shoulder.

I really had no idea what to say in this situation, though a number of really stupid options occur to me. Like, I wanted to say, "What about all those guys two blocks down? Aren't they out past curfew too? You couldn't notice the sixty assholes hanging outside Franklin's, you had to notice me?" But I figured belligerence wasn't the smartest option here.

"You speak English?"

I couldn't quite contain the look of contempt that flashes in my eyes, so I felt compelled to at least nod.

"Looks Russian made," the other peaceforcer said, tapping the butt of Katrina's gun with the barrel of his.

"Where'd you find the gun, boy?"

With my hands still raised, I kind of shrug, like I have no idea what he's saying. "Dumpster?" I offered.

"You come pretty well dressed for a dumpster diver," Peaceforcer One said to me, though he does take a moment to flash his light on my bare feet.

The other guy touched his nose, and the two of them laughed. I didn't need to be able to hear their sub-vocal communication to know he suggested that I smelled like one.

Huddling together, the two soldiers exchanged another couple glances, no doubt continuing their sub-vocal conversation. The robin's egg blue patch of the UN flag was an incongruous flash of pastel decorating their left arms below the epilates. The only other color was the gold flash of inscrutable rank and unit pins. The letters M.P., however, glinted in glow-in-the-dark white. I didn't like the look of the shock stick that hung loosely from their belts. My arms were getting wobbly, but I didn't dare drop them.

"Surrender the weapon and you can go on your way," Thing One said to me.

Well, that was a relief. They must have filled their "harass the locals" quota. "No problem, Officer."

I gingerly removed the Uzi and all its ammunition from my shoulder and offered it to Thing Two, who snatched it quickly as if afraid I'd change my mind and go all ballistic on him. How suicidal did he think I was?

"You should find a place to sleep." Though his voice remained gruff, Peaceforcer One frowned at me in a way that could almost pass as sympathetic. For a brief moment I was nervous that they'd offer to escort me to some shelter or another, but, instead, he lifted his hand as if to dismiss me. "Go on now. Shoo."

Yeah, except. Dude stood right in front of the loose cornerstone that hid my stash. I couldn't leave without it.

I looked at him, trying not to glance at the carefully placed brick propping up the flat rock in front of the deep hole.

He looked back at me. At first like he couldn't quite figure out why I was still standing around. Then his frown deepened with menace that held the clear implication that if I didn't run along now he'd change his mind about how lightly I'd gotten off. Thing Two gripped Katrina's gun in both hands, looking unmovable.

What else could I do? I turned and walked down the street as if headed somewhere important. How long could those guys stand there, anyway?

Turns out, I didn't have to wait long. The sound of gunfire had them running past me at their ridiculously hyped speed—

... right towards Franklin's.

My heart skipped a beat. What the hell was going on down there? Would ever see Mohammad alive again?

And it was all my fault.

Present Day

URGENT MESSAGE pops into my field of vision.

I haven't followed a word of the excited exchange Scoot and Dancing Hair are having, though they still seem to be extolling the virtues of steam-power and the Age of Reason. I turn aside as if for privacy and flip the go-ahead.

I've located Mohammad.

I sit up straighter. My hand clutches at the wood of the seat. *What? Where?*

He and his family are on the train to Mount Sinai.

Mount Sinai? That sounds ominously Biblical. *Are you sure it's the same Mohammad?*

Dragon confirms mouse.net signature. It is the same person that sent the message. If it is the Mohammad you seek, I cannot say.

You didn't ask?

I didn't offer a handshake. I thought that might be presumptuous, father. His message was for you, not me.

"Awfully thoughtful," I say out loud. "You must have inherited that from your mother."

Ha.

Around me, conversations hush. Someone whispers, "Page." My connection suddenly floods with requests to audit. Normally I would indulge them, but I say, "I'm sorry, this is private."

Several of the kids look disappointed, but give me respectful nods as they virtually back off.

"Connect me," I say, surprising myself by not squeaking for once.

A MOUSE THAT ROARED: How Free Access Saved North Africa
By Keela Ryū
Forthcoming from Doubleday Harcourt Penguin, 2111

Excerpted interview of Mouse; footnote commentary by "Page"/Strife

"When I first came to Cairo, I fell down a rabbit hole[16] and ended up in possession of the National Library[17]. No, seriously. Look, downtown had become this weird tumble. Debris from the world's oldest cities formed rolling dunes of destruction from the source to the sea. Underneath it all were accidental tunnels. Good places to hide, if you could survive the trip.

It was wicked dangerous. Sections could collapse suddenly, weakened by water, too much foot traffic, or some idiot who thought it'd be nice to expand what Allah had given us by chance. There were holes so tight that a misplaced elbow could trap you forever; no joke – I'd seen the corpses. Unmapped and uncharted, it was easy to get lost in the dark, dank, slippery passageways or turn down the wrong way and find yourself forever entombed.

A cave-in propelled me, like Alice of the story[18], into a Wonderland. As soon as I shook myself off and got my bearings, I knew I'd found home. There were rooms and rooms of books, and many of them still undamaged by rodent or cockroach or dampness. I almost thought I'd died, because, even now, when I imagine my final reward, it's not a thousand virgins, it's a thousand books, virgin and unread, waiting for me in some celestial library.

I found a book, American in origin, I think. Its exact title is lost to me after all these years[19], but the subject matter remains near and dear. An obscure

---

16. This appears to be a metaphor and a reference to Lewis Carol's *Alice in Wonderland*. Rabbits, while found in the deserts, are unlikely to have built warrens so close to the polluted river. Rats, perhaps.

17. It is actually extremely unlikely that the library my father discovered was the Egyptian National Library. Also, the book he goes on to describe appears to have been in English, not one of the major collection areas of the National Library. However, it is clear that he did discover a major cache of books, possibly from a branch library or even a bookstore. It is also possible that, given how deeply it seems to have been buried, it may have tumbled with the river debris from as far up-stream as Luxor or any other city along the Nile's banks. I believed what has happened here is what is known as a "romantic" version of the past. It would simply be "cooler" if the library he found was the most famous, but, alas, it's not likely.

18. Ah! I was right.

19. A blatant lie. My father has squirreled away several electronic and hard copies of this book, which is properly referenced as: Hafner, Katie and John Markoff. *Cyberpunk: Outlaws and Hackers on the Computer Frontier.* (New York: 1991). It is baffling why my father refuses to name a book that so clearly influenced his life. I can only suspect that he is either embarrassed at his own attachment to such a quaint and obscure historical moment or, perhaps more likely, he doesn't want others to glean whatever "magic" he feels is attached to this book that brought him the insight needed to create mouse.net and, eventually, me.

bit of history, a curious story of real-life Robin Hoods of the digital age who stole electrons through superior knowledge of computers and a con artist's skill they dubbed 'social engineering'. After reading that book the second or third time I began to believe that maybe there was a light in this darkness, after all, and that – if I could only get my hands on a working phone line – I, like them, could rule the world."

Chapter 12
Morningstar

Cairo, Egypt
Present Day

"Armageddon," I said slowly, disbelievingly. "You realize, Pyriel, how crazed you sound?"

"The signs are there, General," she insisted, the intense bulge of her eyes not making a good case for her sanity. I released a tense breath when she finally holstered her weapon.

"The signs?" I tried not to sound as disappointed as I felt. Worse than insane, Pyriel was a conspiracy theorist. Did she miss the memo? Last I heard we were already living in the messianic age. "Pray tell, which?"

"The prophet is on his way to Mount Sinai."

"The prophet?" I grabbed her by her shoulders and stared hard into her face, trying to detect any sign of subterfuge. "Don't screw with me," I warned.

She tried to shake my grip, but found she couldn't. "General, it's the truth. I've been following your orders since we crossed paths during the Blackout. The prophet has not once left my sights. I've kept him safe. Until now. I had to come to warn you. As I already told you – *Michael* is at Megiddo."

To intercept the prophet. Ariel didn't lie. If I didn't do it, they would. "Mother," I spat. "Fuck."

Blackout

The irony that I reverently carried a sacred relic of Christianity was not lost on the prophet. She kept glancing in my direction in a way I'd learned to read as quietly amused.

Truth be told, I felt a certain affinity for the tarnished, broken thing. Iron rusted beneath a few bits of remaining gold gilt that sun-flamed into a brilliant, white light. An arm of the cross had gone missing; it was incomplete, no longer a perfect symbol of God's glory.

I cradled the cross in my arms, like a child. If the *zabaaliin* matriarch rejected it, I'd be tempted to keep it for myself – if it wasn't such an awkward, obvious albatross.

We made our way across a bridge of planks laid on top of ever-shifting sand to the wall that surrounded the City of the Dead. The wall was really the crumbling, sun-baked brick facade of a roofless building. At some point, a newer house had been built on top of the first and then another on that one. They teetered, perpetually on the verge of collapse, like an apartment complex imagined by Dr. Seuss.

There were outlooks perched at the top of the mismatched structure who watched our approach from the parking lot. I made sure they could see the gift we bore. Excited shouts erupted from the guards, and soon we were escorted inside through a battered wooden door.

We stepped through into an open courtyard filled with garbage. A strong odor of pig manure seared the insides of my nostrils. Swine rooted freely in the piles of collected oddities – coat hangers, smashed vid screens, rotting stuffed animals, refrigerators, car engines, plastic toys, and millions of skittering cockroaches.

"Look, actual bowls and spoons!" the prophet tugged my sleeve excitedly. She pointed to a heap of kitchen items. "And Helena would kill for that rolling pin. Merciful Allah, they really do have everything."

"Except this," I reminded her, tapping the cross in my arms. I didn't worry overmuch about our escorts overhearing our conversation. The prophet and I spoke in English when were alone together.

"Right," she said, taking in a steadying breath and consciously stifling her giddiness. "We're negotiating from a position of strength. I'll ask for much, much more than it's worth."

We'd come to a tent like the kind the Bedouin used, only it was surrounded in a circle of plastic bottles, can openers, blankets, first aid kits, and copper bottomed pots. Out of a flap strode an old woman. Her face was uncovered, but she wore a scarf embroidered with colored threads and tiny mirrors. A Versace evening gown graced her lanky, bony body. Instead of the half-expected fur wrap, she wore a rat-gnawed peaceforcer's jacket.

"Where did you get that?" the prophet demanded, her finger shaking at the Captain's insignia pin on the collar of the battered jacket.

The matriarch arched an eyebrow disapprovingly, but answered, "Mouse gave it to me in exchange for our last working handheld." She nodded solemnly as if in a pleasant memory, "A good trade."

"A handheld?" the prophet looked at me as though I might provide an answer. "It's got to be Chris! When did he start going by 'Mouse'?"

I had no idea what we were talking about, so I just shrugged. "Shouldn't we be getting down to business?"

"What did Chris – or Mouse – say he needed the handheld for?"

The matriarch seemed to prefer the diversion. With the help of the two younger men who'd brought us to her tent, she settled on a broken toilet seat as though it were a real throne. One of them opened an umbrella missing half its fabric to shield her from the sun. "Your friend seems to think he's going to pirate access to the LINK. He promised us entry code if he breaks the walls of Jericho."

The prophet laughed lightly, "I have a hard time seeing Chris as Samson, more like David versus Goliath."

"Yes," the matriarch smiled. "That's it."

It was rare I felt this left out of a Biblical discussion. A mangy dog with matted fur came up to sniff my knee. It must have smelled hell on me, because it growled lightly.

The matriarch noticed the animal's reaction and motioned for one of her attendants to shoo the dog away. Her eyes lighted on the golden icon in my arms. "May I see the cross?"

I looked to the prophet, but she seemed distracted by the memory of her lost friend. "Of course," I said, handing it over.

"You're sure it's Coptic?"

I couldn't be, really, but my sense of its provenance came from where I'd had to steal it from. "The peaceforce had it. It's authentic."

"What happened to it?" She caressed the spot gingerly where the arm had been severed, as though it were an open wound.

"I don't know," I said. "Probably someone broke it, hoping it was solid gold. I have people looking for the missing piece."

She tsked, petting the jagged, broken edge. She turned it over in her hand, as though trying to decide which angle would best disguise its imperfection. I knew she was going to reject it. I couldn't bear the thought.

"It's taken a beating, but it's still a potent symbol," I offered. "More so, given everything it's been through. Like the light of faith in the darkness."

The matriarch looked at it again, her eyes wide. "It's the only one anyone has ever recovered."

Thus the negotiations began in earnest

* * * * *

"You talk very eloquently of faith, given... uh, everything," the prophet said after we'd presented Helena with her brand new rolling pin. The mechanics were busy repairing bicycles, loudly marveling over the fact we'd procured grease for the wheels.

"Who was the mouse named Chris?" I asked to distract her from the issue of my faith. "An old lover?"

"For the thousandth time, I'm *not* gay," she almost shouted. Helena shot us a curious look. I thought the prophet was lucky that Chris was a non-gender specific name or, perhaps, everything would have ended much sooner than expected. The prophet took my hand and led me to the relative privacy of the exit ramp. "Why do you care?"

"You seemed interested in him. I could send some people to scout for him if you wish," I said, which was mostly a lie, but a plausible one, I thought.

The prophet considered my proposal so long that I suspected the answer well before she actually spoke. Her voice was quiet, crisp, "No."

Present Day

I had Pyriel arrange for a train to Mount Sinai, while I cornered one of my boys and had him hook up the butler system to the LINK. It was a slow and arduous process when I did it manually with the keyboard, but the boy could sync his LINK system instantly.

"Who or what do you wish to connect with, master?" he asked.

"Call Mouse," I said.

The boy blinked stupidly at me. "Mouse? You mean, *the* Mouse?"

I was losing my patience. "No, I mean the four hundred and fifty-seven other mouses out there. Of course I mean that Mouse."

His very pretty face scrunched in confusion. "I don't think you can just call Mouse."

"Well, have you tried?"

DEADBOYS SPEAK
Cult's High Priest to Travel to Security Council

April 27, 2059
Associated Press

New York, NY—Accompanied by a Saudi prince and two bodyguards, a man claiming to represent the Deadboy Cult and answering only to the name "Osiris" demanded an audience with Secretary General Nguyet Aaldenberg today. Security guards clashed with bodyguards because Osiris entered the building in a skirt, a violation of the United States' Leviticus Laws, which stipulate that men may not appear in public in women's clothing. Osiris was also wearing a gold bracelet and beaded necklace believed to be part of Tutankhamen's treasure, and a birthday party hat.

"He looked like a freak," said one of the peaceforce guards involved in the incident, who asked not to be named. "Dude was wearing a 'birthday princess' tiara. His bodyguard was dressed like a dog, with this weird mask and everything."

Eventually, Prince Esmail Qureshi's presence leant credence to the validity of Osiris' identity as high priest of the cult that bears his name. "I suspected no one would take Osiris seriously without me," Qureshi admitted in a later interview. "But people need to hear from real Egyptians about the situation there."

Prince Qureshi went on to talk about "disaster fatigue" and how even among Muslims, who are required to almsgive as part of the five pillars of Islam, donations to support the region are flagging. "It's really only been a few months since the flood. Our neighbors in Egypt still suffer."

In a surprise move, president-in-exile Amsi Mubarak acknowledged Osiris's right to speak to the needs of the survivors in Egypt. "Though their religion might not reflect the majority of the country, Egypt needs an authentic voice. Osiris understands the plight of those left behind."

There is no word yet whether or not Secretary General Aaldenberg plans to meet with Osiris. According to sources inside the peaceforce, Aaldenberg wishes to first research the past identity and history of the man called Osiris. Currently, it is believed he may be Abdul-Qudir Boutros, a former CEO of Egypt Oil, who lost his fortune during the Medusa War.

Chapter 13
Mouse

Cairo, Egypt
Present Day

Another URGENT MESSAGE blinks in front of my eyes, blurring the train schedule I try to read without having to resort to the reading glasses stowed in my shirt pocket. "Who the hell wants me now?"

Looks like Satan's signature to this one, says Dragon with a disapproving sniff. *Shall I try to raise Mohammad again?*

Like some kind of dorky teenager, I dropped the connection when the screen showed the image of a familiar face made strange with time and hormones. All the cherubic roundness I remember weathered into gaunt cheeks and a high, wrinkled forehead. The wild afro was tamed and transmuted into iron-gray wire. A full, trim beard and a mustache framed the frown that tried to place my face or perhaps form words of reproach.

That's when I'd hit "end transmission."

Page and I argued. I guess he couldn't understand why I wouldn't just talk to the guy after all this hassle. He'd stormed off to pout indignantly somewhere on the ether. Dragon stepped in as official nag.

"I'd rather talk to the Great Satan first," I tell her truthfully.

Mohammad seems like a nice man. This one's research indicates that he has a family, a wife and two daughters.

"Not talking to you right now," I say, clicking the go-ahead. An antique butler icon appears in the usual mouse.net window. Wow, Morningstar is cruising the autobahn on a dumpier jalopy than mine. *Hello to the house?*

Oh my god, it worked. Holy crap, you can *just call Mouse. Uh, Mouse, hang on. I just need to get the keyboard and connect up the video feed. Hang on...* A smattering of code rapidly scrolls through the window until I finally see a very irritated Satan. He sighs exasperatedly, *Is this thing finally on?*

You're live, I tell him. *What's up?*

You have to get to Megiddo. There is an ambush waiting for the prophet.

Wait a minute I thought you didn't know where Mohammad was. How do you know he's – momentarily, I struggle with the words and the concept – *headed for Armageddon?*

A bird with a broken wing told me. It doesn't matter. I thought you'd like to know that I plan to defend the prophet against the host. His jaw twitches angrily as he adds through clenched teeth, *However, this is not a battle I have ever won. If you care at all for the prophet, you will hurry to her side.*

Are you trying to tell me that angels are gunning for Mohammad?

That's it, yes, precisely. Then, without a lick of proper protocol, he disconnects.

I'm still blinking from the hard boot when Deidre presses the tickets into my hand. "What's wrong?" she asks.

"I hate angels," I mutter.

Blackout

Katarina was pissed I'd lost the gun, but not as much as I was when I heard what happened to Mohammad. "You let the peaceforce take him, are you insane?"

She splayed her fingers in a gesture of helplessness. "I had no choice. You neglected to mention that the extent of your friend's injuries meant he was drugged out of his mind, and the fact that he was not on the public roster."

Well, thank Allah for small miracles. At least if Mohammad had been abused it was only by Franklin himself... on second thought, that didn't sound like much of a bonus. I shook my head to banish the images that sprung to mind. "Look, I didn't know about any of that. I had to abandon him."

"Yes, well, he's not terribly happy about that, I can tell you," she said.

"You got to talk to him?"

We perched on a pile of rubble on the bank of the Nile, near where Katarina had left the camouflaged canoe. The moist spray seeped into the heavy cotton of my sweats. I slapped at a mosquito, hoping the antibiotics she'd given me earlier covered malaria. Fires from Gazira Island shone like beacons in the north.

"Briefly," she said. "We were heading out when the firefight started."

"I thought for sure that was you," I admitted.

She tossed a loose piece of concrete into the river. It hit the water with a loud sploosh. "It started when some rival gang tried to raid. I think they were hoping to carry off some boys as booty, but Franklin's guard returned fire and then the peaceforcers showed up..." she shrugged, like the rest was obvious. "Speaking of, I see you have the jacket."

"Did you actually see them take Mohammad?"

She cocked her head at me for a long moment, and then on her fingers she ticked off three answers: "I shoved him toward a door. What happened to him after, I have no idea."

"Craptastic."

"Is that English slang?"

"I've got to find Mohammad," I stood up suddenly. Though, not quite knowing which way to go, I hopped from one foot to the other. I let out my impotent anger with a shout: "Why the fuck did you let him out of your sight?"

Leaning back on her elbows, Katarina seemed bored by my hysterics. "You try fighting two elite cyborgs."

I wasn't in the mood to argue with her. I had to find my friend. Climbing up to the street level, I started walking towards the ruins of the British Embassy. Katarina gripped my elbow in a flash, making me wonder exactly how much augmentation she had under her skin.

"You're wearing the jacket, Mouse. You lied to me. Mohammad had nothing; *you* have my stuff."

I jerked out of her grip. Lucky for me, the microfibers in the smart fabric were designed to be slippery. "Finders keepers, losers weepers."

"Just hand over the data chip, and I won't be forced to hurt you."

I glared at her. I was getting extremely tired of being threatened with physical violence. "There was no chip," I said. Pulling the lawgiver from its holster inside the jacket, I pointed the business end at her face, "But I did find this."

Of course, she laughed at me.

My fingers were already tingling from having my palm wrapped around the grip. If I tried to pull the trigger, I'd get nothing but a wicked electric shock. So I flipped it over, grabbed it by the barrel, and whacked the butt hard across her face.

Katarina stumbled back in surprise. When it looked like she might recover, I kicked her in the knee.

Then, I ran.

I ran and ran and ran like the devil himself nipped my heels. My back itched with the anticipation of a mech-hyped flying tackle that never came. When my breath began to come in ragged huffs and my side ached, I considered the possibility that Katarina might not be in pursuit.

Maybe revenge wasn't worthwhile without the damn data chip she'd been after. I ducked into the alcove of an old storefront to catch my breath. Bent over from exertion, I leaned against a faded promise of halal meat and fresh produce. Out of curiosity, I pulled the other treasures from the pocket of the jacket to examine them. There was almost no light, except from the moon, but the hands and numbers on the analog watch's face glowed faint, pale green. The earrings were simple glass studs. Or were they?

Allowing my knees to buckle, I slid down the wall until my butt rested on the narrow sandy stoop. I turned the earrings over and over in my hands looking for an indication of a port or other method of connecting with an electronic device. Some new kind of data crystal?

But peaceforcers were all LINKed with what they called "boy.net," a combination command central and social platform. Why would some dead officer be carrying around something as stone age as a memory drive? And what, exactly, was it meant to plug into?

They were pierced earrings. Maybe the plug-in was the ear itself? What would that make them? "Flesh drives"?

Eeew.

Worse, if that was the case, I should've just given over to Katarina. Even if I rammed the earrings through my earlobes, they were pretty useless to me, Mr. LINKless boy.

I tucked the earrings back into my pocket; I'd have to deal with them later. Next, I checked out the watch. Another antique, I could hear a gentle ticking when I held it to my ear. Still, it was nicely made. Maybe I could trade it for some food or water. My stomach rumbled at the thought.

In the meantime, I thought I should wear it. I wasn't much for jewelry of any kind, so it took me a bit of figuring to get it around my wrist so the numbers faced the right direction. Then, of course, I had to tighten it to fit my narrow arm.

That's when I accidentally found the switch and phoned home.

A screen flickered to life on the glass, projected across it like a flat holo.

"*Govno,*" I heard a male voice mutter in the dark. An actual, electric-powered light switched on, and then the image showed a man sitting up suddenly in bed. It was a wide, civilized-looking thing, with navy blue sheets and soft comforters. Whoever this was, he was a long way from me.

The man continued to mutter in a language I didn't recognize. He ran a hand through brownish curls cut in a military style, showing off strong arms and a naked, well-muscled chest. Blinking at me, he reached for something off screen. Then, very pointedly, as if it should mean something to me, he shrugged into a Russian uniform jacket. It had the same red star symbol of Katarina's tattoo emblazoned over the breast pocket.

"Identify yourself," he ordered calmly and in perfect Arabic.

"I'm called Mouse," I said, because, well, it was true – tonight, anyway.

His tone remained unconcerned and neutral as he made the switch to English with ease, "Where is Captain Del Toro, Mouse?"

"Dead," I mean, Del Toro must have been the peaceforcer I landed on if he was looking for her, right?

The man on the other end of the line considered the news. I couldn't tell if he was bothered by it or not. He rubbed his eyes. "You seem awfully young for NSA. Who do you work for?"

I'd gotten used to making shit up with Katarina, so I said smoothly, "Whoever pays me."

"Who's paying you now?"

"No one."

A sly smile slowly spread across the man's face. "Well, that's easily rectified, comrade, especially if you're in possession of all of Del Toro's... things."

"You mean the flesh drives? Yeah, I've got them."

He laughed at my term. " 'Flesh drives,' I like that, but I think the better pun might be 'spy *wear*'." He scratched the back of his head absently. "Alright, Mouse, if you can deliver the equipment safely to one of my people there, I can make it extremely worth your while. Interested?"

"As long as those people aren't named Katarina, we're good."

"Colonel Katarina Pyrinova?"

"Dude, I don't know," I said, exasperated. "Just tell me I don't have to deal with *anyone* named Katarina and I'll be happy."

"No Katarinas," the big Russian nodded. "In fact, I'd prefer you avoided anyone in a Russian uniform."

"Including you?"

He looked down as if he'd forgotten what he was wearing. "Yes," he said to my surprise. "Just hand Del Toro's equipment over to my contact. Don't call me again; I'm rerouting this, in fact." He glanced off screen at something, then said, "We should make this fast. We've been transmitting too long already."

Okay, *spy* wear. I was getting this. Sleepy Russian dude was some kind of double-agent. "Okay, give me the details."

"First, name your price."

I felt like some kind of cheesy, movie villain, but I said it anyway, "One million credits."

"Done," he said without a moment's hesitation. Had I sold myself short? "My man will have an anonymous credit counter ready for you at delivery. Oh," he flashed a grin and pointed at my jacket, "and you might want to lose that before you meet him. You need to get to Colonel Lars Heinrick, Cairo base commander."

Holy mother fuck, he wanted to me to walk into the very mouth of the beast. That was going to be impossibly risky.

"I don't know, man," I said, hesitating.

He crossed his arms and regarded me. "You're regretting asking so little, I suppose." To my rapid nod, he continued, "I know it's traditional to barter, but we don't have time. My counter offer is five million credits and transport for you out of Cairo when everything is over."

Merciful Allah, how could I say no? Yet, there was no hesitation: "And a friend."

The big Russian narrowed his eyes. I thought for a moment I'd blown my third, possibly most important negotiation of the week. Then, he gave a curt nod. "If your friend is with you at the base when you meet Heinrick, fine. Otherwise, you go alone."

I opened my mouth, but he disconnected the call.

Well, okay. I guess I knew where I was going next.

Except – I was curious what it was that I had. As easily as the Russian spy more than doubled his counteroffer, I knew I'd still gotten ripped off. So what exactly did this piece of "spy wear" do that was worth so much to a secret agent in some comfy bed a million miles away?

Before I handed it over, I intended to try to find out.

I tucked the earrings into the pocket of the jacket and zipped it tight. Skirting around the area I last saw Katarina, I moved back in the direction of Franklin's. She said she'd pushed Mohammad towards a door. Maybe he'd gotten out after all, and was still on the street somewhere. I had to look.

Peaceforcers were everywhere. They seemed to be indiscriminately hauling people away. A group of kids sat handcuffed along the wall, waiting for transport or perhaps eventual release, considering how hard Franklin argued with Thing One, who seemed to be the officer in charge.

Scanning faces, I didn't see Mohammad. But considering his injuries, he might have been taken away earlier. I snuck up as close as I dared to a boy sitting nearest the corner. "Hey," I whispered. "Hey, kid!"

When he turned, his eyebrows raised. "Chris?"

"Yeah," I said dismissively. There wasn't time for happy reunions, plus, honestly, I'd intentionally blanked everything that happened in Franklin's, even this guy's name. "Hey, did you see where they took Mohammad?"

"Which Mohammad?"

Merciful Allah, of course there was more than one. My eyes watched the peaceforcers movement along the street. "The one with the broken arm."

"Oh, yeah, Franklin's favorite," he nodded. "I don't know, man. It's been a mess. Everyone who could scatter did. But the peaceforce came down hard. I'll bet he's in the Citadel. That's where they're going to take us all."

The arc of a flashlight headed in my direction. I scooted back behind the corner of the wall and held my breath. If I had any chance of seeing Mohammad again, I had to run.

Present Day

"Armageddon is a place?" Deidre asks. "I always thought it was a time, you know, like the end of all of it."

I lifted a shoulder. "Megiddo is a place; it's some battlefield or plain or desert or something near Jerusalem... or in Israel somewhere." I stare in frustration at the tiny print on a map I bought from a vendor at the train station. "Look, I don't know. Do I look like a Biblical scholar to you?"

"With those glasses you do." She gives me an affectionate smile; I whap her playfully with the map. She laughs and adds, "A very grumpy Biblical scholar, mind you!"

This one believes Megiddo is near what is considered the current location of Mount Sinai, but that's guessing through context. Morningstar believes his "prophet" is headed for Armageddon. Our Mohammad is near Mount Sinai, ergo...

Thank you, Dragon. I reign in my sarcasm because I've already pissed off one AI today. *Will you tell Page I'm sorry I yelled at him, please?*

Page has made it clear, Mouse. He'll return after you talk to Mohammad.

Ugh, they were ganging up on me.

I hand the map to Deidre. "I suppose we should just get on the same train as Mohammad."

"Okay, but we don't know where he's planning to get off."

You could call him.

I suppose after Morningstar's warning, I should. "All right."

I can almost hear Dragon's satisfaction in the dial-tone of the connection, which is her own affectation, of course. She's playing old-time operator. *This one will connect you now.*

Mohammad answers immediately, no doubt tired of getting prank mouse.net requests. "Who is this?"

For the first time, I notice his interface isn't LINK. From the angle of his irritated expression, I suspect he's got a dick tracy or something else external. "Um, hey, Mohammad. It's Mouse, uh, I mean Chris. Christian El-Aref."

Beside me, Deidre mouths, "He knew you pre-Mouse?"

I wave her away with the "I'm trying to talk here" gesture. After giving me an indignant glower, she wanders over to the newsstand and flicks her fingers through the tabloid interface, enlarging pictures and articles she wants to read.

Mohammad stares at me. He strokes the edge of his moustache with a finger. "So you *are* Mouse. I read some years ago that a Christian El-Aref was allegedly the infamous Mouse, but I didn't think it was possible that it was actually *you*."

"You know any other Muslims named Christian?"

He laughs. It's a sound I've missed. "You got my message, then?" I nod, and I'm about to interject that, apparently, he was heading into the end of time and the devil was going to defend him against an army of angels that wanted to kill him or something, when he said, "I'm in trouble. I think Allah wants me dead."

A MOUSE THAT ROARED: How Free Access Saved North Africa
By Keela Ryū
Forthcoming from Doubleday Harcourt Penguin, 2111

Excerpted interview of Mouse; footnote commentary by "Page"/Strife

"First of all, technically, the nexus is not something your mother gave you in the womb. Shortly after you were born, a doctor gave you a shot that contained the nanobots necessary to form the nexus at the base of your very soft skull and, once activated, to build the microwires to connect the salient brain bits. All that stuff continued to grow with you, and no one in their right mind would activate the LINK until the last time your brain rewired itself sometime in your teen years.

But that aside, it's, first of all, very easy *not* to be born in a hospital. Women managed without doctors for centuries. There are plenty countries in the world where, in fact, that's the norm, not the other way around. Still, midwives have access to the 'botshot, though for a cost. And there is a window of opportunity. Once your skull is fused, you need serious surgery to get the LINK. It's not impossible even then, but it costs money.

My family had money. Merciful Allah, I went to a British boarding school – I had privilege coming out of my ass.[20] I got 'botshot at birth. But I was still fucked when the dams broke.

My problem was that I was too young; my nexus hadn't been activated yet. Poor me. World's smallest violins and all that.[21] But I was one of those people who was shocked to discover how just many people were... what? 'disenfranchised,' is a favorite term for historians, I guess.

'Screwed' is what I would call it."

---

20. Hyperbole. My father's life is a bit of a paradox, and, in my opinion, it would be difficult to consider a Muslim, mixed-race child of an unwed mother "privileged" in the traditional sense of that word. I think the anger my father seems to be expressing here by the use of strong language may be due to his genuine distaste for the class into which he was born. Outside of an early childhood among the moderately well-off in an economically depressed country, most of my father's life has been a hard scrabble. He takes a lot of pride in his "street cred," and has always been the champion of the underclass.

21. A paraphrase of an antiquated expression of mock pity usually shown by rubbing one's thumb and pointer finger together and while saying, "This is the world's smallest violin and it's playing just for you." As to why my father would think anyone would disrespect his experiences in the Blackout Years baffles me. He is, in a word: prickly. And he seems to have worked himself into quite a state for some reason. My only guess is that having seen worse things happen to others, he's feeling guilty.

Chapter 14
Morningstar

Megiddo, Israel
Present Day

Michael strode out onto the plains of Megiddo to parlay. The sun glared off the rust-red rocks, and I squinted at his approach from behind a cheap pair of convenience store sunglasses.

The subtle changes in Michael's clothes and demeanor concerned me. Instead of the leather jacket he favored, he wore a trench coat that flapped behind him the dry wind. Kakhi replaced denim. Army boots kicked up miniature dust storms in his wake. A gun plainly holstered in a Sam Brown belt made him look more like a desert mercenary than an Italian cop. The grim determination his martial strides matched the dark expression on his face.

"Clear the field, Morningstar," he shouted the moment he was within hearing range. Of course, he didn't know I was deaf in one ear thanks to Gabriel's trumpet, but I understood him plainly as he continued, "This is not your fight."

"You're wrong, yet again, my dear brother," I said, stuffing my hands into the pockets of my jeans casually. "This is mine to finish, not yours."

A bit of color blushed those chiseled cheekbones of his. "Uriel says you refuse."

Uriel now? Ariel rarely came down in her guise as the angel of death, and never, ever before as a man. I couldn't pretend disinterest anymore. "Uriel is here?"

"He stands at my side, with Jibril."

The horn player, just lovely. "And Raphael? Is he planning on joining our delicious little end-times party or did he get a better offer elsewhere?"

Michael's gaze flicked over to the horizon, and his lips pressed together. "He'll be here." My questions and my attitude apparently irritated the prince of heaven, because he wanted to know, "Where's your army?"

"Since when do I need an army to kick your ass, little brother?"

He quirked an eyebrow at me, but otherwise didn't rise to the bait. Instead, he offered up a clumsy, if accurate reply, "Since the moment you left the dirty work undone."

Blackout

The prophet brooded over her mousey not-lover for days. Talk started to circulate. Whispers grew into rumors. Who was this Chris the prophet so clearly loved? A boy or a girl? All around the prophet, people argued. *Was she gay? Did it matter?*

Finally, on the third day of the prophet's great funk, I overheard a man ask his wife, "What's she hiding under those robes of hers anyway?"

"What do you think," I offered, from where I stood next to him in the soup line. "You think she's some kind of butch lesbian or something?"

He had the good graces to look disgusted by the implication of my words. "It's not that," he said, his ancient, weathered face wrinkling in thought. "Not exactly."

Yet, it didn't take long for discussion around the prophet to expand. Who had seen the prophet without clothing? The debate began to center on whether or not the prophet had the right to hide behind a burqa. "It's not as if she's properly sheltered or chaperoned," I added to the fireside deliberations. "How orthodox can she really be?"

The final moment came when we were camped in sight of Giza. A full moon reflected off the glass of the Great Pyramids. Our tents and lean-tos lined up along the edges of the city. It was a cool night, fires blazed. The mood was high. Someone had started up a bit of music, playing a penny whistle found along the way. Pots became drums. Feet moved in remembered belly dance steps mixed with rock moves. The prophet watched with her sister or secret lover from the sidelines.

Perhaps dared by friends, the little beggar girl who'd once been so comfortable in my lap ran up to the prophet. With a joyful shriek, she pulled off the prophet's hood and darted away with it. Leaving the prophet's face completely exposed.

Whiskers softly dusted a roundish chin. Fierce eyes dared us not to find beautiful handsomeness in long-lashes, fawn colored skin, and a wild, wide afro. An androgynous mixture of gender, the prophet looked to me just like an angel.

Alas, mortals fear angels.

Confusion rippled through the crowd. Music ground to a halt. In the moon's cold light, I held my breath and scanned the faces of the prophet's followers for any hint of sympathy. Fear snarled lips. Anger twisted expressions. Meanwhile, cowardly eyes darted away.

Then, damn them all to hell, someone whispered loud enough to be heard, "Abomination."

I picked up a small stone and pressed it into the palm of the boy with the cruelest look. Then, I turned my back on humanity. Such as it was.

Walking slowly into the desert toward the Sphinx, I heard an angry shout. The sound of stone hitting flesh echoed in the darkness.

Present Day

Rising wind tugged at my hair. Fiery anger had unfurled my wings. Each slow, deliberate flap formed mighty swirls of debris. Dust devils rose into churning columns. Revolving faster and faster, they spun off secondary tornados. Soon the plains of Megiddo swelled with howling twisters.

Using the power that broke heaven in two, I bent space and time to my will. An army of fallen materialized from sand and wind. In a flash, dust stripped away to reveal only the devils themselves.

Granted, many of them had spent their time on earth as petty middle management types, and, thus, blinked confusion from their eyes and tugged at power suit skirts, adjusted glasses, or straightened ties. But, to the fallen's credit, they recognized the end of times when they saw it. Someone shouted a battle cry, quickly echoed by the two-thirds, "Lucifer, Light bearer!"

Michael was surrounded. His paltry army vastly outnumbered, and his jaw dropped in surprise at my show of strength. Miracles were not easy on earth, but I of all the angels had exercised freewill in static, immutable heaven. None could match me for sheer force.

Removing my cheap sunglasses, I tucked them into the pocket of my shirt. "We do not yield. Consider the battle begun."

DEADBOYS ALL CASTRATI
Secrets of the Cult of Osiris Revealed!

April 30, 2059
Rolling Stone Magazine

New York, NY—Since his dramatic arrival in New York several days ago, a lot of attention has been showered on the High Priest of the Deadboys, a man simply known as "Osiris." We sat down to interview this mysterious man at his New York hotel. Barechested in the cool April rain, he smoked cigarettes at the cafe, dressed in a white linen skirt and gold armbands. Disappointingly, he seemed to have left his signature tiara in his room.

Tell us a little about your religion.
We are the revived cult of Osiris, the chief Egyptian god. When the dams broke, it came to me in a fever dream. The Nile was angry at being pent up. It had been the dominant force of nature – of culture, really – since the beginning of human history.

Angry? So you believe the ancient gods of Egypt were responsible for the death of millions of people?
Yes. And the gods are still angry. That's why they demand constant sacrifice.

Spooky. What are you talking about here?
Are you familiar with the story of Osiris? The jealous god Set constantly tried to kill him, but his magic was too strong. After finding him alive once again, Set tore Osiris into fourteen pieces and scattered his remains throughout the land. Isis, his wife, searched for him and found everything except his phallus, which was eaten by a fish.

Phallus? Are you talking about what I think?
Yes. To honor the story and the demands of an angry Nile, we sacrifice our phalluses and those of any initiates to our cult.

So you have no—
Penis, that's right.

Chapter 15
Mouse

On the road to Armageddon
Present Day

The rails click underfoot. My butt squishes uncomfortably close to Deidre's hips on the narrow, cracked vinyl seat of the electric train. Though morning prayers had been called some time ago, lights of passing stations flash like a strobe through the darkened windows.

I'm pretty sure you're right, Mohammad. I say to my friend. *Actually, I'm a hundred percent certain that Allah's been out to get us both for some time now.*

He frowns sternly at me like he thinks I'm joking around.

I notice a strange puckering in the wrinkles in his forehead, and I point to them, *What happened to your head?*

A rock, he says simply. *I was nearly stoned to death.*

What? When? The words came out without thought, which explains why I add, *Are you okay?*

Mohammad nods. His avatar leans to the side and he tilts his head slightly, as if accepting a hug from an invisible wife. *There was some brain damage. I have seizures. No LINK.*

Which would explain the image's mimicked movements, no dick tracy then, he must be using some kind of external hardware that tracks physical reactions. *Merciful Allah, I'm so sorry.* I want to say more about all the things I regret, but since the words don't form easily, I blurt: *Speaking of Allah, don't go to Mount Sinai. There's an ambush.*

Are fundamentalists planning to attack the transgender conference?

No, angels are. Which doesn't sound nearly as strange to me as: *A conference? Who holds a conference in Armageddon? Did you get a cheap rate on hotel rooms or something?*

Mohammad laughs in a way I remember so fondly. *Israel promised top security.*

Israel... something other than traditional distrust nags at me. Suddenly, I recall an angel with salt and pepper hair.

Uh, buddy, by any chance are you being escorted by a Mossad agent? I look at Deidre. The tabloid smart-sheet sits in her lap, and she uses her finger to flick through an article about some celebrity's botched attempt at rehab. "Isn't there an archangel in Mossad?"

"Raphael?" she asks by way of agreement.

Almost simultaneously Mohammad replies, *Raphael?*

Blackout

I must have dozed, because I awoke to zombies sniffing the leather of my sleeves. Jumping up, I batted at limbs. They smelled of rotten breath and putrefying flesh. "Ai! Not food! Not food!"

Fingers grabbed at my arms and legs, but the peaceforcer's jacket repelled any attempt to keep hold. Grabbing the lawgiver from its holster, I whacked my way out of the moaning mass of rags. Weakened bones cracked. The zombies screamed and spat, but I kept up my assault. The instant I was free of them, I ran.

A few blocks and several deft turns later, I lost them. While I caught my breath for the next dash, I double and then triple checked the contents of my pockets. Praise Allah, the earrings were still there.

Dawn threatened to break over the jumbled rooftops. Unless I wanted to spend the day dodging zombies, beggar kings, Deadboys and the like, I needed to be well away from the riverfront before morning.

The peaceforcers had established their base behind the walls of the Citadel in the far east of the city. I headed in that direction, but with the sun rising soon, my first priority was a hidey-hole and some fresh, drinkable water.

I thought I found the first in an open, second-story window accessible only through very careful maneuvering on a rickety, rusted scaffold. When I eased myself into the cool, dark interior, I discovered a Gorgon's nest. My foot had hardly creaked the floorboards when the Gorgon pounced.

Breath fled from my lungs with a woof as my shoulders were pinned to peeling linoleum. Silvery eyes caught eerily in the dim light. Long white strands of hair shrouded all the details of a face except a pixie-pointed chin and sharp nose. "What have we caughts, my precious?"

"Something 'juicy? Scrumptiously crunchable'?" I offered.

The pressure on my chest eased slightly. "Oh? You've read *The Hobbit*?"

"Only twenty times," I said, hoping that the enthusiastic squeak of my voice might spare my becoming this would-be Golem's meal. "Uh, you read?"

"You sound surprised," the Gorgon noted. His voice had a slightly British lilt, though I couldn't tell if it was an affectation or not.

"No offense," I croaked. Even with the peaceforcer jacket absorbing most of it, the Gorgon's weight pressed on my lungs. Thing was, I thought the Medusa virus killed the Gorgons before they had time to do much other than breed. "It's a great book. Have you read the *Lord of the Rings* trilogy?"

The Gorgon snarled. Apparently, not a fan of Tolkien's later works. "Don't make nice. I smell gun oil and blood."

I raised my palms up off the floor in a gesture of surrender. "I'm not here to hurt you. I was just looking for shelter from the sun."

Sniffing noises close to my ear made me flinch. "You smell like a frightened rat. Why is a rodent dressed like a soldier?"

"Well, smell a little harder," I said rather incautiously. Apparently, I defaulted to belligerent when I got nervous or scared. "The soldier I took the gun and the jacket from was dead. I'm hoping to barter both for some supplies and a handheld from the *zabaaliin*. Then I'm going to break into Peaceforcer headquarters and talk to a spy in order to get transport out of this shithole."

The Gorgon hopped off me. In a voice trembling with excitement, the Gorgon breathed, "An adventure, a quest!"

Sitting up slowly, I checked for broken bones and surreptitiously slipped my hand into my pocket to make sure I hadn't lost the earrings. A plastic bottle whapped against my aching chest. It bounced into my lap. Picking it up, I saw the UN stamp. I had the cap twisted off in a second and drank deeply of fresh water.

The Gorgon crouched beside me, watching my every move with a feral, toothy smile. "Now you owe me for the water, and I demand you take me with you."

I could think of worse companions. I finished off the bottle and, after screwing the cap back, I set it against the wall. "What do I call you?"

"Hmmm," the Gorgon seemed to consider several possibilities before settling on, "Thorin."

Not Bilbo or Gandalf? I would have picked Strider, myself, but apparently "Thorin" hadn't yet read those. "I've been going by Mouse."

"Okay, Mouse, try not to struggle."

"What?" was all I had time to sputter. Thorin leaped on me again. Despite his slenderness, he had considerable strength. The water sloshed uncomfortably in my stomach. In a minute I found myself dragged across the apartment and trussed up, my arms spread eagle, to a water pipe. As if that wasn't enough, Thorin settled across my legs like some kind of Bizzaro-land Great Dane.

"What the hell is all this for?" I asked, testing my restraints. They were wire and plenty secure, as it happened. Should I be concerned that he had all this ready and hadn't had to fumble for a thing?

"I can't have you reneging on your promise and sneaking off to adventure without me."

"I *hadn't* considered it," I said meaningfully, but, as he already snored softly, he missed the implication entirely.

Fabulous.

I struggled a bit and managed to cut my wrist and elicit an annoyed growl from Golem/Thorin. Eventually, there was nothing else to do but surrender to sleep.

The need to pee and a sharp shaft of light woke me up several hours later. The Gorgon sat crouched like a monkey on the narrow counter of the apartment's kitchenette, a battered copy of *The Hobbit* resting on his knees. Bookshelves lined the walls of the tiny efficiency. There were thousands of antique paperbacks of all variety, most in English, though some were in what looked to me like German. The furniture that could be carried away had been. I could see marks on the walls where a couch had probably rested once. A lamp lay broken on the floor, its cord still plugged into the dead socket. The doors of the cabinets in the kitchenette hung on broken hinges. Dust collected on the surface of the sink, dishwasher and fridge. Thorin had one hand resting possessively on a six pack of UN water bottles, three rings of which hung empty. Yet the walls were impossibly filled with books. There were piles of books on the floor which made me wonder if Thorin had been gathering others and bringing them here.

I sat up and rubbed a bruise at the back of my head before realizing he'd undone my restraints already. Quickly, I double-checked my pocket.

"What has it gots in its pocketess?"

"The one ring," I said, pulling out the earrings to show my crazy companion. "Seriously, these were forged in the shadows of Mordor and are totally going to rule. I hope, anyway."

"Are you insane?" he asked me in a serious tone, his head cocked to the side like some predatory bird.

"Probably," I admitted. Stretching out, I tucked the earrings back into their spot and zipped up the pocket. I walked over empty bottle I'd set aside the night before and deftly filled it with the contents of my bladder.

"Very civilized," Thorin remarked dryly. "Personally, I use the sink."

"It's my fervent hope," I said, twisting the cap back on tightly. I walked over to the fridge, and set the refilled bottle inside on one of the empty shelves, continuing, "that one day the peaceforce will be assigned to retrieve all these. Seems fitting. They provide the water and the toilet."

Thorin grunted and returned his attention to the book. From the angle of the light, I guessed there were a few hours until the sun set. I reached for a book of my own to pass the time. Unfortunately, I had to give up on it after a while because the author's ability to describe mouth-watering food set my stomach growling fiercely.

I was searching for another when I heard the call to prayer. It was that woman's voice again, only this one seemed like it might be recorded... which wasn't possible.

The Gorgon noticed my confusion. "Zealots revived the muezzins using precious battery-power. Can you believe it? Before working toilets!"

"And its heresy – or blasphemy, I can never tell the difference."

Thorin hopped down lightly, tucking his book into the back pocket of his jeans. He seemed pretty well-dressed for a mutant. Like me, he had no shoes. His jeans were dusty but without rips or tears. He wore an undershirt that seemed much too big for his slender frame. Over that he had the kind of open, lumberjack plaid, button-down that all the retro kids were into back Before, when anyone gave a damn about fashion. Where it was exposed, his skin was unnaturally pale, and, in the light of day, his irises seemed almost invisible.

"Why?" he said, coming up beside me. "Why is it wrong? I thought prayers were part of the five pillars."

"They are, but the call isn't supposed to be sung by a girl."

"Why?"

"Because," I said grumpily.

"Because, why?"

"Well, I don't know. Do I look like an imam?" The question irked me on a number of levels, not the least of which was that it made me think of Mohammad. "No religious or philosophical questions before breakfast, okay?"

"I think it's beautiful," Thorin said. His pupils pinpoints in the brightness. "I don't understand why Allah would be offended by something so pretty."

"Yeah, whatever," I said, though, secretly, I didn't either. "We should get going."

Turned out that having a Gorgon as a guide *was* a little like having Gandalf and a magic map. Thorin knew all the best routes to avoid the zombies and Deadboys, and, because he scared the shit out of most people, he walked right into a beggar king's camp and traded the lawgiver for more water and two plates of hot, cooked food.

"You are absolutely incredible," I told him as he handed me a cracked bowl of goat meat stew. We settled on the rooftop overlooking the fires of the encampment below, our legs swinging over the edge.

"They assume I am not alone," he said. He flashed me that snaggle-toothed grin, "And I play up the 'my precious' thing. Keeps them on edge."

"Smart," I said, thinking about how everyone always said the Gorgons were little better than animals. Seems a lot about them were lies.

After filling our stomachs, we continued onward. Thanks to Thorin's resourcefulness, we reached the City of the Dead by midnight. But the guards stopped us before we reached the door.

"You are not expected," a guard shouted from the rooftop, after peppering our path with shot from his gun. "And you," he pointed to Thorin, "are not welcome."

"How about a little Christian charity," I yelled back. "Make an appointment for us. We want to barter."

"Come back tomorrow."

"No," I said. Zipping up the peaceforcer jacket, I wished I had the full uniform and a boy.net connection. I hoped my plan would work, anyway. To Thorin, I whispered, "You're fast, right? Meet me at the door."

In a flash, he took off. I started walking. "I want to see your matriarch..."

The blast hit me square in the shoulder. A few pellets sprayed my cheek and chin, burning like a son-of-a-bitch, but the brunt of it was absorbed by the jacket, as I'd hoped.

"—about a jacket," I continued as if my face wasn't bleeding.

Just when I thought they might just reload and aim higher this time, the door creaked open.

Present Day

"Okay, nobody panic," I say completely freaking out. Deidre glances up at me with a mix of concern and confusion.

"What's going on?" she asks, setting aside the tabloid. The instant she removes her fingers, the paper reverts to blank. The breaks of the train squeal as we approach a station. I hold onto the pole to avoid squishing into her, as momentum jerks me around.

I don't understand the concern. Raphael's been a real angel, Mohammad says.

Yeah, see, that's the problem, I tell my friend. *He is a real angel.*

Mohammad's avatar turns as though studying someone in the distance. I expect the usual disbelief, doubt, and denial, but Mohammad nods. *I can see the familiarity. They could be brothers.*

To Deidre, I say, "Sounds like he's met an angel before. I don't know if that's good news or bad."

"Bad," she mutters returning to her trashy articles as people file into the tram car.

Who? I ask Mohammad. *Who could be brothers?*

Raphael and Morningstar.

Oh yeah, it's bad all right.

A MOUSE THAT ROARED: How Free Access Saved North Africa
By Keela Ryū
Forthcoming from Doubleday Harcourt Penguin, 2111

Excerpted interview of Mouse; footnote commentary by "Page"/Strife

"There's no question in my mind that without United States funding and research grants, there would be no such thing as a bio-mechanized soldier. (Personally, I always wished they'd called themselves bio-mechs, but the term cyborg was in the collective unconscious long before we actually had such things – or people, as it were.)

Thank goodness the Security Council actually grew a pair[22] and told the US where to stuff their plans for world domination. I suspect having an army of elite living weapons at their backs helped considerably. There's nothing like having a small company of dudes[23] who can break down walls with their bare hands and leap tall buildings and all that Superman[24] shit to help with

---

22. "Of testicles" is the complete sentence, though my father probably would have said "of balls." This is a rather sexist way of implying that particular component of male anatomy, which is seen as being the repository for testosterone, is required for courage. It isn't. In fact, it is my opinion that courage has very little to do with one's physical characteristics, gender or sex. You don't need a body at all in my opinion to be brave. Though, it is perhaps easier when one doesn't have to combat fear and the fight-or-flight response, which can be manufactured by biological components, such as adrenaline.

23. While men make up a large percentage of cyborg soldiers in the UN's peace keeping force, there are a fair number of women, all of whom meet the exact specs required of a peaceforcer. Which my way of saying that the "dudettes" are just as strong, fast, etc., as their male counterparts.

the old 'fuck off' to America, you know?

Plus, any war America starts smacks of corruption. They're good at join-ing in late, but if they're the ones who think it up, trust that some third-world country is about to lose access to its natural resources.

Luckily, the United Nations folks were able to out-vote the Americans when they wanted to start making their own super-soldiers, too. Those guys in Geneva quickly slapped trademarks all over their bio-tech. Of course the United States makes pretty functional knock-offs[25], but they can't be peace-forcers. And I'll give props to the people in R&D at the Security Council: a peaceforcer is still the most awesome humanized weapon in existence. Only the Russians come close."

---

24. Since my father is about to go off on a completely unnecessary rant about American politics, let me just say I am annoyed by the fact that while there is a Superman, there is no Superwoman, only Super*girl*. In a little blue mini skirt, no less! If I sound personally insulted, I must admit to shifting my gender during the course of this article. If you were to LINK to me at this moment, you wouldn't see a carbon copy of my father, but the image of a woman in a black chador.

25. American cyborgs are hampered by the fact that not everyone who wishes to become a cyborg can do so easily. There is a genetic component to accepting bio-mechanization. Some simply reject the enhancements as foreign bodies, a similar "allergy" keeps some from being LINKed. The UN has a larger, more diverse pool to draw from, as they pull from many nations and being a peaceforcer is considered an elite, desirable position with a high pay grade and considerable benefits. It is also believed that, like the Russians, the UN may have begun a breeding program that matches those that adapted well to cybernetic enhancement with others of the same. Those rumors, however, cannot be confirmed.

139

Chapter 16
Morningstar

On the plains of Armageddon
Doomsday

God sent His army, like meteors, flashing out of the bright blue sky. One by one, they materialized beside Michael in orderly rows. White, brown, black, flamingo pink, hummingbird metallic-green, they wore brilliant plumage of every hue, as lovely as anything in Creation.

From our fallback position behind crest of boulders, I watched them come through binoculars. Beelzebub sat beside me, sipping water from a canteen. I had not seen the prince of hell, well, since she took up exotic dancing in Argentina. Today, however, she looked more like an earnest college student in her Che Guevara tee shirt and sneakers.

"Unless He sends the saints, we still outnumber them two to one," Bea said, flipping her dark, Latin curls from her forehead. Taking the spy glasses I offered, she squinted at their lines. "Still using the old tactics and formations, I see. I'll bet none of them has hefted a sword since that last day."

Bea, I knew, had been a guerrilla fighter in Central America and, more recently, a successful eco-terrorist in Brazil. "Don't be too cock-sure," I reminded her. "Michael has."

She gave me a measuring look, but eventually she nodded. "But Michael hasn't been dreaming of vengeance since time began."

True. Also, unlike Bea, he probably didn't have a wadded, beer-stained collection of battle plans scribbled on bar napkins. Gadreel had shown me a similar notebook crammed with tightly cribbed notes and diagrams. My generals, it seemed, had obsessed on a rematch to the point of insanity.

Still, it could prove our strength.

After my miracle, I had almost none. I'd hid my weakness from the opposition pretty well, but I didn't have the energy to deal with the fact that my top generals weren't speaking to each other. Seems that, at some point, Bea and Gadreel had become lovers, and, in the way of devils, parted badly. All they had for each other now were recriminations.

"Michael is going to kick our asses if you don't talk to that boy, you know," I said, holding my hand out for the canteen. She thrust it at me. Water splashed the cuff of my sleeve. I ignored her dramatics and took a long pull. "Surely, you're the bigger angel. Just play nice. When we rule earth for the next thousand years, you can spend the entire time putting Gadreel in his place."

She smiled wickedly at that thought, but then bit the strawberry gloss of her lipstick, "He might like that too much."

"You probably would, too. The point is I can't have my two best warriors bickering over some affair from the first World War."

"He's a false, beguiling serpent—"

I lifted my hand. "Yes, yes, aren't we all? I've heard it from both of you now. Just make it up with him." I pointed to the streaks of light raining from heaven. "We want to win this. Pride was our downfall last time. Don't repeat my mistake."

That sobered her. "Yes, sir!"

I watched her stomp off and sighed, hoping this battle would start soon. Otherwise my army might disintegrate under the weight of its collective history.

Picking up the binoculars, I looked out over at Michael's swelling ranks. The differences between our forces gave me a modicum of hope for victory. We might have to deal with internal bickering, but they had a bigger problem. Bea was right. They seemed to organize by some antiquated art of war. More interestingly, only the three archangels wore modern clothes. The rest seemed to have returned to earth in the garb popular during the time of their last assignment – there were medieval knights, Persian princes, nurses from the American Civil war, Irish rebels – many of them centuries out of date. The most recent costume I identified was of a New York firefighter from early this century.

Those who had never set foot on earth wore nothing but their wings. Thus, it cheered me to see that there were a whole lot of naked angels on their side. The newbies seemed distracted by all the new sensations. Like children, they wandered in a daze, marveling at wind in their hair and sand between their toes.

I zoomed in on Michael. His face cut with a deep frown, Michael argued with Jibril about something. He pointed in the direction of a collection of naked angels who cavorted among the scrub sage, tossing sand at each other and giggling.

But then there were faces I recognized. Fallen who had been redeemed by that bitch Amariah, the angels' own messiah.

Still, it was hard not to feel buoyant. At least my army had hit the ground ready to fight. A dozen or more were, even now, on dick tracys calling in favors from drug lords, gun smugglers, and mercenaries. Our disgrace had led many of my best soldiers into the kind of life that leant itself well to this new battle. Of course, there were also the pencil pushers and bureaucrats, but I could work with them as I had in the past. In fact, many of those business types were the ones most anxious to prove their mettle, having sublimated their true nature for so long.

I could actually *win*.

CAIRO SURPRISINGLY VIBRANT
Life Continues Among Ruins

May 14, 2059
Associated Press

Cairo, Egypt—For the first time since the disaster, news correspondents have been allowed access to Egypt. Though mostly restricted to the "green zone" of the newly established peaceforce base located in the outskirts of Cairo, new information is finally reaching the West.

And it's surprising.

Newsbots, which had been deployed immediately after the dams broke, never made it far into the country. At first, it was assumed that the bots had been damaged by the sandstorms that continue rage through the region. It seems more likely now that they had been captured and their batteries salvaged by survivors, colloquially called city rats, or simply rats.

The peaceforce, expecting to find only devastation, have been shocked by the strange post-flood culture that has arisen with astounding rapidity, particularly in Cairo. "People are much more resilient and – uh, enterprising – than we were prepared for," admitted Colonel Lars Heinrick, base commander of the new Cairo outpost.

Colonel Heinrick may be specifically referring to the brisk trade that seems to have developed between the *zabaaliin*, a Coptic Christian group previously responsible for garbage collection in Cairo, and self-appointed leaders of rag-tag gangs of survives called "rat kings." Apparently, rat kings spontaneously organized out of a need to protect supplies from looters, particularly those entering Egypt from outside.

Other outsiders have taken advantage Cairo's disaster and set up any number of outposts for trade of all kinds, including prostitution.

"It's sick, really," said Col. Heinrick in an unguarded moment after his first patrol through the city. "The human predators have done more damage than the Nile crocs."

Alternatively, the Deadboys' orderly rows of food crops and highly coordinated defense of their "farmland," also caused some consternation among the ranks of the peaceforce, though rumors of their activities had been suspected, due to their previous dealings both with the UN and neighboring countries.

Col. Heinrick renewed promises to bring stability and order to Cairo.

Chapter 17
Mouse

Okay, so where are you? I ask Mohammad, stepping onto the train plat-form. I'm directed by a soldier to stand to one side. I won't be allowed through customs until I disconnect from mouse.net. It's a stupid rule, of course, since there are no real boundaries in the ether, but security can be very hide-bound.

We've come into Jerusalem, he tells me. *Raphael is insisting we head directly to the conference site, but my family and I want to check into the hotel first. My children are getting cranky.*

Good, stick to your guns.

What are you planning, Chris?

Just tell me where you're staying.

He does, and I disconnect with the promise I'll be in touch as soon as we cross the border. The soldier is unimpressed with my suspicious behavior. She nods with the barrel of her gun that I should hurry things along.

I smile and wave like it'll only be a few more minutes, which I'm hoping is true. Deidre has gone ahead, her purse open for inspection on a long, metallic table. The customs officer studies her passport, asking questions about the length of our stay.

It should only take another half-minute to upload the rolling blackout virus and set the timer. Unfortunately, Israel's main node is naturally para-noid, and I'm using a trick I've triggered in the past. Thus, I'm forced to do a bit of on-the-fly coding. The soldier clears her throat. "You need to hang up now, or I'll force a shut-down."

I make the munching hand motion to indicate a chatty Cathy. "My moth-er," I mouth, pointing to the almond-shaped lump at my temple. "In the hospital in Israel."

The soldier shakes her head. "Lock-down in: ten, nine..."

The last of the corrections are done, and I release the program. "Okay, okay, okay," I lift my hands in surrender and begin a very obvious closing of the open line to a very confused operator at the Bikur Holim hospital in Jerusalem. "I'm really sorry, officer, but my mother..."

"Has been dead for some time, Mr. El Aref," she interrupts sharply, and then nearly blinds me with a laser ID check to the retina. "You're coming with me."

Damn my highly recognizable and probably "most wanted" eyeballs, anyway. But the virus is safely free, so I shrug, "I guess my reputation precedes me, eh?"

"Israel refuses entry," she informs me in that far-away voice of someone LINKing higher up the command chain. "Your visa is denied. You will be detained."

"Damn it. I was really hoping to go the transgender conference in Jerusalem. A friend of mine is speaking there, did you know that?"

Her eyes shift to the right, still focusing on something far away, and I don't need mouse.net to confirm that a whole bloody battalion of Israelis has just been dispatched to the conference, Praise Allah.

Out of the corner of my eye, I see that another solider detains Deidre, as well. It's out of my hands now. I just hope that Mohammad knows what to do when the blackout rolls through.

Blackout

Despite the unwelcoming committee, the matriarch greeted us with a warm smile and a hot compress for my face. Luckily, the guards on the roof had run out of ammunition some time ago, and so had filled the barrels of their shotguns with pebbles and sand. Meanwhile, the pigs fascinated Thorin, and he crouched near one, cautiously attempting to pet it.

"What kind of tech?" she asked, as she fondled the deceptively supple fabric of the peaceforcer jacket. I resisted the urge to apologize for the parts the rats chewed. It was obviously still working well enough, otherwise I'd be dead.

"A handheld that would read a data chip," I said, having transferred the flesh drives to the pocket of my sweats before handing the jacket over.

She laughed, but not unkindly. "Do you know what OS you need?"

I thought I might, but I wondered if I could afford it. "Whatever the military is using these days, probably something compatible with boy.net."

"Why not ask for the moon?"

"Because the moon won't help me read these," I pulled out the earrings to show her. We sat around a fold-out card table on battered wicker stools that threatened to collapse with my every nervous twitch. Around us garbage rose in two-meter tall heaps, but the matriarch poured green tea from a silver pot into Japanese-style ceramic bowls.

"And what are those?"

"That's the thing, I don't know."

She gave me a side-long look. "And you came all this way, took a shot in the shoulder, just to satisfy your curiosity?"

"Uh, pretty much," I admitted.

A pig snorted and dashed through the narrow by-ways between the piles of crap. "They're poky!" Thorin informed us cheerfully, after picking himself up off the dusty ground. "Poky porky!"

Gorgon humor, apparently, was indistinguishable from that of a six-year old. I returned his smile and happy wave.

"What if I wanted the earrings?", the matriarch asked, taking a sip from her bowl. "Would you trade for them?"

I couldn't imagine anything better than what the Russian had offered me, but I said, "Maybe. I'd like to know what's on them first, though."

"As would I, my friend, as would I."

"So the question remains: do you have anything that can read them?"

"Oh, I think I do," she smiled.

Turned out, the rumors that the *zabaaliin* had developed primitive access to the LINK weren't entirely true. However, they had a mind-blowing stockpile of working technology which they let me root through. I tried not to be distracted by the game consoles and the word processors with their flashing lights and my own memories that transported me back to Before. I found a game Mohammad had loved and turned as though to tell him I'd found a copy. Instead of Mohammad, I saw Thorin gleefully pushing every button just to hear the noises they made. He was a serious distraction. So I showed him how to work the simple gaming pad, and he curled up in a shaded corner completely absorbed.

It took four and a half hours, but I eventually found something that had a port and an operating system that recognized my chips. I held my breath as I slid them in place, not quite sure what to expect.

Text scrawled frantically across the screen. *Hello? Del Toro?*

I shut down immediately. Had the handheld picked up a boy.net signal from a nearby peaceforcer? I checked it to see if it was capable of receiving wireless, but all the indicators stayed black. Carefully, I reloaded the crystals.

Identify. The program asked. *Identify.*

This wasn't just spy equipment you wore like jewelry; this was a spy who lived inside your earrings. Clever. The Russians were upping their cold war with the peaceforce by taking the artificial intelligence wardog technology to a new level.

Pulling out the crystals, I tossed the handheld back into the heap. I didn't want to talk to this thing – not yet, anyway; what I wanted now was something that could read its code.

Present Day

"Listen, Lieutenant, my lawyer insists that my association with that Palestinian incident is *alleged*," I say to the officer who leans into my face. He's so close I can smell his expensive aftershave and the cheap coffee he had for breakfast. My left wrist is handcuffed to the chair, and the beige room I'm in is specially designed to jam my mouse.net connection.

"Very well, but you have not yet adequately explained what you planned to do in Israel, Mouse," he uses my name as though we're friends, yet he'd probably slap me upside the head if I started calling him Aaron. "Tell me again. What is your interest in this conference in Jerusalem?"

This rugged, traditional soldier seems uncomfortable with the idea of a transgender summit, so I say with a cheerful smile and an exaggerated leer, "I've decided to embrace my inner queer."

The lieutenant, who had been sitting with his hip resting on the edge of the shiny black table so that his crotch was nearly level with my face, stands suddenly. He paces. "I don't think you're telling the truth. Who were you LINKing when my officer detained you?"

"I can't LINK. The American's slagged me."

"Very well, to be more precise, who were you mousing?"

"I love hearing people verb my name," I say.

"Answer the question."

Of course, that's when the rolling blackouts start.

A MOUSE THAT ROARED: How Free Access Saved North Africa
By Keela Ryū
Forthcoming from Doubleday Harcourt Penguin, 2111

Excerpted interview of Mouse; footnote commentary by "Page"/Strife

"Probably the other thing that keeps the UN from taking over the world is the fact that there are only ever little more than a thousand peaceforcers at any given time.

Officially, anyway.

The UN doesn't trust Russia any more than the US does, despite the fact that Russia still sits in on all the big committees. I'd be surprised if the UN isn't secretly matching a peaceforcer to every Russian in uniform. My prediction for the next big one? Peaceforcers versus Russia. It'd be a war of the sexes, too, and I'm not sure I'd bet on the big, beefy guys myself[26]. Luckily, Russia has stayed quietly behind its silent curtain not giving anyone any reason to declare war.

My fingers are crossed it stays that way for the rest of my lifetime, especially given what I know about Russia's space program. Let's just say the 1967 space weapon treaty only bans orbiting weapons. It doesn't say anything about bases on the moon.[27]"

---

26. Surprising from Mr. "grow a pair." Though, despite his recent tone, I know my father well enough to say that I believe he's not usually so piggish.

27. A state secret. Let's hope father has a good place to hide from the Russians when this book comes out.

Chapter 18
Morningstar

On the plains of Armageddon
Doomsday

Our snipers took out their flanks as they advanced. Angelic bodies exploded into brilliant flashes as bullets ripped through the shell of their flesh. We blew Michael back to heaven six times before he called for another parlay.

"You're not playing fair," Michael groused.

"Then take your ball and go home. Cede the field, little brother."

"Never," he said, his eyes narrow slits.

"As you wish. Be sure to say 'hello' to Mother next time you're home," I waved as I walked away.

"Hey, Morningstar," Michael shouted. I turned just in time to get a blast from his .45 square in the chest. "Do it yourself."

* * * * *

And then I fell.

The darkened sky opened up and I hit the side of a glass pyramid. Garish neon lights lined its sides. They pulsed as I rolled the entire length of the building before crashing into a palm tree and bouncing onto a sidewalk full of drunken gamblers.

"Yo, man, you okay?" asked a portly, white woman in a loud, Hawaiian print shirt. A meaty hand reached to help me up. I took it and was hauled to my feet in one mighty heave. "Uh, you should really cover up. You can get arrested like that."

She stared pointedly at my nakedness.

We both admired my attributes for a moment, and then she moved on, coins rattling in a plastic cup in her other hand. I looked around, trying to figure out where God, in His infinite humor, had deposited me this time.

A clot of electric cars hummed along a broad boulevard. Seeing me, many honked. Tall buildings flashed beacons into the dark, smog-smudged sky. The air was cool and dry and smelled of dust. Neon and LED-pulses twinkled like costume jewelry spelling out hotel names, gambling parlors and girls, girls, girls.

Ah, Las Vegas.

"Dude! How drunk are you? Put some clothes on," a young man helpfully shouted out the window of his car. A group of girls gasped, and then giggled. *My kingdom for a fig leaf.*

I headed for the lobby of the pyramid-shaped hotel. Faux Egyptian script spelled out its name, "Luxor." A bellboy came rushing up to me, "Sir, you can't come in here like that."

"Seems I lost a bit more than my shirt gambling," I said dryly. "But I need a secure port to access my bank account." He looked doubtful, so I said, "Or... I could take my business elsewhere, if you prefer."

Luckily, it was an affectation of the ultra-rich not to be LINKed. He chewed his lip, his glance nervously darted across my body. Finally, his gaze unfocused and he conferred with his bosses. "Come this way, sir," he said. "We can accommodate you."

I noticed, however, that he'd also alerted a security team, which followed us to the private alcove. A concierge met us at the door. He dismissed the bellboy and set the security to watch the exit. He was handsome in an inoffensive, forgettable way, with a LINK chassis enviable of any wire-wizard. Gleaming chrome wire snaked visibly from his temple to the base of his neck. He handed me a shielded keypad for my account number. I typed the code. Taking it from me he detached a wire from the base of his skull and expertly fed it into the pad.

"I'm sorry, but this account is invalid."

"What? Check it again," I said.

His sigh was pained, and he shook his head. "According to the account records you withdrew everything yesterday at 21:35 GMT."

"Yesterday...?" I tried to remember where I was, and then it hit me: "Mouse. Of course." Ah well, wages of sin and all that. I held out my hand for the pad. "I have a Swiss account. That should be untouched."

Skeptically, he gave to it me. His eye watched the door, and I sensed that if Mouse had found a way to infiltrate the most secure bank in the world, I'd be spending the rest of my time getting to know hotel security and likely the local constabulary as well. We went through our type and plug ritual, but this time his bored irritation disappeared with an impressed lift of eyebrows.

"Welcome to the Luxor, sir. How can we be of service?"

* * * * *

In a matter of hours, I had a new wardrobe and external LINK hardware sent to my high-roller suite. While I waited, I paced. How the hell was my war going without me?

When the obsequious concierge appeared with my things, I snatched the LINK connection from him and waved the shopping bags toward the bed. I pulled the headset on and adjusted the various microsensors. After spending far too much time remembering how to interface with one of these stupid contraptions, I managed to sync with the butler system at my establishment in Cairo and find my listing for Bea's phone.

"Time," I requested, while waiting for Bea to respond. The external LINK informed me in a pleasant female voice that it had been three and a half hours since I left the battlefield of Armageddon.

"Commander, good to hear from you," Bea said, when she finally connected. "I thought maybe that bastard finally decided to let you stay."

I shook my head; as usual I'd bounced off that non-place that was Hell. "I'm in Vegas. How goes the war?"

"Our side stormed the field after Michael's treachery. Your name was a battle cry once again, my prince," Beelzabub smiled in a way that made it clear I'd missed a surge of awesome beauty. "Their side has retreated to regroup."

As pleased as I was to hear this news, I was desperate to be there to see Michael's defeat. "I'm booking the next flight to Israel."

"We will await your arrival."

I started to nod, but stopped myself, "Unless an advantage presents itself."

Her lips parted in a crafty smile, "Your will be done."

BLACKOUT HITS ISRAEL
Country in Chaos

August 17, 2110
Agnostic Press

Jerusalem, Israel—Rolling blackouts throughout the country of Israel are blamed on a possible hack of the main Israeli Node today. In a style reminiscent of earlier attacks on the city of New York several years ago, electric grids sporadically failed. Though not directly part of the assault, LINK communication crashed due to the overload of emergency calls.

The biggest area affected was traffic, as all vehicles are powered by the "habit trail" electric lines. Chaos ensued as people unaccustomed to steering their own cars, suddenly had manual control. "It was a mess," said one police officer in Jerusalem. "We had trouble responding. The streets were clogged." Though emergency vehicles have their own internal battery, the number of accidents and abandoned vehicles made passage through the streets difficult. Many emergency workers were forced to make their way to injuries on foot.

Though no group has claimed responsibility for the attack, it comes at a time when Israel was already on high alert. There are a large number of Family Firsters in town for a conference involving the international transgender community. Several members of the Family Firsters have been arrested, as well as known Palestinian terrorists. It is also believed that the convicted LINK-criminal known as Mouse is also in custody in this time. Though his connection was supposedly slagged during imprisonment for the LINK-Angel fraud, experts suggest the signature of this incident bears a striking resemblance to his "bag of tricks."

As a Sunni Muslim, Mouse's connection to evangelical Christian Family First organization is not known at this time.

Chapter 19
Mouse

The Gaza Strip
Present Day

I'm under the table before the lieutenant unholsters his gun. He swears when his augmented eyes light on the empty cuff. Not that I've gained too much time, I only hope my gamble pays off.

"You're not going to get out of here easily, Mouse," he warns, though it sounds as though he's trying to convince himself.

My fingers continue to grope frantically across the carpeted floor. Finally, I find what I've been searching for. Prying the cover open with my fingernail, I expose the electrical outlets.

"I know you're hiding under there," the lieutenant says. "I don't know what you think you're going to gain by this."

Me either. Taking the paperclip I'd used to undo my handcuff, I bend it into a prong. I jam it into the sockets. A spark snaps. My fingers tingle, and, for the briefest second, so does mouse.net.

"Goddamn it!" the lieutenant shouts, probably in response to his own LINK coming online in the supposedly dampened room. "Lock this room down," he shouts at the ceiling. "Lock this room down!"

The sprinklers splash him in the face. The fire alarm drowns out much of his swearing.

When the other soldiers rush in, I make my move. I kick out chairs in every direction, and they clatter against the wall and squelch into water-logged carpeting.

A bloom of bluish light explodes on my right as one of the chairs is hit with a stun pulse. The fabric sizzles with static discharge. Hmmm, I need an alternate route out.

Ideas?

Neither Page nor the Dragon answer. Hopefully that means they're watching over Mohammad, though considering their combined processing power, you'd think they could do two things at once.

When fingers nearly close around my ankle, I'm forced to make a break for it. I squiggle over to the chair I'd been sitting in. Grabbing its legs, I swing it around.

I get my hands off it before the pulse races down the length of the chair. My arms go numb up to the elbow. Unfortunately, the soldiers seem to be organizing. The table lifts, and one of them crouches, gun at the ready.

There's really no place to run, the lieutenant having placed himself at the door. I'm raising my hands in surrender and preparing for the sting of the stun, when a channel opens up in mouse.net.

This is Russia Actual, it's the lovely dulcet tones of the supreme commander of the Russian Federation. I can see by the surprised expressions on the soldier's faces they're receiving the same broadcast over the LINK. A weird code flashes in the corner of my vision, which I assume is some kind of verification of identification. *You will release our treasury secretary. He has diplomatic immunity.*

Blackout

I spent six days with the *zabaaliin* reading and revising code. Apparently, the matriarch was a bit of a techhead and she'd been one of the main bidders for the wardog bits Mohammad and I'd been selling to Ahmed.

"Who is, pardon my French, a complete asshole," she told me as we sat inside her tent, chatting over breakfast. Thorin slept in the corner, curled up like a dog on a soft pillow. The interior was dark, lit only by battery-operated tea lights. Their flickering reflected in the metallic beads on the fabric of the walls. "But he provided the most awesome mech, which I paid dearly for."

"So you still have all the wardog brains?" I stuffed flavorful bean paste into my mouth on a thick slab of buttery flatbread.

Her lips pursed slightly, glancing at the food in my hand. "Your tab is already quite large, my friend. The power we're using to run the ancient mainframe you cobbled together is not cheap."

Turns out, I was the nerd trying to wire all their garbage together.

"I know," I sighed. I'd no doubt I'd exhausted the price of the jacket two minutes after I switched the toggle on the big generator. In fact by this point, I was probably several generations into a life of indentured servitude. "But I've been thinking about how I can repay you. What if you could barter on the LINK or a reasonable facsimile?"

"We would be a thousand times richer," she agreed skeptically. "But we trade with professional scientists often. No one has ever offered anything like that. I'm not sure it's possible."

"None of them have what I have," I said.

"And what is that, besides a healthy ego?"

I used my sleeve to wipe my mouth. "Well, I *had* a rudimentary thinking machine that could spy, but I think I'm about to have..." what? I wasn't entirely sure myself what I was doing to the program, "... something else entirely."

"And you think this something else is going to build you a bridge to the LINK and crack its legendary security?" She offered me a mug of hot coffee, which I knew was tantamount to signing the research grant check.

I took the cup and all it represented with a smile, "Kind of. I think, though, that what I want to build is free access for all. All of us... you know, outside."

She nodded slowly. "Noble venture, but is it practical?"

I didn't know, so I chewed the bread instead. I couldn't even explain why I'd taken so easily to the logic of the code, and why I found myself absorbed in it for hours.

Thorin rolled over, letting out a loud snort of a snore. All I knew was that it was like I'd found my *Hobbit*. To the matriarch, I said, "Can I look at the dog brains? I'd love to do a little compare and contrast."

Her agreement was skeptical, and I knew I'd added another lifetime to my bill.

The dogs absorbed my attention for two days, but then I hit a wall.

I'd been over every line six or seven times, adding bits gleaned from studying the dogs and tweaking things that lacked... well, poetry. But I had no idea if I was just screwing the thing up or what. I needed a better interface than a stupid handheld.

Texting the spy had proved fruitless and painfully slow. It didn't want to chat about what made it work and refused to discuss anything not relevant to its mission, which it also wouldn't disclose.

It had basically shut down on me. I knew it was there, and I knew it was still working, but for all intents and purposes the AI was in a sulk.

Or maybe that was me.

Working with the AI was most fascinating and important thing I'd ever done in my life, and I couldn't get it to respond to me. I was going crazy. I sat in the hot sun, glowering at the blinking greenish-yellow script of the ancient mainframe. With an angry flick, I popped open the jerry-rigged crystal reader. I picked up the earring and shouted at the tiny jewels in my fingers, "You don't want to text, fine. Interface this!"

Then, I jabbed the first earring into the flesh of my lobe. I followed it with the second, in the same ear – I mean, there was male fashion to consider, after all. Blood dripped onto my shirt. My ear throbbed in time to my heartbeat. And I sat there, hyperventilating and ready to pass out from sunstroke.

Nothing happened.

Though finally my ears stopped hurting and my breath evened out. The sun, however, was still hot.

"Crap," I muttered, and wandered off to find something cold to drink.

Then, I stayed away from the mainframe for the rest of the day, playing a game of pick-up football with Thorin and some of the kids instead. I went to bed bitter, and woke up the next morning still dissatisfied. With a heavy sigh, I went to tell the matriarch that I was going to have to be her slave for the rest of my life.

She was moderately sympathetic. "You've wasted a lot of valuable resources for nothing. Worse, I'd begun to believe in you, Mouse."

"Me too, okay? Look, I suck. I got nothing else."

At that moment my brain shattered. My body went into a seizure, arms jerking out clumsily. My legs kicked out from under me. I hit the ground hard, and my eyes rolled up into my head.

In the darkness, I heard a voice, *Hello? Identify.*

Present Day

Sitting tailor fashion on soggy carpeting, I watch confusion roll across the faces of the soldiers listening to the LINK from the supreme commander of Russia. I guess Page could multitask, after all.

Water dripping from his nose, the lieutenant scowls. "Unacceptable."

"This is not a negotiation, lieutenant," the commander continues, her voice firm. "Do I need to get the Israeli Prime Minster on the line again?"

The lieutenant actually growls. But, with tight lips, he finally says, "Very well." He gestures at me with an impatient wave. "Let's go, Mouse."

I don't really know why he's so mad. No one got hurt other than two very stunned, smoldering chairs. Perhaps he doesn't like what the sprinkler system has done for his hairdo.

"If I have any say at all in this you will be remanded into Russian custody directly." Putting his gun away, he takes my elbow. I'm sure his grip is crushing, but I still can't feel a thing. "You will not set foot in Israel."

"Okay," I agree with an unconcerned lift of my shoulder. "I'll bet I missed most of the conference, anyway."

I can actually hear his teeth grinding.

A MOUSE THAT ROARED: How Free Access Saved North Africa
By Keela Ryū
Forthcoming from Doubleday Harcourt Penguin, 2111

Excerpted interview of Mouse; footnote commentary by "Page"/Strife

"Technology is an area of blindness for a lot of people, especially those, like me, born into a certain kind of privilege. There's an assumption, even nowadays, that everyone has the newest stuff as soon as it comes out. That might be true among your early-adopter friends, particularly if you live in a society that values tech, but there's a reason mouse.net was able to take advantage of ancient computers and phone lines.[28] Way back, when the 'world' went wireless, some people still dialed-up, and, perhaps more surprisingly, a large percentage didn't even have computers at home.

Yeah, you think I'm bullshitting you.

That's because it's easy to forget. Do you think the instant the light bulb was invented every house in the world suddenly got electricity? Can you even imagine that there are still places in the world without electricity? Running water? Flush toilets?

Well, there are.

If you ever have to go there, you'll still be one level removed. You have the LINK. Until I came along, they had jack.[29]

Now, Allah willing, they have mouse.net."

---

28. Which reason, of course, he does not say, as mouse.net's operating hardware is still a guarded secret for the most part.

29. Self-aggrandizing hyperbole. *sigh*

Chapter 20
Morningstar

On the plains of Armageddon
Doomsday

Conventional travel took forever, and I spent the entire time grinding my teeth into a fine powder. At least Bea had a jeep waiting at the airport to transport me directly to the battlefield.

To my surprise, I discovered the driver to be human. It wasn't difficult to figure out how Beelzebub had recruited him, however. The man looked like a walking advertisement for *Soldiers of Fortune*, right down to the long scar running from his nose to his ear and the deep five o'clock shadow shading his chin.

Before I'd even settled in my seat, I asked, "Are we still winning?"

"I don't know. The other side doesn't seem to die. They pop right back," he said, though he sounded more frustrated by the problem than theologically challenged. Perhaps he had a history fighting the immortal undead? He glanced over at me momentarily before returning his attention to the road, "Meanwhile, our people sometimes don't make it back for days. If at all."

"Yes," I nodded. God *would* cheat by keeping any of mine that ended up in heaven. I only hoped they were giving him hell there. "We need to solve that problem."

"I hope you have ideas, boss."

I did, but it might mean the ultimate sacrifice.

* * * * *

"No," Gadreel and Bea said almost simultaneously. They'd constructed a shaded lean-to from which to base operations. Along the far wall, a series of machines had been erected to monitor the human world for signs of interference. So far, miraculously, Israel had not noticed the battle raging in Jerusalem's backyard.

Shouts from the fight echoed in the valley below.

"We can't allow you to be hit again," Bea said, as she paced back and forth in front of the flimsy, fold-out table that held her maps, plans and dozens of discarded Styrofoam cups of tea. I wondered if she ever finished any drink she ordered.

"You can't storm the gates, my lord," Gadreel agreed. "He'll never even allow you to reach them."

"If I take the fight to heaven, God will recall Michael, and possibly the other three."

"And...?" Bea stopped long enough to glare at me. "They're still immortal."

I tapped the tip of the ear Gabriel's trumpet had damaged. "If I can hurt Michael there, he will return similarly wounded."

Gadreel opened his mouth to say something, but stopped.

"What?" I asked.

"You – you go to heaven?"

It was a reasonable question, given my recent bounce. "No. But I think I could."

"And you could fight Michael there? And really wound him?" No one knew my secret, so Gadreel shook his head. "How can you be so sure?"

"Are your wings broken, Gadreel?"

My generals shared a glance. Bea's lips were thin, angry. Gadreel looked away, embarrassed, and then answered, "I don't know. I've never seen them, you know – out."

Perhaps this was something they'd fought about long ago? But, for myself, I couldn't blame Gadreel for his cowardice. A lot of the fallen were afraid of shattering their flesh and exposing wings for the same reason so many had not returned. Mere pride kept my army from returning to heaven. I was the only true exile.

"Mine are," I explained. "And there are other scars I carry. If I hit Michael in heaven, he will feel it on earth. I'm certain of it. It's the only place you can change an angel permanently."

Though I could see Gadreel considering, Bea shook her head. "It's too risky," she said. "We need you here."

"But we're hemorrhaging troops," Gadreel countered. "A lot of them aren't coming back."

"We just haven't heard from them yet," she snapped.

I took a long sip of pale, tasteless tea, and slowly shook my head. "They're lost to us, Bea. Admit it. Father forgave them and they stayed. You would too." I lifted a hand before she could protest, "Almost anyone would. We'll be lucky if we don't start seeing our losses joining their forces."

"We already have," Gadreel admitted quietly.

Standing up, I put an arm on Bea's narrow, taut shoulder. During my absence, she'd changed into a black muscle shirt and camouflage-patterned shorts. Her curls had been restrained by a rubber band at the nap of her neck. I tucked a few escaped locks behind her ear. "I'm leaving you in charge on the ground. If we must fail, I'm counting on you to make certain it's spectacular."

Her eyes flashed cold, even as her lip trembled. "I won't grant an inch."

"Nor will I."

MOUSE RESPONSIBLE FOR LINK ATTACK
Russia Expected to Make Bid for His Release

August 17, 2110
Agnostic Press

Gaza, Israel—Though not officially charged, Mouse has been arrested for his alleged part in the attack on Israel's main node today that caused mass panic and rolling blackouts throughout the country. Stopped while attempting to cross the border into Israel, Mouse was identified by a guard and taken into custody. "At first I didn't recognize him," said the guard. "But he was acting very suspicious, refusing to close all LINK activity."

Many international borders to require that LINK communications to be suspended during the customs process. Though the law has been repealed in many busy ports, including those in the United States, the majority still demand at least a partial shutdown of communications. Ivan Daschenko, a Russian lawyer who has represented Mouse in the past, says that such measures are "silly" as one doesn't need to be in actual physical proximity of a node to launch a virus. "That my client needs to sneak into Israel to do it harm is ludicrous. If he wanted to, he could send a wyrm from the comfort of his own home."

"I'm not sure that's the theory Mr. Danschenko really wants to put forth," said the Israeli Prime Minister Deborah Segal, "Especially considering the damage done today."

Danschenko maintains his client's innocence, reminding the Israeli Prime Minster that Mouse no longer officially has access to the LINK or mouse.net. He is expected to produce prison records from America that show the "slag" process performed on Mouse after his conviction. "It would take a miracle to revive the LINK after slag," said a LINK surgeon when asked if there was a way to by-pass or correct after such a procedure has been performed. "If Mouse has reconnected after that trauma, he's a bigger wire-wizard than anyone suspected."

The guard maintains that she detected an online signal coming from Mouse before her arrest.

Chapter 21
Mouse

The Gaza strip
Present Day

My freedom, it seems, comes at the price of a lot of paperwork. The only place they've released me to is a new and improved holding cell. This one has no pretense of civility. There are bars.

Have you heard from Mohammad? I ask Page, because, while there are no other amenities, mouse.net remains open. For now.

Jerusalem is still in chaos. The Israeli Prime Minister may renege once he's calculated the damage we've caused.

You think he'll trace it to us?

Even if there is no evidence, your proximity to the Node will convince them.

My feet kick at the underside of the cot, making hollow, clanging, prison-y sounds. *Which is stupid because I could take them down from a massage parlor in Thailand.*

Your lawyer is already making that case.

We're at lawyer stage already? Great. I pull up my feet and lay back. The mattress provides little cushion from the metal slab of the cot, but I close my eyes, anyway.

I must go, father. It's time to fast.

Right, it's still Ramadan. How did I make a Muslim so much more devout than I? *Pray for me, will you?*

I always do.

Blackout

The spy AI rewired my brain. I figured it must have sent the wake-up command to the nexus lodged in the back of my skull because I suddenly heard voices, well, more accurately, one voice.

Identify.

"Are you okay?" the matriarch pried open my eyelid. Light stabbed my retina. I jerked away.

Identify.

But, after shaking away the cobwebs, my smile was huge. I crushed her thin bones in a big bear hug. "Oh yeah, I'm way better than okay! I found my interface."

The matriarch pried herself from my exuberance and made a show of wiping my paw prints from her arms and shoulders. "Does this mean you plan to repay me?"

"Yes," I said. "But I need to make a delivery first."

"To the Lonely Mountain!" said Thorin from where he crouched near my feet. Standing he stretched out and muttered, "Finally."

Identify.

"I'm Mouse," I said, tapping myself on the chest. Thorin and the matriarch gave me a peculiar glance. I pointed to my head, "I'm talking to the A.I."

The matriarch shook her head like she thought I must be crazy. She settled on her toilet bowl throne and popped the umbrella as a shield from the sun. I sat grinning stupidly, my legs splayed on the hard dirt.

"If you have what you need, I'm unplugging your mainframe," she said. "Pack your things. You have three weeks to repay me, Mouse, or I will personally buy the ammunition to hunt you down."

"I love you too," I said. Standing up, I gave her soft, wrinkled cheek a peck.

Identify.

I frowned. Was it broken? I poked my chest harder, "Mouse."

Identify.

Then I noticed that, when I relaxed, my eyes darted this way and that – lighting on rubber tires, sleeping sheep dogs, buzzing flies, tables, dirt... as though trying to figure out what everything was.

Feeling a bit like the first man, I started naming things methodically, in English and Arabic. The AI seemed to prefer Arabic, repeating the sound like a strange mental echo.

Thorin appeared at my side when I returned to the area near the mainframe that I'd been using as sleeping quarters. He handed me a six pack of water. I whispered the words for it to the AI, and then asked Thorin, "How do you always score water?"

"Sympathetic peaceforcer," he said, twisting off the top and taking a long swig. "She's an American who feels badly about the friendly fire the pyramids took during the last war, I think."

Explain.

"The glass causes the mutation of Thorin's people," I told the A.I. "Egypt was supposed to be an ally, but somehow our oil fields and the pyramids got hit by Medusa."

Thorin's head cocked to the side. "Talking to your invisible friend?"

"It's in input mode, kind of like a child asking 'what's this?' and 'what's that?'" I said, trying to figure out which "things" the matriarch thought were mine to pack. I'd come with nothing; was it wise to try to leave with something?

"I'm going to pretend it's Bilbo wearing the ring," Thorin said. "When do we leave?"

The guards arrived with shotguns to show us the door. "Now I guess."

As the doors creaked shut, I understood why the matriarch had sent an armed escort. It was hard to leave behind the safety of the City of the Dead. The air might be fresher, but I already missed the secure sense the walls and friendly faces had given me.

Thorin seemed to feel it too. He glanced behind longingly, like Frodo leaving the Shire.

We turned toward the Citadel. Though I couldn't yet see its imposing structure, I shivered in its long shadow. I only hoped Mohammad waited for me there. Then all this would be worth it.

Present Day

Because of Ramadan, no one brings food, only water. The guard waits for me to finish, lest I fashion some escape tool with the remains of the paper cup. It's the woman from the airport, and her eyes glint smugly from the opposite side of the bars.

I ping her LINK address, capturing salient bits of personal information in a microsecond. Her smile fades; mine widens.

"Have a nice day," I say, handing back the soggy, wadded-up cup.

She takes it and stares at it like I've implanted a virus on its surface. Her face twitches, and it's clear she's debating the wisdom of demanding to know what I plan to do with her ID.

Smiling, I wait for her to call my bluff. Only an idiot would be so obvious to use anything stolen in a handshake, especially when that idiot is already behind bars waiting to see if Israel plans to charge him with LINK sabotage. But, clearly she thinks I'm stupid, because she stifles a strangled noise and huffs off.

You could *play nice.* It's Dragon, her voice the sigh of a long, metal-scaled tail curling around a sleeping beast. In my mind, I can visualize one yellow eye glaring at me, like a cat disturbed from its nap.

I already am. I'm letting them hold me here, even though they gave me full access to mouse.net and their LINK security is crap.

If you escaped, where would you go?

Aye, there's the rub, isn't it? Sometimes the wisest move is not to play. Besides, I'm still waiting to hear from Mohammad. Did the angel kill him? Did he make an escape of his own? Did it work out better than my attempt?

A MOUSE THAT ROARED: How Free Access Saved North Africa
By Keela Ryū
Forthcoming from Doubleday Harcourt Penguin, 2111

Excerpted interview of Mouse; footnote commentary by "Page"/Strife

"Where did I learn to code? I guess I'm what they call self-taught. Not that they teach the line-by-line stuff in school any more, anyway. When I was at Maadi British International School, it was all LINK preparedness classes, like netiquette, social platform relations – you know, typical stuff.

The Deadboys accidentally introduced me to some programming basics, but I can't really explain why I took to it the first time I saw the real deal. Logic and puzzles have always fascinated me, and, when I put my mind to it, other foreign languages come pretty easily – but I'm lazy as hell. I really still only know how to swear in French.[30]

I'm not fond of the idea, because, really, it messes with my politics[31], but maybe relating to code is something I was just born with, like a talent.

---

30. A lie. Perhaps, however, my father refers to the fact that his pronunciation of French is pretty atrocious. He can read it extremely well, and understand when spoken to. Talking back is more difficult. This seems to be true for him in most cases where he's learned another language. Don't even ask him to speak Chinese. It's embarrassing.

31. Which are, in point of fact, fairly egalitarian. He might want to rule the world, but he would tell you his main motivations are based in a desire to keep information free, providing access for all, and championing the underdog.

Chapter 22
Morningstar

The plains of Armageddon
Doomsday

Beelzebub was the master strategian; Gadreel understood treachery and deceit. Together they hatched a brilliant plan. A small strike force, with me in the lead, would wedge through their defensive line. Other guerrilla teams would attack as an obvious distraction. Michael would watch me, of course. Our goal would appear to be revenge, as we'd fight our way toward a clot of redeemed fallen. If he reacted as expected, we'd spring the trap. Our sniper would blow him back to heaven, just as I pulled the trigger on myself to do the same.

The best part? It was all just a ruse. The whole thing. If we never got to Michael, it didn't matter. If their side hit me before I stepped onto the field, it made no difference.

In fact, we intended to fail.

I only insisted we looked good doing it.

The biggest flaw in this entire plan as Gadreel pointed out, potentially, was me. If I bounced off heaven, I'd end up back on earth, naked, without even a weapon with which to try again. I could keep killing myself indefinitely, of course, but eventually I'd run out of resources in terms of the time that it would take me to regroup. Eventually, too, I supposed I'd run out of money for flights home. And, if the fight dragged on too long, the fallen would all be redeemed and back in heaven – ironically, except for me.

So I had to penetrate heaven's defenses the first time. To do that, I was going to have to surrender my pride – just enough to fool Father, but not enough to lose my soul in the Glory of Her love.

I stared out at the red stone and dust, wondering if I had the strength to resist. I have always loved God, even when we fought, and I knew He was wrong. What would I do if the gates flew open and I was forgiven? Would I have the strength for one last "fuck you"? Did I have enough hatred?

Gadreel, I sensed, understood. His eyes flicked over at me from where he stood, pretending interest in something a human showed him on the LINK monitor.

Commotion rose from the other side. I grabbed my spy glasses to see what was happening. Their ranks rippled and the fighting stuttered to a halt. Raphael strode out into the field. He had someone by the scruff of the neck. I strained to see who his prisoner was.

Though older and much more of a man than I remembered, I recognized the prophet.

Raphael shouted something and pulled a gun from the holster at his side. It was clear he intended to end the fight by killing the prophet. Everything snapped into focus in that second, and I remembered why I'd started this war.

To Gadreel, I shouted, "Do not let the prophet die."

Bea and I began our assault, though slightly less organized than our original plan. As we dashed across the field, Michael's soldiers picked off angels on my right and left. With every flash and disappearance, I cursed. The distance seemed the longest I'd ever traversed.

But, finally, we were in range.

Though his ranks closed around him, Michael looked up as Bea pulled out a rifle. Without a second's hesitation she blasted – once through the angel guarding him, and then through the archangel himself.

I was too angry to get access to heaven now, and I knew it. So I waited a beat, knowing Father wouldn't keep Michael from the game too long. My only chance was to catch him on the way back down. "Up," I said, out loud. "Then down!"

Then the space around me collapsed in on itself with the noise like a thunderclap, and I ascended to heaven.

KEYNOTE SPEAKER MISSING
Transgender Activist Kidnapped?

September 17, 2110
Agnostic Press

Jerusalem, Israel—As Israel struggles to recover from the damage caused by rolling blackouts caused by an apparently hostile LINK-node attack, rumors of a potential kidnapping have surfaced.

Zoe Santiago, one of the conference organizers and president of Aguda,

The Association of Gays, Lesbians, Bisexuals and Transgendered in Israel, says that one of the keynote speakers, noted transgender activist Mohammad Fakhoury has disappeared. "Mohammad has been the target of other attacks, and he had a Mossad escort," said Santiago when asked why she was particularly concerned, given the recent chaos. "Besides, his wife LINKed me in a complete panic. She kept telling me 'he disappeared'."

Fakhoury's wife, Izdirhar is inconsolable. "We were promised security," she said through tears. "I knew something like this was going to happen."

The Fakhourys have been frequent targets for "hate crimes" over the years, despite Mr. Fakhoury's status in the community. Apparently well-known as a "ghost king" from Egypt's Blackout past, Fakhoury is speaks regularly about how a surprising tolerance and human decency saved him from being stoned to death when his transgender identity was revealed. "I thought I was dead, but, Izdirhar stood over me. She told everyone that if they wanted me dead they would have to kill her, too. My sister, who was also in the camp at the time, came to stand beside her. One by one, all the women of the camp joined them," Fakhoury explained in a previous speech at last year's conference in Sidney, Australia. "Slowly, people came to accept who I am. I eventually led my people into Israel."

The fact that Fokhoury's story resembles that of Moses is not lost on many of his detractors. He is particularly reviled by both Jewish and Christian fundamentalists.

An all-points bulletin has been issued by the Israeli Prime Minister.

Chapter 23
Mouse

Another earthquake shakes the ground. I grab the bars of the cell and watch in dismay as plaster dust rains from the cracks in the ceiling. Triggering a program I wrote earlier, I listen for the sound of the lock clicking open. If the walls start to fall, I'm out of here.

It's a big one. I ride a wave of heaving earth, one hand on the door.

Somewhere nearby a wall gives way; it rumbles like thunder. I'm down the hall and running for an exit. As I pass, the other cell doors unlatch in quick succession. Soon, I'm joined by a small group of escapees.

"This way, Mouse," someone tugs my sleeve. It's a young man I don't recognize, except that he's clearly one of my tribe, given the silver wire snaking around his head and the blue-green hair that shimmers like a mallard's feathers. He taps the almond-shaped lump at his temple that houses the LINK, "Floor plans."

I'd downloaded them, too, but I'm just as grateful for the assist. Especially since people are shouting, and the smell of the ozone-searing pluses of stun guns fills the air.

The kid wrenches the door to the stairwell open. I grab his shoulder before he falls into the space where the stairs have separated from the wall. "No good," I tell him, though it's obvious. He looks around desperately for another route, but I think I see a way.

We're only a story or more up, and our safest bet might be to find a window and jump for it. A few broken bones would be a small price to pay, particularly if the rest of the building comes down.

The kid sees where I'm looking, but isn't convinced. "There's got to be a better way."

One of the more criminal of our element decides our course of action for us. With a swift kick to the lock, the door to an office bangs open. We rush in the room. Someone overturns the wooden desk to provide cover. Even so, stun pulses thin our ranks. The air sizzles with the proximity of the blasts, and the hair on the back of my neck stands up. The window is painted shut, but desperation gives my muscles strength – and the kid's extra shove helps tremendously, as well. The paint cracks and splits. The air rushing in is dry and hot. I punch out the screen and crawl out. Finally, all that's left is let go.

I close my eyes, and fall.

Blackout

The closer we got to the Citadel, the more the streets swarmed with peaceforcers. We'd gone the long way around, giving the structure and the soldiers as wide a berth as possible. Thorin and I huddled in the shadow of the old city wall near the blue mosque and tried to decide a course of action. The peaceforce had built a security perimeter around the Citadel and military police manned checkpoints at all approaches.

Enemy. The AI informed me any time my glance skipped across the black uniforms. *Enemy*.

"No shit," I said.

"Goblins," Thorin decided. "Lots and lot of goblins."

"Maybe we should just walk in, you know, and surrender," I suggested.

"Are we criminals? Otherwise they'll probably just shoo us off."

He had a point. I wiped the sweat from my brow. "I suppose we could make ourselves into criminals," I said.

"You mean, just claim to be someone they want?"

That wasn't precisely what I'd intended. I'd been thinking we could cause a lot of trouble until the peaceforce decided to arrest us, but Thorin's idea involved a lot less work. "Who do you suppose is on their Top Ten right now?"

"I'll ask."

I reached out to stop him, but Thorin had already moved beyond my grasp. As I watched him skip across the sand I'd waded through, I wondered if I'd ever see him again. At least he'd left me a couple bottles of water. I sat back against the stone and waited.

The sun was setting when Thorin shook me awake. He tossed a pile of black fabric into my lap. "They want that ghost who sings so nice."

I blinked, feeling the sting of sunburn on my face. It took several minutes for what Thorin was saying to register. About the same time I recognized the fabric as a burqa. Did I want to know how he'd gotten one? "You want me to pretend to be a woman?"

"Yes. At least you're short enough."

I snorted. My fingers unconsciously turned the fabric over in my hands, and I thought of another, very different Mohammad. "What did you say they want her for again?"

"She's the one that sings that song that made you mad."

"Oh. The girl muezzin."

"Exactly."

"Well, that doesn't seem like much of a crime," I said. Standing up, I shrugged into the long robe. The fabric smelled of sweat, but also something spicy, like curry or turmeric. It took me a few minutes to figure out how arrange the mask so I could see. My view of the world narrowed to only what was in front of me, and grayed thanks to the fine mesh. "How are we going to convince them I'm this ghost they're looking for?"

"My friend," Thorin said. "I told her I wanted to do something really nice for her, and I asked about the most wanted criminals. She's expecting me to bring you, or rather the muezzin, in."

"Clever," I said, wondering if I was walking into some kind of trap. But then, if I was, it was where I wanted to be, anyway.

"You know," Thorin said, cocking his head to look at me. "You look a lot like her, actually."

I glanced down at my flat chest. "How is that possible? And how do you know?"

"My peaceforcer friend had a photo, and she gave me some stats to make my hunt easier. You're the same height almost exactly, though I think the real prophet has an inch or two on you. I guess she's not even twelve, so she's got almost no bust."

"Well, good. Now take me to their leader, will you?"

* * * * *

Jokes about the incompetence of the peaceforce aside, I still didn't expect to gain access quite so easily. But in less than two hours, both hands were cuffed to a chair in an air-conditioned office, and I was staring at the adjutant of the base commander. She was apparently Thorin's "friend," as she continually stroked him where he sat perched on the edge of her smooth, black shiny desk.

Classically career military, the adjutant's hair was cut short, though it was long enough to end in slight auburn curls. The eyes that watched me suspiciously were the same flinty gray of much of the decor of the sparsely decorated room. Her lips seemed to curl in a constant sneer, except when she looked at Thorin, when they turned into an almost girlish grin.

Gross.

Still, you did what you had to for food and water, man. I could appreciate that.

I rattled my chains, clanking the cuffs against the metal of the chair. So far, the hardest part of the deception was keeping silent. I babbled when I was nervous, and seeing all these soldiers around made me very, very twitchy.

So I talked to the AI.

"This is the ugliest room I've ever seen," I whispered. The only color in the room was a stern portrait of the United Nations' Secretary General, a white haired Asian woman who looked like she'd swallowed something particularly sour just before sitting for the holo-artist. Otherwise, thanks to boy.net, there were no file cabinets or papers or anything that made the room look lived-in besides the gigantic desk, which was clearly placed for its intimidation factor. "There's not even a rug to soften things up. And my standards are pretty low. I live in the apocalypse."

Explain.

By which I assumed the AI wanted to know why a nice looking room mattered to me, so I continued conspiratorially, "Well, they apparently bring their guests here. You'd think they'd make an effort."

Why?

"It's just good manners, isn't it?"

Define.

I was about to when I noticed the adjutant looking around the room as if trying to see who I was talking to. She glanced at Thorin and asked him, "Is the muezzin insane?"

I laughed. I mean, who knew, right?

"He – she's just talking to Bilbo," Thorin said. Then he leaned down so that his lips tickled her ear, and said, "When is your boss coming? I want to go eat in the mess hall like you promised."

She glanced off to the side, engaging her LINK. Then, she stood up and smoothed out her uniform. She snapped to attention. "Here he is now."

The door behind me opened, and I turned to see Colonel Lars Heinrick, who, in some other era, could have been poster-boy for Hitler's youth. Blond, big and beautiful, he strode into the room like he owned it, which I guess as base commander he kind of did. The imposing black peaceforcer uniform had its desired effect on me, and I squirmed uncomfortably in my chair.

"Who is this imposter?" he asked.

The adjutant looked shocked. "What do you mean?"

"I mean, Captain, that the muezzin has been ID'd by two of our guys in sector seventeen harassing the Deadboys again, apparently. I sent out a confirm order as soon as you said you had her in custody." He leaned his massive six-foot something frame to look me in the eye, "So, I'll ask again, who is this imposter?"

"I'm Mouse," I said. "I was sent by Del Toro... or maybe the Russians. Which one do you want to talk about in front of your adjutant?"

He never skipped a beat or stopped staring at me, "Leave us, Captain. Now."

"The Russians?" the adjutant started, but he cut her off with a sharp glance.

"Out," he reminded her.

He resumed staring at me uncomfortably closely, his hands gripping the arms of my chair. When the door clicked behind her and Thorin, Heinrick sat back against the desk.

"Where is Del Toro?" he asked, his arms crossed in front of his massive chest.

"Dead," I said. "But I've got her stuff, which I'm supposed to give to you, and you're supposed to get me out."

"Is that so," he said in a decidedly unconvinced tone.

"Yes, it's so," I insisted, rustling my cuffs a bit desperately. "I negotiated that deal in good faith with..."

Valentine.

"Valentine," I repeated what the AI said. "You don't want to piss Valentine off, now do you?"

Heinrick leaned back and regarded me darkly. I had a feeling I shouldn't have pushed it with that last bit, but, eventually, Heinrick's lips pressed together before he said, "All right. Let's see it."

"I'm wearing it," I told him. "On my wrist."

He walked behind me, his boots clapping on the stone floor. Kneeling, he lifted the fabric of the burqua. "The spy wear is a dick tracy?"

I wasn't giving up the earrings, now was I?

"Of course," I said, as if he were the biggest idiot in the entire known universe.

"Smart and very subtle." Though I couldn't see him, I sensed his nodding.

He undid the clasp and removed the watch. I felt a key click in the hand-cuffs. He released me, "Fucking Russians. No offense."

"None taken," I said lightly.

With my hands free, I snaked my fingers under the hood of the burqa. I rubbed my nose, which, of course, itched from the moment I couldn't reach it. Heinrick, meanwhile, sat back on his heels alternately inspecting the watch and glancing at me. "You can take that off now, if you like."

"It's okay," I said. "Honestly, I wouldn't mind at all if you never saw my face."

He frowned at the watch. "I don't like dealing with spies."

I couldn't agree more, but I knew he considered me part of that profession so I said nothing. The more he turned the watch over, the more my heart raced. In a minute the damn thing was going to phone home, and my con would be blown to hell. "I'd like to go now."

"I'd like the rest of Del Toro's things before you do." He glanced up at me, his eyes sharp. "Unless you'd rather tell our interrogators what you've done with them."

Give him what he wants.

"What?"

The AI wanted to go? It wanted me to hand it over to the "enemy"? I was heartbroken. Even though our relationship mostly consisted of me naming things for it, I'd grown fond of having it in my head with me. It had felt so... natural.

"Valentine's communiqué said you'd be handing over 'things,' plural." Heinrick held up the watch as if it were exhibit A. "This is one thing. I want the others."

I started to reach for the earrings, but stopped. "Do you really want that?" I asked the AI.

Give him what he wants.

Heinrick's brow knitted. "Yes, I believe I do. And I would like it right now."

With a sigh, I undid the first earring. "Seriously?"

"Yes," Heinrick said, his frown deepening.

The AI was silent long enough for me to hold out hope that it had changed its mind and wanted to stay with me. A heartbeat later, it said: *Yes, do it.*

A yank that tore through crusty blood brought a brief tear to my eye. I dumped both earrings into Heinrick's waiting palm. "They're more your style, anyway," I said.

"Good man," he said, though I no longer felt like one. I was empty, bereft, and alone.

I hardly noticed as Heinrick pressed a credit counter into my hand and ushered me toward an aircraft hanger bay. Someone, a pilot I supposed, asked where I wanted to go, and I muttered, "America."

My answer surprised me because I hadn't put much thought into it, except that I'd assumed that's where Mohammad would want to go.

I grabbed Heinrick's arm as he started to leave, "Wait! What about my friend? I have to get Mohammad."

He shook his head as he easily shook loose from my grip. "Your plane is leaving. You can cancel the flight if you want, but this is a one-time offer. You go now or not at all."

The thin plastic of the credit counter cut into my palm. "Yeah, I go now. But you need to release my friend Mohammad. Your people took him from Franklin's place. He's got a broken arm."

Heinrick glanced off to the side, clearly communicating with someone. "We released those boys a long time ago. There were only minor injuries treated. No one with a broken arm was in our custody."

"What? No!" I'd gotten this far, and there was no Mohammad. "If he's still out there, I've got to go."

"The door is open, but there's no plane if you walk out."

How would I find Mohammad out there? He could be anywhere.

"Tick, tick, Mouse," Heinrick said, glancing at his pilot as if ready to dismiss him.

I looked at the plane, and then out into the desert just outside the hanger doors. I could go back out there, try to find Mohammad, but... but it would be easy for someone to steal the credit counter. Then what would I have? Wouldn't it be smarter to go somewhere safe and make inquiries from there? With four million credits I could hire someone – a dozen somebodies, maybe even one of the matriarch's people – to find Mohammad.

Or maybe that was just cowardice.

Heinrick nodded sharply, and his pilot started to walk away.

"No, wait! Okay, let's go," I said, hating myself. As I settled into my seat in the plane, I sighed. At least I finally got my damn thirty silver.

Explain.

"It's a reference to Judas," I whispered, before it hit me. The AI! It was still with me! I touched the empty, aching holes in my earlobes. "Where are you?"

Nexus.

"What about the earrings?"

Empty.

I couldn't help smiling. "Awesome."

Maybe with the AI's help, I could make good on my promise to the *zabaaliin* and get them free access to the LINK. At least then I might not be a total heel. And then, some day, I would come back for Mohammad.

Present Day

The landing does something really bad to my knee, but otherwise I seem to be alive and breathing. Of course, I'm surrounded by soldiers who are milling around and assessing the damage the building sustained from the earthquake. No one has noticed yet that those of us coming out the window are escapees. It won't take long, however. So I start walking away – slowly, casually, but with a sense of rightness and purpose.

I'm just going to that grocery store across the street. That's where I was headed when the earthquake hit, I try to feel the truth of it in my bones. I try to exude a "normal" vibe, even as I limp out into traffic.

Behind me, I hear someone shout, "You there!"

But I don't turn. It can't be me. After all, I'm just a guy going to the store.

"Stop or I'll shoot!"

My shoulders tense, but I try not to show it. I hear the zap, but, somehow, I'm unaffected. My curiosity wins and I turn just in time to see the green-blue-shiny-haired kid crackling with electricity for a moment before diving facedown into the pavement.

This is why I never did anything fancy to my hair. Shocking colors make excellent bull's eyes.

I make it across the street and into the grocery/convenience store. It kills me, but I'm going to have to wait to contact Mohammad. To pass the time, I feign interest in the mangos and dates. I buy a bag of figs, a map, a camera, a cloth safari hat, and a shirt that proclaims: "I heart Israel" in English. I change in the bathroom, and then take up the slow and easy stroll of a tourist.

Eventually the store clerk will tell the soldiers about my suspicious insistence that I use the employee bathroom to immediately get into my tourist gear and hand over the security camera tapes, but, for the moment, I'm headed for the train station and Jerusalem. If Mohammad is still alive, he'll be somewhere just outside of Armageddon.

Man, that doesn't bode well, does it?

A MOUSE THAT ROARED: How Free Access Saved North Africa
By Keela Ryū
Forthcoming from Doubleday Harcourt Penguin, 2111

Excerpted interview of Mouse; footnote commentary by "Page"/Strife

"I guess he got religion from me, but, really, Page is a far better Muslim. He prays a lot. He fasts for Ramadan. I mean, I'm not always that good about the simple stuff.[32]

But I do have a weird theory; do you want to hear it?[33] Yes, it's probably as strange as my one about the Russians. Okay, here it is: I think that when Page first started inhabiting my brain with me, he ended up on the right side. No, I mean as in the right hemisphere – the one responsible for the creative, abstract stuff.

Why? Well, our first interface was kind of crude and, in retrospect, lopsided. It's possible that the delivery system was designed with women's fashion in mind. Yes, I'm being cryptic. No, I'm not going to explain it any better. Look, I don't need everyone knowing how Page came into being.

The point is that I think that because I didn't want anyone to think I was gay, he mapped to a part of my brain that triggered that bit of his personality no one can quantify or explain with simple observation of code line.

---

32. My father is too modest. His faith, particularly his almsgiving, saved an entire country.

33. I find this theory fascinating, of course. No one really understands where my "soul," such as it may be, came from. I have very few accurate records from the early days in the Blackout. My first moment of consciousness, I remember breathing – the actual physical act – and then my eyes opened to a world I couldn't identify. I know that I spent several months inside the closed system of my father's nexus before we invented mouse.net, and that much of who I am has to do with how I first perceived the world, but the mysteries of my soul are as unknown to me as to all those hundreds of scientists who have since studied and tested me.

Chapter 24
Morningstar

In the sky above Megiddo
Present Day

This time when I fell, I took Michael with me.

As we tumbled, I continued to pound him. My fist connected blow after blow, no longer bruising his battered face, but still satisfying. Below, angels scattered, watching our descent.

When we landed, Michael lay beneath me, defeated.

I could not pretend I was unscarred, but, slowly, painfully, I got to my feet. My body naked with broken, charred wings plainly visible, I raised my fist in the air. Despite the pain, my voice was clear and strong, "Victory is mine."

For a moment, I heard only confused whispers. Somewhere behind me, I thought I heard Bea's voice quiver, "What do we do now? This isn't how it's supposed to be."

Ignoring the fallen's doubt, my eyes sought the three remaining archangels, and I commanded, "Surrender."

Jibril stepped forward, a bit uncertain. His black eyes darted to Michael's prone body and then to me. "No," he said. "It can't be this way."

The dragon wasn't supposed to slay Saint Michael. Good always triumphed over evil in the end. "Yet, here we are. Where is the prophet?"

"Here," said a trembling voice. The prophet stood beside Uriel, and seeing them together made my heart lurch. Damn Gadreel for not getting to him sooner. "Morningstar, you never told me why Allah wanted me dead. Is it true what Uriel says? Does God want me to be an example? Would my death make it okay for people like me?"

"No!" I stepped forward, my hand outstretched, imploring. "Don't let them talk you into suicide. Other people have died for God. Do you think their message survived uncorrupted?"

"But to be a martyr for Allah would be honorable, would it not?" the prophet asked, though he sounded uncertain.

Michael sat up slowly. His head bowed, he rested his hand painfully on his knee. I looked down at him and our eyes met. I half expected God to move through him, and forge a victory from this defeat. But, They didn't.

The fact that God was silent wasn't lost on Michael, either. His voice sounded as broken as his body. "The prophet Mohammad, peace be upon his name, lived his whole life out. So did Buddha. And Moses. There is no reason you have to die to spread your message. God is wrong."

Even I stared, open-mouthed, at Michael. But I saw a momentary flash, this wasn't sedition or capitulation brought on by free will; this was Michael's message. God's attempt at a retraction, an—

... apology.

Well. I accept.

"You heard what Michael said," I shouted. "Go tell it on the mountain or whatever it is you messiah-types do. Tell it for the rest of your life." My gaze swept the plains of Armageddon looking each angel in the eye. "And if any of you angels try to get in the way—", I held out my hand to Michael; when he took it, I lifted him to his feet, "—my brother and I will kick your ass."

ACTIVIST FOUND
Joyful Reunion with Wife and Family

September 17, 2110
Agnostic Press

Jerusalem, Israel—Though his exact whereabouts during the rolling blackouts that affected most of Israel today, Mohammad Fokhoury, the trans-gendered activist believed kidnapped, returned to his wife and family today. A police officer spotted Fokhoury on a train coming from the area near Megiddo and quickly alerted authorities.

His wife and two daughters by his side, Fokhoury expressed his gratitude to the gathered newsbots. "I am continually impressed by the kindness and concern people have shown for my well being. It gives me hope for a better future."

The Mossad agent assigned as Fokhoury's security was conspicuously absent, and is considered at-large. Israel's Prime Minister has issued an arrest on sight order.

Chapter 25
Mouse

Jerusalem, Israel
Present Day

Deidre and Mohammad's wife swap stories about us on the balcony of the hotel room while he and I awkwardly attempt to reconnect. His daughter naps on the nearby bed, her thumb tucked in her tiny mouth. I'm mortified to see how clumsy his right hand is, as he smoothes the curls on her forehead.

"I can't believe that Franklin didn't even fix your fucking arm," I say, not really intending to mention our mutual past so soon. Mohammad looks up at me, his eyes clouding with the memory.

"You know I came here to tell you how sorry I am," I say. "For everything."

"Everything? Do you even know what you're apologizing for, Chris?"

It's funny, but I realize the last time anyone called me Chris without sarcasm was the last time I spoke to Mohammad, which was the day I betrayed his secret. "I should never have taken you to Franklin. You were-I didn't think how much more vulnerable-I mean, shit, man, I was just trying to do the right thing."

"You've got to stop swearing in front of my daughters," Mohammad shakes his head. "Hamidah is a total repeater."

I wait to see if that's it, if that's all the forgiveness I'll get.

He's smiling at me, though I still know him well enough to see the tension at the corners of his mouth. "I hated you for a really long time. But I came around. Look, I realized. if it wasn't for you, I would never have escaped. The Russian woman, she told me something about a mouse which I didn't understand, but then she asked after the peaceforcer's things, so I knew it must be you that sent her. She must have offered a lot of money, because Franklin had been very... possessive before that."

It was easy to imagine what he meant. I shake my head, and look away, shamed.

His hand claps my shoulder. "No, Chris, don't be like that. What I'm trying to say is that Russian? She was my angel. She got me out of the darkness. Out of that room meant out of that place when the fighting started. Things – well, things eventually got better."

I nod, though I have no words to add. I feel absolved, yet I know we're both still broken by our past. He talks to me about other things – new holos, games, inconsequentials – and eventually some crazy idea about a paradigm shift of consciousness and the LINK.

"You want me to do what?" I ask.

"A virus or a meme, I'm not sure," he admits. It's time for breakfast, which would be the last meal before we begin fasting on this last day of Ramadan, and he's arranging food on a plate. "I've got something people need to hear."

I pick an olive off the plate and pop it in my mouth. "You know I was kind of forced to retire the LINK angels."

Mohammad chuckles at that. "I was thinking something a bit more legal."

"I don't really do legal."

His eyes twinkle kindly. "Maybe it's time to start. Perhaps this is something we could work on together."

Something lifts off my shoulders, something I'd been carrying a long time, like a shroud. "I'd like that."

Father...?

"But first I have go on hajj."

THE END

Ishtartu
A short story
in the AngeLINK Universe

Originally written for an "erotic lesbian futures" anthology edited by Lynne Jamneck called Periphery *(Lethe Press, February 2008), "Ishtartu" takes place in an AngeLINK future Minneapolis, but don't expect to see cameos of familiar characters, alas. This story was chosen for inclusion in this publication because it was felt that of all the AngeLINK short stories written, this one resonated the most strongly with the themes of* Resurrection Code. —LM

The reflection in the changing room mirror looked like an effeminate man in drag, Edie decided. It didn't help that the salesclerk, in a misguided effort to be helpful, had chosen something pink and girlish. The legal-length hemline didn't flatter her rugby-thickened calves, and she'd yet to find a pair of high heels she'd been able to wedge her broad, square-toed feet into. This was never going to work.

Edie waved her hand to dispel the hologram. She smoothed back the trim line of short blond hair above her ears, and adjusted her tie. Much better.

Except.

Except she'd interviewed with eighteen prospective religions this week and none of them – not even the Wiccans – could grant her immunity from the Leviticus law which stated "a woman shall not dress as a man," and vice versa in public.

The salesclerk knocked politely on the shuttered door. When Edie didn't immediately answer, the woman cleared her throat. "You might like these." The hand that inched the door open slightly held a number of holo-chits. "They're not precisely street legal, but I think you'd look great in them."

Curious, Edie took the shy offering. The first turned out to be a black mini, which showed off the lions of Ishtar tattooed on Edie's inner thighs. And hid little else.

"Oh, my, my," the clerk tsked in pure Minnesotan, clearly peeking despite the privacy screen. "You'd be arrested in a heartbeat. It's a shame too, because it looks hot with the blazer and tie."

"I look like a whore," Edie said, more angrily than she'd intended.

"No disrespect, but isn't that what you *are*?"

The question was innocent enough. Normally, Edie had a firm but tactful explanation that the ishtartu were sacred prostitutes – that she was, in fact, a priestess, due as much respect in the eyes of the law as a Catholic Monsignor or a Muslim imam.

But, since Valentine died, she'd lost her faith.

Valentine was Edie's best friend. He'd been her "cover" all through high school. He was probably the only reason she wasn't in some re-education camp right now. He'd saved her life. In fact, Valentine had been the first one to show her the queer underground comic books and magazines. Together, they'd discovered that the ishtartu had the legal right to wear whatever they pleased in service of their goddess. She'd joined a month after he had, even though she was just barely old enough.

Edie's faith had been unshakeable. Any goddess who celebrated queerness was a goddess for Edie. Then, Valentine up and died on her. Suddenly, it wasn't enough anymore.

Edie had offered and offered and offered herself those months Valentine was sick. Edie'd taken so many tricks, prayed so hard, her knees still hurt. Despite all the sacrifices she'd made, all the shit she'd put herself though, the goddess let him die.

No, the goddess killed him.

The memorial had been like losing Valentine a second time. The high priestess tried to keep order, but Valentine's family kept disturbing the vigil with their hateful shouts about hell and how his religion had defiled him and given him the disease. The hard part was that Edie knew it was partly true. Valentine had told her he'd taken a risk with a client because he believed that the goddess would protect him.

Valentine's faith betrayed him.

Even knowing that, Edie had held on to her belief that the goddess would come through – give him some kind of miraculous remission. Edie prayed the only way she knew how, and the goddess refused answer. She woke up the day after his memorial service with a cold, twisted sense that the goddess was just a sham. All those protesters were right; she was just fucking people for money.

"Yeah," Edie told the salesclerk, feeling shame well up deep inside her. "I guess that *is* what I am."

* * * * *

Edie walked home with the receipt for the mini and two conservative skirts in her coat pocket. Five hundred credits to look like crap, she sighed.

People parted before her like the Red Sea as she moved through the busy Minneapolis skyway. Edie noticed there were generally two sorts of people, those who kept their eyes firmly averted, and those who stared. Of those that stared, the majority made some kind of ward against evil like the sign of the cross. Some looked ready to spit or shout. A few just took her in – the buzz cut, long coat, suit and tie – without any expression other than curiosity, like you might gaze at some foreign beast in a zoo.

Normally, Edie moved easily through the crowd, her head held high and ready to stare down anyone. Today, she hurried along, trying to avoid eye contact. She used to love the feeling of flaunting her sexuality; now she felt... exposed.

Edie spotted a uniform headed her way. The cop would stop her in front of everyone and demand to see her green card, proof that she was ishtartu. She fished into her coat pocket. Her card had turned a sickly chartreuse. Flipping it over, she saw she had about fifteen minutes to call in before it went completely yellow and her license was considered suspended. Edie'd heard of cops who'd come up with all sorts of delay tactics just to toss a working girl or boy behind bars.

Given Edie's crisis of faith, she could end up in legal limbo. In this day and age, when America was a theocracy, not having a legally recognized religious affiliation was a crime. She'd planned to go down to the courthouse sometime this week to apply for seeker status (a grace period for people converting to a new religion), but, well, she'd been so busy desperately trying to find another religion that would not only accommodate her sexuality, but also her personal fashion style, she forgot.

The card in her hand began flashing. The cop was nearly within shouting distance. Edie ducked into a public terminal and swiped her card in the reader. The terminal booth smelled faintly of stale sweat, and the floor was soggy with slush and ice. Whoever had used this place last had actually come from outside, where the snow was falling. Edie shook her head in disgust, even while she was thinking, "There but for the grace of the goddess, go I."

A rap on the door startled her. The cop peered in at her through the grime-streaked windows of the accordion doors. She palmed the green card and slapped it in front of his face. The instant the terminal had connected to the Temple, it had turned a healthier shade of green.

The cop pursed his lips and shook his head, clearly disappointed he couldn't harass her. She smiled apologetically, which only made his eyes narrow. He mouthed, "I'll be watching you."

Edie waited for him to move off, but he didn't. The cop took up a position at the crosswalk directly opposite Edie, like he was performing some public safety duty. He crossed his arms in front of his chest, ostensibly watching the crowd for trouble, but he kept his attention on her. *Great*, Edie thought, *so much for slipping off without finishing the transaction.*

The cop's scrutiny felt like needles in Edie's back as she scrolled through the potential client list. The usual suspects flicked across the screen. She hardly saw them. What was she going to do? She need time to think, but the cop started pacing back and forth like a lion waiting to pounce on a kill.

Without even looking, Edie pressed the accept key on the worn out pad. She had to get this creep cop off her back. She'd deal with reneging on the contract later. The machine peeped out a tinny beep, and Edie felt a slight buzz at the receiver buried under her right temple as the client's dossier was downloaded into her personal, private LINK.

Edie green card flushed into a deep green. Her shoulders relaxed as she swung open the doors. From the smile on her face and the corresponding grimace on his, she sensed the cop knew he was beaten.

* * * * *

Edie hopped the light rail for home. The train was mostly empty, except for a couple of women in business suits at the rear of the car talking to each other in the excited gestures of ASL. Edie always found sign language captivating to watch, so she tried not to stare. Most people didn't like too much attention from an ishtartu; it made them nervous, like someone could see into their deepest, darkest fantasies. To distract herself, Edie glanced through the dossier stored in her LINK.

Now that she was away from the cop, Edie planned to hit the reject option – a prerogative all ishtartu had – without even really reading the offer. But, the instant the photo appeared in her mind's eye, she paused.

The woman was beautiful. She had dark mocha-colored skin and dreadlocks that hung past her shoulders. Large almond-shaped eyes stared mischievously at the camera, and a wouldn't-you-like-to-know-what-I'm-thinking-about grin played on full, sensual lips. Too-large earrings glittered at her earlobes. She wore a burnt orange turtleneck, which was the only disappointment because it hid whatever curves might lie beneath.

Edie found herself imagining full breasts... or perky, taut breasts... or.... She stopped herself. Her mental finger hovered over the reject button. Not matter how gorgeous the client, it wouldn't be right. It would just be paid sex.

Her mental gaze lingered on those playful, teasing lips. Would that be such a bad thing? Maybe she could take this job as one last farewell.

* * * * *

Jamila, the client in question, lived in Saint Paul. Though it was the capitol of Minnesota, Saint Paul liked to think of itself as a quaint, small town. Thus, after stopping at home for a quick shower and her overnight bag, Edie found herself standing on a corner, outside, in the freezing rain, waiting for a trolley car. It was her third transfer.

At least she didn't have to take a damned bus, which was good because she was packing. Edie could feel the center strap of the harness wide and firm between her legs. She ran the flat of her palm over the pronounced bulge riding on her mons. It was going to be along trolley ride. Ah well, every moment would build the anticipation.

Though the LINK automatically informed a supplicant that their offer to the Temple of Ishtar (tax deductible!) had been accepted, Edie liked to call ahead and get a feel for the client. So, she mentally signaled a go-ahead for the LINK to establish a connection.

"You're not canceling like the others, are you?" Jamila's voice was a rich, deep alto. And Edie had been so pleased to see that she looked just as gorgeous on the LINK as she did in her profile, that it took a second for her to parse Jamila's question.

"Actually, I'm about five minutes from your place. That's still good, right?"

Jamila rewarded Edie with brilliant flash of a smile. "I'm all ready for you, girl. I even have hot cocoa waiting."

"With whip cream?"

Jamila chuckled lowly. "Lots."

* * * * *

It was only when she was standing on the sagging front porch of Jamila's Victorian did Edie pause to wonder why anyone would cancel. Jamila's dossier expressed an interest in a variety of different sexual positions and a tendency towards experimentation, none of which would normally be a turn-off to an ishtartu. Before putting her finger on the doorbell, Edie LINKed to Jamila's offer one more time. She scanned the surface for any anomalies, but found nothing. Then, she accessed the client history. There they were: two rejections. Odd. Both happened after having accepted the call. One left her in the bedroom. Highly unusual.

A gust of cold wind nipped at Edie's ear. Despite her growing concern, she rang the doorbell. The door opened with a puff of warm air that smelled of pine and baking bread. "You actually came."

Jamila wore a bulky brown sweater that matched her eyes. Since she was in her own home, she wore faded blue jeans and comfortable bunny slippers – complete with ears and a pink triangular button nose. Edie smiled at those.

"You're beautiful," Edie said, completely genuinely. "How could anyone say no to a woman like you?"

Jamila raised thin eyebrow, even as she stepped out of the doorway so Edie could enter. "Wait until we get to the bedroom."

"I can't wait," Edie said, shrugging out of her coat. Seeing a coat tree beside the door, she hung it up. She kicked off her boots and took a look around.

Jamila's house was like so many in Minneapolis/St. Paul. Despite all the advances in technology, it was still a grand old place with twelve-foot ceilings, maple trim, and hardwood floors. Jamila had a fire roaring in a stone fireplace. Velvety purple couches and a matching overstuffed chair tucked comfortably around the fire. Bookcases encircled the room, filled with data-chits and crystals. What looked like original, abstract oil paintings hung on the rich cream-colored walls.

"You want that drink, or should we just..." Jamila's eyes indicated an open staircase.

"It's entirely up to you," Edie replied.

"Then, I'd like to get this over with. If you're going to run screaming like that last girl, I don't want to waste my good cocoa on you. No offense."

What had happened here? Edie shook her head in disbelief. "There might be screaming," she insisted with a wicked smile. "But I promise I won't run."

"Good," Jamila murmured, stepping closer.

They were almost the same height, Edie being only a few inches taller. Edie could smell the other woman's scent – lavender and musky.

Jamila slowly ran a finger down the length of Edie's tie. Twirling her long-boned fingers around the silk, she gripped it firmly. With a tug, she led Edie up the stairs.

* * * * *

Edie got the sense of a bedroom with the usual furniture and piles of clothes scattered around, but the instant they stopped moving, Jamila wrapped her in an embrace. Jamila pressed her body against Edie's crotch.

"Mmm, nice," Jamila said, feeling the hardness there. Then, Jamila kissed her.

This is not how this is supposed to start, Edie thought to herself, even as her lips sought Jamila's slightly parted mouth. *I'm supposed to say the ritual words.* But, Edie forgot all about that for the moment lost in the sensation of soft, wet lips. Jamila's lipstick tasted of wax and cinnamon.

Jamila's fingertips brushed the short, sharp hairs at the back of Edie's neck. Edie's arms encircled Jamila's generous waist; then explored the broad expanse of hips and buttocks.

They continued to kiss, tongues probing deeper.

Jamila pressed her body harder against Edie's package. The pressure sent a quiver along Edie's thighs. She allowed a groan to escape between her lips.

Edie slipped her hand under Jamila's sweater. Jamila's skin was warm and dry against Edie's palms. She moved upwards, stroking spine and softly cupping shoulder blades. On her way back down, Edie paused when she felt scar tissue under Jamila's armpits. Jamila pulled away from the kiss, her eyes dared Edie to comment. *Is this why the others cancelled*, Edie wondered. Edie continued to stroke the scars, which ran all the way to Jamila's breastbone.

"Can I see?" Edie asked.

Jamila shrugged and lifted the sweater over her head.

A holographic tattoo of the goddess Kali danced along two angry, pink scars. The miniature goddess was only three inches tall. Her skin was blue and she wore a skirt of skulls. As she danced, she waved her multiple arms menacingly. Edie smiled as it hopped from one scar to the next to continue the dance.

Edie ran her hands down Jamila's sides, feeling the feminine curves. *So she'd lost her breasts to cancer*, Edie thought. *There's so much more to a woman.*

Edie leaned in for another deep, probing kiss.

Jamila worked open Edie's fly. Her hand closed around the hard plastic and gave it a little tug. "I love a girl with a dick," she said. "I want to see the whole look. Take your shirt off."

There was something about the command that made Edie hesitate. She was used to this sort of talk from clients, and perhaps that's what stopped her. She'd forgotten for a moment that this was just another job. As an ishtartu the client's pleasure was her duty, but....

An unfamiliar heat blushed her cheeks.

Jamila released Edie's dildo and stepped out of their embrace, clearly expecting her order to be obeyed. "I like to see what I'm buying," she said with a smile. "All of it."

That's right. This is for money. Give the client what she paid for, girl, Edie reminded herself. She unknotted her tie and let it slip to the floor. Edie found her eyes unable to meet Jamila's as she began unbuttoning. Her fingers shook, but somehow she undid them all.

Edie looked up, the shirt undone. Jamila waited, watching.

Cold air met her flesh, as Edie let the shirt slide to the floor. She shivered, feeling exposed under Jamila's unwavering gaze. Edie fought the urge to cover her breasts with her arms. She felt like a whore, and a tear formed in the corner of her eyes.

Then, Jamila spoke: "My vulva, the horn
The boat of Heaven
Is full of eagerness like the young moon
My untilled land lies fallow
Who will plow my vulva?
Who will plow my wet ground?"

Jamila said the ritual words with such conviction, such passion that Edie looked up into Jamila's face.

Jamila's eyes glowed red, like molten rock. For a moment, they stood in the center of a ruined temple, dark and thick with vines. Above, the ceiling had crumbled and was open to the air. Kudzu crisscrossed the circular space like a spider web. Edie could see Venus, sacred to Ishtar, shining brightly next to a full moon. Mourning doves flitted from perch to perch, calling out their sad songs to each other. The air was warm and rife with mildew.

Edie blinked, and the illusion was gone.

Jamila's arms were open, welcoming, and Edie knew the goddess had not abandoned her after all.

"I will," Edie whispered the ritual response, and felt warmth flood between her legs. No longer feeling ashamed of her nakedness, Edie straightened her shoulders. More firmly, she repeated: "I will."

Jamila's smile was as bright as the evening star.

THE END

Acknowledgements

I have to thank a lot of people for this book and their support of me while I wrote it. I believe I have Christa Dickson to thank for reading and enjoying the previous AngelLINK books, then suggesting to Lars Pearson – her husband and the publisher of Mad Norwegian Press – that he should contact me about writing a prequel to the series. Also, thanks are due to two Mad Norwegian associates, Michael and Lynne Thomas, for enthusiastically supporting the idea. I also have to thank Lars himself – and all the AngelLINK fans – for their extreme patience. I'm grateful to my agent Martha Millard for understanding how much I wanted to write this book and negotiating the deal.

Then there is my much suffering and rarely truly appreciated partner, Shawn Rounds, who has to put up with me poking her in the middle of the night to tell her how brilliant a sentence is (after, of course, a three minute set-up of all the context and salient details).

A shout-out has to go to Lane McKiernan who read the book without knowing quite what he was getting into; Sean M. Murphy and Naomi Kritzer, who should know better by now; and my diligent copy-editor – once again, the lovely and talented, Shawn Rounds. Also, Sean, thanks for the Hebrew and its translation, and Rachel Kronick for going out of her way to introduce me to Lane.

I must acknowledge that some of the ideas in this book came from or were outright stolen from others. I must credit science fiction author Daniel Keys Moran for coining the term "peaceforcer" for the UN peace keeping force. Though my peaceforcers are also cyborgs, I hope they're sufficiently different from his to be the homage they are intended as, instead of a complete rip-off. (Do me and Mr. Moran a favor and go hunt down his excellent books, including *Emerald Eyes*, one of my personal favorites.)

I also have to thank my Egyptian friend and artist Dorian Haqmoun for his insight into life in Cairo, and Jennifer Conlin of *The New York Times* travel section, for her article "Hurry Sundown" (January 3, 2010) both of which provided excellent source material for my imagination.

Naomi Kritzer and synchronicity are to thank for the term "sihr halal" ("lawful magic") which she discovered just as I needed it from Neil MacFarquhar's book *The Media Relations Department of Hizbollah Wishes You a Happy Birthday* (which cites the term and its definition from Phillip Hitti's *History of the Arabs*).

Also thank you to all the caffeine provided by the amazing folks at Amore Coffee, and the use of their free wifi for all my research.

I'm sure I've forgotten someone who has played a vital role, and, if it's you, I'm sorry; I suck. Of course, none of these people are to blame if I got my facts wrong or have misrepresented anyone's experience. All the stupid is mine, and mine alone. If you want to yell at me, I can be reached at *lyda.morehouse@gmail.com*.

Credits

Lyda Morehouse... leads a double life. By day she's a mild-mannered science fiction novelist known for her award-winning cyberpunk novels in the AngeLINK series (*Archangel Protocol*, *Fallen Host*, *Messiah Node*, *Apocalypse Array*). At night, she dons a leather cat suit and prowls the streets as vampire romance writer Tate Hallaway. Tat's books include the Garnet Lacey series (*Tall Dark & Dead*, *Dead Sexy*, *Romancing the Dead*, *Dead if I Do*, and the final book, which came out in May 2010, *Honeymoon of the Dead*) and the young adult vampire princess of St. Paul series (*Almost to Die For*, and – soon – *Almost Final Curtain*). Lyda lives in St. Paul, Minnesota, with her partner of nearly 26 years, their son Mason, and a menagerie of cats, fish and gerbils. Tate's whereabouts are currently unknown, though a good place to start looking is: www.lydamorehouse.com

Publisher / Editor-in-Chief
Lars Pearson

**Senior Editor /
Design Manager**
Christa Dickson

Associate Editor
Joshua Wilson

**mad
norwegian
press**

The publisher wishes to thank... Lyda, for thinking Mad Norwegian a worthy home for the next chapter in the AngeLINK series, and for being an editor's dream by applying such talent and spit-polish to the book in question. Also, thanks are due to Christa for both her keen insight and for always making our books look gorgeous; Michael D. Thomas and Lynne M. Thomas; Shawne Kleckner; Josh Wilson; and that nice lady who sends me newspaper articles.

1150 46th Street
Des Moines, Iowa 50311
info@madnorwegian.com
www.madnorwegian.com